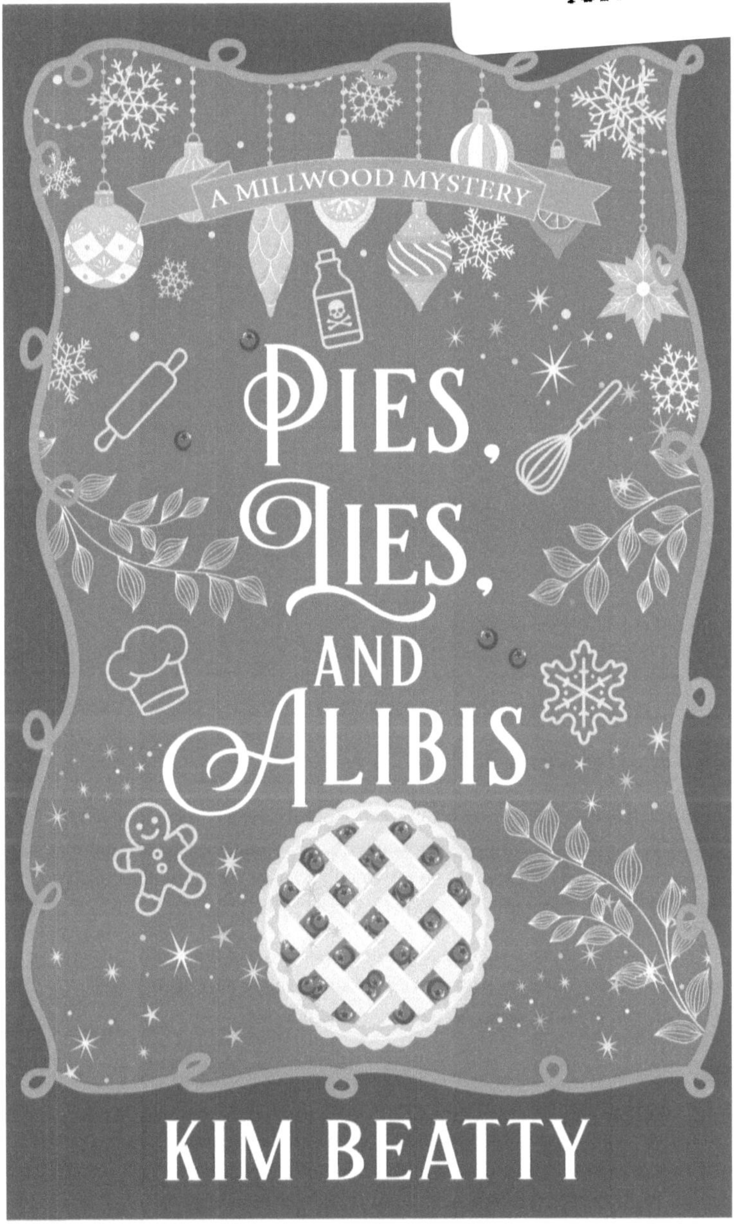

A MILLWOOD MYSTERY

PIES, LIES, AND ALIBIS

KIM BEATTY

To the lovers of daydreams and whimsy; of nostalgia and wonder.

Never give up on your dreams.

Chapter One

"STARING AT THE TIMER ISN'T GOING TO MAKE THEM BAKE ANY faster, Tess." I teased my best friend as she gazed into the oven window, impatiently tapping her finger on the counter.

She sighed dramatically as though I'd asked her to give up chocolate…or wine. "Oh hush, Kendall."

I rolled my eyes and wiped my floury hands on my grandmother's apron, my fingers grazing the embroidered peaches on the pocket. It had been several years already since she passed, but it didn't make me miss Gran Lottie any less.

Some grandkids long for some kind of rare collectables or financial inheritance; all I wanted was my grandmother's homemade aprons, hand-written recipes, and the memories of flour-dusted countertops and the smell of warm fruit wafting from the oven. If I couldn't have Gran here with me, these were the next best things. I liked keeping these mementos visible; she was the inspiration to follow my passions and would be so proud to know my bakery, City of Pies, was successful.

Tess couldn't escape the scent of baked goods very easily, especially since my bakery and her bookstore were separated only by an arched wall. I appreciated her staying after the bookstore closed to help me decide on the winter menu for the bakery, even if she had no self control when it came to freshly baked treats. I preferred to use ingredients that were in season, so cranberry, citrus, and of course pumpkin, apple, and pear all made it into the rotation. This year I thought I'd experiment with some pomegranate recipes... maybe a nice pomegranate glaze over some scones. While the name was City of Pies, I offered a bit more than that; muffins and scones were popular among the morning crowds so I liked to make sure I started the day with a good supply.

"You really need to warn me when you're hungry. Here, have one of these. You can be my taste-tester." I presented a small platter of hand pies and a couple tarts stuffed with fruit.

"Wow, these look amazing!" Tess licked her lips, trying to decide which one to sample; her hand hesitated before her eyes landed on one in the middle, a plump pastry with deep red cranberries tucked inside flaky dough, its fate decided. She bit into the still-warm pie, her eyes closed with contentment. "Yep, these are my favorites," Tess said chewing carefully, savoring every last bite.

"You said that about the cherry ones last week, Tess."

"Well...it's good to keep an open mind. Seriously, these are fantastic. Is this what you're making for the pie social at Willowhaven?"

I nodded in confirmation. "Yep, I just finished prepping the dough and it's chilling in the fridge. I just needed to make a few to see how the filling turned out."

When the holidays rolled around, Tess and I baked pies, tarts, and other goodies for the residents and workers at Willowhaven Care Center, where Gran stayed when she fell and broke her hip. What started as a school community project turned into a labor of love for both Tess and me. Gran eventually moved into the assisted living facility and after visiting so often, the residents became like family; for many of them, Tess and I were the only family still around. With the help of staff, we planned the event so residents would be able to celebrate when traveling to family wasn't an option, and it was one of the things I looked forward to most during the year. Once I opened the bakery I took over the baking… Tess stuck to quality control.

Tess licked crumbs from her fingers as she eyed the plate of baked goods. "I guess I shouldn't eat all the product." She grinned as I slid the plate just out of reach. The oven timer went off and I removed the last batch of scones, arranging them on a cooling rack. They smelled like heaven and would be perfect for the morning crowd.

"I think we'll stick with apple and pumpkin, but maybe we should add something different. Maybe I'll make the custard filling that Barbara likes so much." I drummed my fingers on the counter as I sorted through the stack of cards I pulled from Gran's old recipe box. Tess was being unusually quiet, and when I glanced up, pie filling was smudged across her cheek; a guilty look in her eyes telling me everything I needed to know. *Note to self—make more cranberry hand pies.*

"Sorry…yes, apple. And these cranberry ones for sure. Is that citrus I taste? So good…though they're a little too fancy for the likes of Ernest…it'd be a shame to waste them on such a grump."

"Ernest would honestly eat anything we put in front of him. Last year he tried hiding half of a pie in his sock drawer." I snorted, recalling the exasperated nurse who discovered the contraband. I was concerned it would mean we'd have to stop bringing the treats, but Ernest was just being Ernest: cantankerous and sneaky. "It will be so nice to see everyone without having to rush the visit."

"I know who you're really looking forward to seeing," teased Tess. I narrowed my eyes at her, trying to feign disinterest, but the subtle blush rising to my cheeks probably gave me away. "Don't look at me like that. You know it's true. It's not like he's hideous to look at."

I sighed. It was no secret I had eyes for Sebastian Shaw; in fact,

I was pretty sure the entire Willowhaven staff knew, no thanks to both of our grandmothers. He was tall and lean, with brown hair and eyes that were green as grass. And the dimples…

Sebastian's grandmother, Prudie, lived next to Gran at Willowhaven. She had been living there for several years before Gran moved in, and they grew as close as sisters. They could often be found chatting conspiratorially, only quieting down when Sebastian or I were within earshot. Once I tried to enlist the help of Harold, the resident busy-body, to try and figure out what they were plotting…but all he came away with was the synopsis of the last Young and the Restless episode. I smiled as I recalled the look of suspicion that Sebastian gave his grandmother, and his dimples when he cracked a smile. Tess cleared her throat.

"Uh," I fumbled with the pen I'd been holding and fanned myself with a notepad, smiling sheepishly at Tess. *Thanks, hot flashes, for making it seem extra obvious.*

"Uh-huh…go on and tell me you weren't thinking about him."

"Oh hush. A girl can daydream a bit, can't she?"

"Sure, as long as she doesn't drool on the baked goods." Tess nodded towards a half-eaten hand pie. She tapped her phone screen to check the time, then sighed. "I need to head home soon to feed my cat before he riots and tears the house apart. Tomorrow after we close, want to work your magic and make it look festive around here? I need to stop at Willowhaven to restock their book cart, so I'll grab some food on my way back." Tess cast a glance at the last hand pie on the plate, "Save one for me?" she asked before saying goodbye for the evening. I laughed as I closed and locked the door behind her, blocking out the chilly night.

I wiped the countertops down before looking at the clock. I figured I still had some time to pull down the boxes from storage so I could get a head start on decorating for Christmas. Normally it would be done by now, but with Thanksgiving being later this year, the ramp up for the holiday pre-orders ensured I didn't have much free time to spend fussing with Christmas lights. Still, I wanted to make sure the bakery felt festive and cozy for my favorite time of year.

The worn and ratty cardboard smelled of dust and age; most of these decorations were from my childhood, but I had a few things Gran passed on to me. I lifted the lid from the box with the aluminum Christmas tree and smiled. Silver branches with tufts of tinsel stuck out erratically from the main stalk. It'd seen better days, but I couldn't bring myself to get rid of it. With the vintage ornaments on it and the color wheel light casting its soft glow, people didn't pay much attention to the condition it was in. I always loved hearing customers comment on how they had one growing up, or the photos they have of holidays long-passed with similar trees. Nostalgia was a powerful drug, especially this time of year.

After hanging a few strands of lights around the bakery and getting the tree set up on a table in the corner, I yawned loudly and decided to call it a night, thankful no one was around to hear that unflattering noise. Turning off the remaining lights to the kitchen and making sure the door was locked, I made my way up the back stairs to my apartment just above the bakery. While there were stairs outside leading to my apartment, whoever had the idea to build a set of stairs on the *inside* of the building was my hero; I did not take for granted the fact I didn't have to leave the bakery to get home.

My apartment was a modest space that I tried to make my own. There was a bit of a mid-century modern vibe to the color scheme, and I loved having Gran's Pyrex dishes on display. A large metal starburst hung on the wall above the electric fireplace, the mantel decorated with various vintage treasures I'd picked up thrifting or at estate sales. I made myself a cup of peppermint tea in one of Gran's old mugs so I could wind down, and dearly looked forward to climbing into bed.

Chapter Two

RUNNING A BAKERY WASN'T AN IDEAL PROFESSION FOR SOMEONE who wasn't a morning person, and I grumbled as my alarm shouted at me. Untangling myself from the sheets, I quickly brushed my hair and tied it up into a messy bun before washing my face. Looking in the mirror, I lifted my cat-eye glasses and squinted at my reflection; were those wrinkles? Gran would call them laugh lines; she was never bothered with aging, and tried to instill the same in me growing up. In truth, I didn't mind getting older; I viewed it as a sign of surviving whatever life threw my way. So many women are made to feel less-than as they aged, as if their beauty and worth only existed in their outward appearance of youth; when I turned 43, I felt empowered and ready to take on the world. Even if I'd need bifocals to read the signs along the way. I dressed in my usual outfit of jeans, concert t-shirt, and flannel—hot flashes be damned; even perimenopause couldn't make me abandon my beloved flannel shirts—and headed for the bakery.

Today was pick-up day for holiday pie orders, and I knew things would get hectic in a hurry. I liked to make all my pies ready-to-bake; they remained in the freezer, and once the customer was ready they could simply pop it in the oven to bake before serving. Not only did this save *me* time and oven space, it also made the customer look like they'd toiled away on a homemade pie for their guests. Thankfully Cayden, the college student I hired part-time last summer, was able to come in a bit earlier today to help assemble boxes and make sure each one had instructions attached.

The timer on the pre-programmed coffee maker dinged and I paused for a moment of gratitude, savoring the warm cinnamon scent as I swirled the creamer into the magical brew. I just don't know how people function without a caffeine addiction. I liked to tell folks I was really doing it for their benefit: I was not pleasant in the morning without my coffee.

Cayden was waiting at the door when I flipped the lights on in the kitchen, a bakery box tied with pink twine in their mittened hands. Judging by their rosy cheeks and nose, I guessed the temperatures had gotten lower than expected overnight. I really needed to get them their own key.

"I come bearing gifts," Cayden announced. "I know you bake, but sometimes it's nice to have someone else do the work!" They shrugged off their coat, hanging it on the hook by the door; their tawny hair was slightly staticky from the knit hat once perched on their head.

"You're my favorite shop assistant," I said taking the box from them.

"I'm your *only* shop assistant, Kendall," Cayden replied, flatly. They peered around me to look into the front of the bakery. "When did you even find time to put up decorations out there? Do you ever sleep?"

I was certain the dark circles under my eyes answered that question more honestly than I ever would. We chatted a bit as we munched on our donuts and went over the winter menu choices so the chalkboard could be updated. Since Cayden was working toward a degree in graphic design, I gladly gave them free reign over all things artsy. I eyed the clock while washing my hands; it was already five o'clock and I knew we'd better get busy. Those pies were not going to package themselves!

We worked like a well-oiled machine, and this year it only took us an hour and fifteen minutes to package and label everything—a new personal best. As Cayden closed the freezer for the last pie, I held out my fist for a fist bump—a gesture that was likely deemed uncool by most college kids—which they obligingly reciprocated. If it *was* uncool, they didn't mention it; I liked to think Cayden respected their elders that way. I topped off our coffees and flipped the shop sign to Open, ready to greet the day.

THE DAY FLEW BY, as chaotic as I expected it would be; a steady stream of foot traffic kept us busy and we had to restock the display case with scones twice, thanks to a delivery order to a nearby office. By the end of the day there were only three unclaimed pies in the freezer—I gave customers a few days to either call to arrange pick-up or they'd end up forfeiting the order; in the event they didn't show, I usually took them to the local shelter so they didn't go to waste. Gran would haunt me if I threw a perfectly good pie away!

A few minutes before closing time, Tess arrived as promised with take-away and soon the most mouth-watering smells filled the bakery. I cleared some space at one of the tables after flipping the Closed sign. Lifting the lid on one container, the scent of tikka masala met my nose and my stomach growled. Loudly.

"Good thing the food got here when it did, you sound like you might starve." Tess dished some rice onto a plate, followed by a heaping spoonful of the delicious orange-colored curry. I passed around the stack of naan. If I was honest, that was probably my favorite part. That and the kheer. And those little fried dough balls in that heavenly syrup…I made a mental note to figure out how to make them. I doubted Mrs. Harish would divulge her secrets.

"I heard something interesting when I was at Willowhaven this afternoon," Tess said, tucking a blonde strand behind her ear; having recently chopped her hair to chin-length made it a futile effort. "I stopped to talk with Celeste before I left. She was telling me that a couple of the residents had finally been feeling well enough to rejoin their normal activities; I guess pneumonia made it's way around the unit…anyway, she also said about a week ago some folks were reporting things rearranged in their rooms. Pictures in wrong places, or their belongings in different drawers or cupboards." Tess looked from Cayden to me, waiting for a reaction.

"Ghosts?" I asked, trying to keep a straight face.

Tess threw her crumpled napkin at me. "No, wise guy. They still don't know who it was."

"Hmm. I still think it could be ghosts."

"I also overheard her talking to Debbie, one of the administrative staff, asking about some of the discrepancies in their pharmacy counts," Tess said.

"Well, that's concerning. How does that even happen?" Cayden asked.

"No idea," Tess said, shrugging.

"I listened to a podcast once where a nurse was stealing medication so she could sell it. She was using the money to pay off her student loans, ironically," Cayden mused.

"I only know a few of the nurses, but I can't really picture any of them doing that. Olivia certainly seems to be doing OK, she has all those fancy purses…" I shouldn't have even said the thought out loud; even though my words were dripping with sarcasm I could tell Tess's wheels were spinning. Her brow was furrowed so deeply, I was afraid she'd have a permanent crease there.

"Maybe she's an escort," I offered as if it were the most logical explanation. Both Cayden and Tess stared, unsure of what to say; when I grinned broadly, Cayden groaned and rolled their eyes.

Tess was still quiet, then tilted her head to the side. "Well, she does have someone new to date almost every other night," she said.

"Speaking of dating…have you talked to Sebastian lately?" Cayden pinned me with an intense stare.

"Um, no, why? And why would talking about dating make you ask that? You know we're just friends. That's all," I said defensively.

"Me thinks the lady doth protest too much," Tess said in the most awful British accent I'd ever heard, her green eyes sparkling with delight. I glared at my friend, but once again felt my cheeks growing warm; it was not because of a hot flash, this time.

I knew it was a hopeless case trying to downplay my feelings about Sebastian, especially where Tess and Cayden were concerned. The truth was, I was afraid what admitting my feelings would mean; afraid I would have to come to terms with some rather hurtful lies I'd grown to believe about myself. It wasn't long ago that I felt like I was the problem in most—if not all—relationships, thanks to my undiagnosed ADHD and partners who were less than understanding. People found it easy to gaslight me, manipulate my feelings, and make me feel like I was less-than, forgetful, or difficult. I struggled to regulate my emotions which was overly frustrating, and partners were eager to use that to their advantage.

I knew I was damaged goods and didn't shy away from that; and I knew that anyone who even remotely took an interest in me would have to be okay with that. It took years of therapy to finally get an official diagnosis and find the right medication to help calm my brain, and it was still difficult most days. Through all of that, I realized I really needed to work on myself before considering another relationship, even if it was with someone I had known for years. I had no doubt Sebastian would make a great partner, but I didn't know if I was ready to be that vulnerable again.

Cayden cleared their throat, shaking me out of my thoughts. "Right, well, when you're ready to confess that you've been pining after him for the last few years, we'll be right here. I know it's hard to put yourself out there, especially with past hurt. I mean, look how long it took me to even talk to Max, let alone consider a relationship. And Tess hasn't dated anyone in who knows how long." Tess huffed at that comment before Cayden continued, "We don't want to see you hurt again, but we want you to be happy...and the way Seb makes your face light up, it's hard to deny that boy *definitely* makes you happy."

I felt tears prick at the corners of my eyes; my friends really were the best. And they were right, as much as I hated to admit it. Maybe it was time to rip that bandage off. Or at least peel a corner away. I'd have to give this some serious thought, though—my stomach flipped at the thought of just jumping right into that conversation with Sebastian. "*Hey, Seb...wanna make out? I've got some baggage, but ya know, I'm working on it. I might have some meltdowns, and you may not understand what the heck is going on...but it's fine.*" That did not seem like the ideal way to approach things.

Once we finished eating and Tess cleared away the dishes and containers, I dragged the boxes of decorations into the middle of both shops. Tess reluctantly cued up some holiday tunes—classics mostly with a few contemporary songs mixed in—and we got to work. It wasn't that Tess didn't like Christmas songs, but years of working in retail environments ruined it for her. Her face turned a funny shade of green when the self-proclaimed "Queen of Christmas" started to defrost in early November.

I, on the other hand, danced my way to the front window where I stenciled snowflakes onto them with the frosty white spray I remembered from my youth. I arranged a few artificial evergreen trees and a small grazing deer, creating a winter woodland scene. Gently twinkling lights provided a soft glow and faux snow blanketed the floor of the display window.

Tess was busy hanging garland along the front of the counters, silver bows accenting each peak. Rather than going with traditional red and green holiday colors, we both leaned into the less traditional color schemes of silver, frosty aqua, and salmon pink. Satisfied with the windows, I gathered some empty boxes in various sizes along with scissors, tape, and gift wrap. I unfurled the rolls of vintage-looking wrapping paper across one of the tables in the bakery, eyeballed the dimensions and began to cut; I was sure there was a look of pure satisfaction on my face as the scissors glided through the paper, emanating that 'sshrisss' sound. Tess was ready to adorn them with bows and ribbons—she hated the actual wrapping part, but liked to add the finishing touches. These pretty packages would go on top of the book shelves and on some of the tables around the shop, serving as a nice reminder to patrons that books and gift certificates are always the perfect size.

"Right, I think that's enough for tonight. Any more and it will look like Christmas threw up in here. I don't mind, but I think customers get a little unnerved at the enthusiasm I have for the holidays." I chuckled as I packed up the wrapping supplies and cast an approving gaze around both of our shops. "Once again, we've outdone ourselves, friends!"

"Mittens McGee has some kind of hateful attitude towards anything decorative and will destroy it, so I like to live out my wonderland fantasies here," Tess added, a hint of sarcasm in her tone. Having a cat in her life meant scaling back on anything Mittens McGee could wreak havoc on which meant Tess had very sparse home decor. McGee, though, lived like a king.

"Cats are gonna cat!" I grinned. "I still think we could get him a little elf outfit! Oh! We could do shop Christmas cards!"

Tess rolled her eyes. "Don't expect me to pay for your urgent care bills when McGee decides he's had enough tomfoolery and swipes you with his murder mittens. When do you want to start on the hand pies for Willowhaven? I have a book shipment arriving tomorrow to stock up for the holidays but I have a couple part time helpers coming in so I will have a little more wiggle room to help. Thank goodness for bored college kids!"

Cayden flicked Tess with a fake holly sprig. "What else are we supposed to do? A body can only binge-watch so many episodes of 'Shadows of Frosthollow.' If you don't need me for anything else this evening, I'm going to head home. There is a very fluffy duvet waiting for me."

"I have the dough made for the crusts already so there should be plenty of time to bake everything." A worrying thought crossed my mind, "Maybe I should call Issac or Celeste to see if they still want us to come over; if the residents are still recovering, they may not be up to it." The thought of missing out on our tradition made me sad, but the thought of anything happening to those wonderful people made me more sad.

"Sounds good. I'll be on my way, too—McGee awaits!" Tess waved.

As they both made their way to the parking lot, I locked up the shop and took one last admiring look at the holiday splendor we'd created in a matter of hours. Smiling, I turned off the lights and headed for my apartment; I, too, was ready for a fluffy duvet.

I eyed the couch longingly, the squishy cushions beckoning me to sit for a spell. I kicked my shoes off and grabbed a quick dinner from the kitchen consisting of cheese, crackers, and turkey pepperoni—what did the kids call it these days—'girl dinner?' I plopped onto the couch, munching on my cheese and crackers and catching up on social media. I'd taken a few pictures of the decorations we put up tonight, so I composed a quick post for Instagram featuring the glowing lights and tinsel tree. The next thing I knew it was six o'clock the next morning, and I had a piece of turkey pepperoni stuck to my cheek.

My phone chimed loudly from its resting place right next to my head and I jumped about a mile off the couch. Wiping the sleep from my eyes—and removing said pepperoni—a smile spread as I realized who the message was from...Sebastian.

> Hey, Kendall! I'm sorry for messaging so early but I just wanted to say hi, and I'm looking forward to seeing you. For pie.

Just as I was about to set the phone back on the table, I noticed the three little dots bouncing, indicating Sebastian was typing another message.

> Um, I mean, not just for pie. Um. Never mind. See you later!

I grinned imagining Sebastian rolling his eyes at himself.

> Looking forward to seeing you too, Seb. And pie.

Chapter Three

I<small>T WAS A QUIET DAY AT</small> C<small>ITY OF</small> P<small>IES, FOR WHICH</small> I <small>WAS THANKFUL.</small>
With it being a little over two weeks until Christmas, there were a
few last minute pie pick-ups, and some hungry shoppers in need of
sustenance to keep them going.

Cayden arrived around nine o'clock, just after finishing a
morning exam and wanted to try a new recipe for scones, which
gave me time to enjoy the festive decorations in the bakery. I
glanced at the walls, their soft peach giving a warm glow to the
room under the lights, and the white trim reminded me of a cozy
cottage. The front window allowed natural light to spill in, making
the space feel bright and welcoming. Built-in shelving took up part
of the wall space; I wanted to showcase some of the vintage Pyrex
I'd found from estate sales over the years, as well as some of the
baking cookbooks Tess had in stock.

When we first opened, I was concerned the aesthetic of our
businesses would clash: Tess wanted a dark, botanical academia
theme—which I didn't even know was a thing—lots of mossy
greens, browns, and cream colored accents. Not only do both
spaces fit our personalities perfectly, they pair really well together.
Many customers have commented on how welcoming and comfort-

able both shops were. From this vantage point, I could see the appeal.

As I was checking the delivery schedule to ensure we had none for the day and humming "Silver Bells," the bell over the door jingled and in walked a man I hadn't seen before. I wondered if he was new in town; while I didn't know everyone who lived in Millwood, it was a small enough town it didn't take long for newcomers to stand out. He rubbed his hands together, trying to generate warmth.

"Welcome to City of Pies! Can I get you some coffee or tea to help warm up?"

As he approached the counter I noticed he kept glancing toward the bookstore.

"Ah, are you looking for Tess?" At the mention of her name, his eyes brightened.

"Actually, I am. But I'll still take you up on that tea if you don't mind. Have any Earl Grey by chance?"

"You got it! Any room for milk?" I always liked to ask before I poured; there was nothing worse than trying to slurp scalding hot tea or coffee out of the cup just to make room. The expression on his face indicated I'd made a grave mistake asking if he wanted milk in his tea.

"No, thanks. Just straight up Earl Grey."

"Kendall? Where the heck are my glasses?" Tess's voice echoed from somewhere in the bookstore. I glanced up at Mr. Earl Grey and caught a smirk on his face.

"Did you check to see if they're on your face already? Or on top—"

"Never mind! Found 'em!" Tess interrupted me. She came around the corner then stopped dead in her tracks when she realized the man was standing there.

"Uh, that's three dollars for the tea," I said before I'd completely lost his attention.

He paid, then turned to Tess and smiled. "Thought I'd stop by," he said.

"I see that," she replied. She nodded for him to follow her, and I was disappointed to lose my entertainment.

About 30 minutes later, he strolled from the bookstore through the bakery, out the front door. "Thanks for the tea," he said before closing the door behind himself.

"Tess…"

"He was standing there when I asked where my glasses were, wasn't he?" she asked. I laughed; I hadn't seen Tess this flustered in a while…especially where a man was concerned.

"So who is Mr. Earl Grey, No Milk?"

Tess went on to explain how they'd met a couple weeks ago at the CSI Night hosted by the high school; he was there in a professional capacity. "They had various interactive stations where kids could do some basic crime scene analysis. They even had a station set up that mimicked blood spatter." Tess shivered at that memory.

"So he's an investigator…Detective Earl Grey? Does he live in Millwood?"

"His name is Jordan Fox. You can call him that instead of Earl Grey. And yes, he lives in Millwood. Has been here for a couple years, so he's still trying to get a feel for small town living."

"I take it he's from the big city where they're too refined for milk in their tea," I teased. She threw a wadded ball of paper at me.

"You're so annoying," Tess grouched. "We met there and have been talking on and off since. That's all."

Satisfied with that explanation, I refrained from teasing her further…goodness knows what'd I'd get in return.

❧

AT LUNCHTIME I walked down to the hardware store to finally get a key made for Cayden; they'd been working with me long enough that I trusted them with it. Plus, they wouldn't have to wait on me to unlock the door when the temperatures really dropped.

Mr. Larsen estimated he'd have the copy done by the end of the day, and sure enough shortly before five o'clock, he stopped into the bakery to drop it off. I wrapped up a couple scones for him to take as a thank you for the personal delivery. I knew Mrs. Larsen liked blueberry the best, and I just happened to have two remaining. I handed off the key to Cayden, who look like I'd just given them a key to the city.

The light outside was beginning to fade, typical for December in the Midwest. Street lamps were flickering to life, and the glow of the holiday lights from the front window made me want to curl up with a book and blanket for the night. Maybe after I made sure there was dough for tomorrow morning...and double checked with Issac and Celeste we were still on for the pie social.

To my utter delight, Cayden had already prepared some dough for the morning's scones, and even left a note on which muffins they'd like to make. I added my own notes about adding a few tarts using the pomegranate I just picked up at the store and locked up for the night.

I grabbed the keys to my vintage Beetle (Betty) and pulled my coat a little tighter as I stepped outside. In addition to the recipes she'd saved for me, Gran also passed on her 1979 Volkswagen Beetle, which she purchased new and treated like a member of the family; she treasured the car. Like Gran, I passed many milestones in this car: learning to drive, getting my license, stalling it in the middle of a busy intersection and only having a mild panic attack about it. Sure, creature comforts were nice for long trips, but for puttering around town she was perfect. Being of an older generation, Betty required a little extra time to get moving...very relatable. I let the engine run for a bit before taking off.

It was a quick drive to Willowhaven and the parking lot was mostly empty. I was able to park close to the doors; a blast of icy wind hit me as I opened my car door reinforcing my decision. I pushed through the front entrance and checked in at the security desk. The man handed me a visitor's badge and had me sign the registry.

"When did you start doing the visitor badges?" I asked, realizing he spelled my name incorrectly. For the amount of time I would be here, it wasn't worth correcting him.

"Just within the last week, ma'am." The way he said *ma'am* made me feel ancient, and definitely indicated this conversation was over. I thanked him and proceeded to the residential wing.

Issac waved as I made my way towards the nurses station. "Hey, Kendall! How are things at the bakery?" Issac Parker was in his 30s and worked at Willowhaven for about 15 years, working his way up to his current role as department lead. He helped Gran when she was in the rehab facility and around the time she moved to the assisted living facility, Issac transferred departments. He was so kind and gentle with the residents, I couldn't think of anyone else I'd want looking after my loved one.

"Hi Issac! Things are going alright! Busy, but good. Everyone behaving themselves?" I glanced around the common area, noticing it was quiet. "Where is everyone?"

"Ah, they just started a new film club so they're having their opening reception. Even Harold went, though I suspect it was mostly to keep tabs on everyone. You know how he is." Issac rolled his eyes but smirked. Sometimes if it wasn't for Harold's nosiness, the staff wouldn't know half of what goes on around here.

As we were chatting, Olivia approached the desk; her long black hair was pulled into a severe pony tail that swished with each step. For someone who works in patient care, she seemed to be lacking the "care" attribute; her face was set in a nondescript expression, though it bordered on annoyance. Being the night-shift nurse meant she usually started around seven o'clock in the evening; I glanced at the wall clock behind her and realized she was about an hour and a half early.

"Oh, hey Olivia. How are things?" Issac greeted her.

"Hey, Issac. Kendall." she replied as warmly as a cup of coffee that's been left for hours.

"Hi Olivia. How are you?" I didn't honestly expect a response, which was good because I never got one; just as Olivia looked about ready to reply, her cell phone rang. She quickly looked at the display and curled her lip in disgust before walking away without a word. *She's so pleasant.*

"Must be a new beau. That girl, honestly," Issac huffed. "If she paid as much attention to her work as she did her dating schedule, it'd be a miracle. It's been weird having her around during the day." Issac went on to explain they'd had to juggle the scheduling a bit due to the holidays, and Olivia actually volunteered to work days for the last couple of weeks.

I was getting ready to ask Issac about the items that had gone missing when the doors to the common area opened and the residents came spilling back into the room, chatting excitedly about the film club. Ernest veered off and made a beeline for his room, grunting a "hello" as he rolled his chair past Issac and me. He was the most cantankerous man I'd ever met. He convinced everyone his hearing was gone, but he always managed to eavesdrop on conversations. Alvin and Elenore pushed a cart of left over snacks and drinks, while Barbara wrote on a whiteboard the name of the film and everyone's rating. Harold fussed with the remote on the TV before settling on the local weather channel.

"Well, Ernest didn't think too highly of your movie," Issac laughed as he read the 2-out-of-5 rating.

"It's Ernest, does he ever think highly of anything? I did catch him smiling a time or two, so I suspect deep down he actually didn't hate it." Alvin chuckled. "Kendall! How are you, dear?" Alvin was a widower who moved to Willowhaven shortly after his wife died; he didn't want to be alone, or want his kids worrying about him. You'd never know he was in his mid-70s to look at him —he was fit as a fiddle and flirty as could be, especially with some of the other residents.

"Hi Alvin! I'm doing OK!" I replied, then addressed the larger group, "How was your movie club?"

Everyone talked excitedly about the movie—a rom-com about a couple who started out as enemies in rival businesses but ended up falling in love—which they all voted on watching. As I looked around the group I noticed one familiar face was missing.

"Hey, where's Prudie?" I asked.

"Prudie said she wasn't feeling up to the film club and decided to stay in her room to rest. She's been awfully tired lately, and complaining about some dizzy spells. And I didn't want to say anything to alarm anyone, but she looks pale. Don't you think, Barbara?" Elenore wrung her hands as she spoke, her voice full of concern. Barbara nodded in agreement.

"I noticed yesterday she looked too pooped to poop," Harold added. We all just stared at him in wonder at his colorful description. "Well, she did."

I shot Issac a worried look, and pulled him aside as the residents went back to munching on their snacks and chatting about the film. "Was Prudie one of the residents who came down with pneumonia?"

"She did mention a few symptoms she was having, so we kept her comfortable to make sure nothing serious developed. She hated sitting out on some of the activities, but she wanted to make sure she was well enough for the pie social," Issac reassured me.

"I'm so glad we can go ahead as planned! I'm making a special treat just for her!" I said my good-byes, and tried not to worry about Prudie.

Just as I passed through the doors to the main hallway, I heard

Olivia speaking in hushed tones. Her voice was low and quiet; I could just pick up bits and pieces of what was being said.

"...it's weird being here during the day. No, not yet. Well it better be there! Let me..." Olivia's voice grew distant as I saw her walking briskly toward one of the stairwells, her back to me. *What better be where, Olivia?* It did not sound like a conversation someone would have with a new love interest, though who really knew with a girl like her. It was strange, and left me feeling like she was up to something.

I dropped the visitor's badge off at the security desk and pushed the door open. I pulled my scarf tighter; in the time I'd been inside Willowhaven the temperature dropped a bit and the chilly air sent a shiver through me. As I looked towards my car in the parking lot, I barely had time to register someone directly in my path. I stopped abruptly, just short of smacking into the man in front of me.

"Oh my gosh! I'm so sorry!" My words seemed to shake him back to the present, and he looked at me as if seeing me for the first time.

"Sorry, didn't see you. Guess my mind was wandering. You OK?" The man asked, and seemed concerned, and a little confused. The wind whipped around us, the ends of my scarf flipping me in the eye, immediately causing it to water.

"I'm fine, thanks. Going to visit someone?" I asked. Why did I ask that? It's none of my business.

"Uh, no...I work here. I've seen you around before. Sorry, I don't know your name. You're the pie lady, aren't you?" He scratched the back of his neck, eyes shifting between me and the door. I could tell he hated small talk as much as I did, so I'd release him from this torture.

"Ah, sorry. I'll let you get inside where it's warm. And yes, I'm the pie lady...in fact, I'll be back with some tomorrow for the pie social! Stop over in the assisted living wing and make sure you get something!" I smiled and stepped aside.

The man nodded in appreciation but didn't say another word. I inhaled deeply, the cold air tingling my nose; as I exhaled my breath came out in a frosty mist. In the shelter of my car—it was by no means warm in there, but at least it blocked the wind—I turned the key in the ignition and allowed the Beetle to warm up before making my way home.

Chapter Four

ALL NIGHT LONG MY DREAMS WERE PLAGUED BY WEIRD IMAGES OF Olivia lurking in shadows and whispering into her phone, Harold trying to goad Prudie into wheelchair races, and the man I encountered as I was leaving. Glancing at the clock, I decided to get up, even though it was three-thirty in the morning and I knew I'd regret it: tonight was the pie social and I'd need all the energy I could muster. It was definitely a day for lots of coffee. I waited until a decent hour before I sent a text to Tess asking if she could swing by The Steamed Bean to get me a triple-shot sugar cookie latte. An hour later, she arrived, coffee order in hand; Cayden was right behind her. I grabbed the cup with eager hands and sipped carefully, savoring the warmth; I swear I felt the sweet, sweet caffeine pulsing through my veins.

"I talked to Issac yesterday when I stopped by Willowhaven," I shared the details of the conversation about Prudie being under the weather as I made myself comfortable at one of the high-top tables in the bakery.

Tess unpacked some special book orders while we chatted. I took a little time to enjoy my coffee before grabbing my apron and washing my hands. I wanted to make a few more hand pies for tonight, and prep some things for tomorrow morning.

"I know it's hard not to jump to any conclusions. You know Prudie, she can't sit still for long and I'm sure she's run herself ragged with some of these new clubs they're putting on. Issac and Celeste will keep a close eye on her." Tess stacked books on the counter as she spoke, and I resisted the urge to sniff the new pages. "Hey, I know that look. First sniffs belong to the customers!"

I laughed, "How did you….never mind. I don't want to think about you being able to read my thoughts." I took a draining gulp of my coffee, sad it was gone. "Oh, and when I was leaving, I ran into some dude who works at Willowhaven, but I'd never seen him before. He seemed a bit scattered…" I trailed off, trying to think of how to describe him.

"It was most likely one of the nurses in a different unit. It's the holidays, I'm sure they've got people covering all hours of shifts," Tess said.

"That's true. I even saw Olivia there…and overheard a weird conversation." I shrugged, then realized eyes were on me. "Did I not mention that?" I relayed that part of the visit as well and how it crept into my dreams somehow. Even now, I felt uneasy about the whole thing, though I couldn't pinpoint why, exactly.

At about two-thirty in the afternoon, the baking was done. Rows of hand pies stared back at me, the edges all neatly crimped. Tess brushed the last one with the sugary glaze while snitching spoonfuls of leftover filling as we worked.

"Want a refill?" I asked, pointing to my mug.

"Ugh—no. I've realized the older I get, the earlier I have to cut myself off otherwise I won't sleep for days. I don't know how you do it; I'd be a zombie if I drank as much coffee as you!" Tess stifled a yawn, as if to prove her point.

"I think I'm just immune to it. I've read that people with ADHD have an easier time concentrating with higher levels of caffeine in their systems. It doesn't seem to work for me, but I'm willing to keep trying. For Science!" I raised my mug in the air triumphantly.

"Oh, before I forget... I just received notice they need to do some maintenance on the duplex and the water will be turned off for several days. Would you care if McGee and I stayed with you while they work?" Tess asked, her eyes looked like saucers and I swear she batted her lashes at me. "I'll keep him in the spare room with me, so he's not underfoot."

"You know both of you can stay with me; I'll get the spare room spruced up for you."

"You are the literal best! I'm not sure when they're starting, but as soon as I find out I'll let you know. I considered staying at a hotel, but I don't think McGee would do so great there. He actually likes you; I don't need to risk hotel staff being scratched because they so much as breathed in the same room as him."

"It's really no problem; there's no reason for you to spend money on a hotel. Just let me know when you need the room ready, and I'll make sure it's good to go!"

"I have to go home to change for tonight, so I'll see if there are any updates. Then I'll stop by to help you load up the pies," Tess said as she brushed the tiny flecks of paper dust from her jeans as we walked to the back door of the bakery.

"I'll have them packaged and ready to go!" I replied, thankful for her help.

Upstairs, I debated far too long about what to wear. I wanted something comfortable, so I grabbed one of my lightweight sweaters and paired it with dark jeans and some flats. I made sure my hair was presentable—it was not, currently—and swept it up into a messy bun to keep it out of my face.

A KNOCK on my door let me know Tess was ready for Operation Don't Drop the Pies. There'd be no way I could fit them all in the Beetle without risking a mess; I'd have to stack them and that was tempting fate a little too much for my liking. Tess brought up the rear with the last of the desserts and huffed as she leaned against the car. "Are you sure you have enough? I feel like you could have made at least another dozen."

"Are you implying that we went overboard? We would never." I pretended to take offense at the suggestion. Double-checking we had everything and it was securely stowed away, we departed for the care center.

We pulled into the Willowhaven parking lot where Cayden was waiting for us. Issac and Celeste met us with a cart and began loading the boxes of treats. "I am so excited for this," Celeste said, peeking inside one of the top boxes. "Ooh! Hand pies!"

"How is Prudie doing, Issac?" I tried to wait before asking, but curiosity was getting the best of me.

"She's just fine! Her color's returned to her face, her blood pressure was low but within an acceptable range, and she's just as sassy as ever. I think allowing her to rest a few days really did the trick." He smiled, hoping to reassure me. I sighed with relief—at least that was one less thing to fret over tonight.

Since Issac and Celeste were with us, we didn't have to stop at the security desk. The same serious man who issued my visitor's badge yesterday was there again today. I smiled, and waved a hand toward the cart of goodies.

"We have plenty, so feel free to grab a snack!" That seemed to soften him just a bit; he smiled and nodded his thanks.

We made our way to the dining hall, where two long tables were set up for the pies and other treats, decorated with floral arrangements donated by The Daisy and The Bee, our local florist. Pinecones dusted in glitter were scattered across the table; strings of lights were draped in the windows and battery operated tea light candles added a soft glow and helped chase a bit of the chill away.

"Everything looks so magical!" I beamed at Elenore and Barbara as they added some more cups to the drinks station. There were large dispensers for coffee, and tea, as well as a warming carafe filled with spiced apple cider. Cans of soda were lined up on the counter next to the ice machine.

"We spent the afternoon gluing the glitter on these blasted things," grumped Ernest, glaring at a pinecone. "I almost stuck my fingers together!"

"Well they look fantastic, Ernest," I said, patting his shoulder.

"I'm just glad I had a light lunch; there was no way I'd fill up on that goop when there was real dessert to be had!" Harold said, eyeing the hand pies as I opened the boxes and added the labels for which flavors were available. It warmed my heart that they put so much effort into making this a special evening. Even Harold and Ernest.

***

ISSAC AND CELESTE gathered all the residents and staff around. "First we want to thank everyone who could make time to be with us tonight. And to Kendall, Tess, and Cayden for all their hard work in making these magnificent goodies, and for helping us continue this tradition." Issac nodded in our direction as the residents started to applaud. "The holidays can be a difficult time for some of us, but this helps ease those feelings and allows us to celebrate the warmth of found-family."

I waited for the murmurs of agreement and applause to die down a bit before speaking, taking a moment to compose myself; I knew I'd start blubbering given the chance. "I know I say it every year, and this year is no different—this tradition started with Gran Lottie, and continues with you. While we may not be blood relation, we're definitely a family, and I love you all." I smiled warmly, looking around the group taking in each of their faces; my breath hitched when I caught sight of Sebastian wheeling Prudie towards us. His tall form was a stark contrast to Prudie's, but you could see the similarities in their eyes—green and full of joy. I definitely didn't notice how the dark indigo sweater vest he was wearing made his eyes that much greener…not at all.

"Prudie! I am so glad you're feeling well enough to join us! It sure wouldn't be the same without you tonight." Tess gave her hand a gentle squeeze, then looked to Sebastian, before turning to me, waggling her eyebrows. I immediately felt my cheeks warm. I glanced away, hoping no one noticed but when I turned back, Sebastian was smirking. *Ugh…not the dimple…*

Issac continued his speech, thanking the staff for their continued help, and praising the residents for pitching in like always to help out. "OK, gang! Let's eat!"

Cayden and Tess helped the residents get their desserts; the chatter replaced by quiet chewing. After settling Prudie in with warm cup of cider and half of a blueberry hand pie, Sebastian came to stand next to me. I caught a scent of his cologne—something a bit spicy like cloves mixed with a hint of citrus. My stomach did a little flip.

"Hey, Kendall." His green eyes twinkled as he smiled down at me.

"Hi, Seb." I smiled, trying to come up with what to say next. Small talk was not my forte; I think I'd rather go to the dentist… well, maybe that's a stretch. "I'm so glad to see Prudie is doing better."

We talked for a bit; Sebastian apologized for texting me so early the other morning. "I was on my way to Crooked Pine and just felt like saying hi. Hope I didn't wake you up." He grinned, and even if I would have been annoyed by it, all traces of that floated away.

"Ah, no. Well, yes, but I had to get up early anyway so no worries at all. How are things in the tech world?"

Sebastian's was one of the few computer-related businesses in the area, often getting calls from neighboring towns. He specialized in information security and computer networking, but also helped folks with repairs and the like. After working for several years in the city, he moved back to Millwood to be closer to Prudie.

Right before he could answer, we heard voices coming from one of the hallways just beyond the nurse's station. It was hard to make out what was being said, but it sounded serious. All the background chatter faded away as the loud voices grew closer.

"Look, I don't know where it went. I just know it's missing," a man's voice said. He sounded flustered.

"When was the last time you had your badge?" a woman—I realized it was Celeste as she came into view—asked.

"I know I had it this afternoon when I was refilling meds. The only time I take it off is when I change to go to the gym," the man said, then added, "I remember clipping it on when I came back."

Issac tried to divert attention away from the situation by inviting the residents and their guests to sing Christmas carols; they started out strong, but it quickly fizzled out as residents began yawning and nodding off. I couldn't blame them, to be honest. Sebastian and I helped Issac get residents back to their rooms, offered treats in take home bags for the visitors who joined us, and finally began cleaning things up before saying our own goodbyes.

I WAS COMPLETELY EXHAUSTED by the time I climbed the stairs to my apartment; my legs felt like they had sandbags weighing them down, and my back ached from being on my feet for so long. Kicking off my shoes and hanging my keys on the hook by the door, I wanted nothing more than to collapse into bed. I finished washing my face and brushed my teeth quickly before flopping onto the bed; I was fast asleep in no time at all.

A loud vibrating noise startled me awake. Squeezing my eyes shut, I hoped it would stop, but unfortunately it just kept making a racket as the phone rattled against my bedside table. Blindly feeling for the offending noisemaker, I brought the phone within an inch of my face, cracking one eye open to see if I should bother answering. When I recognized Sebastian's contact picture, I sat bolt upright and answered the phone.

"Hey, Seb, is everything OK?" I asked, voice scratchy from sleep.

"Ken, I am so glad you answered. I…it's Grams. Something has happened to Grams. Can you come to Willowhaven as soon as possible?" Sebastian's voice shook with emotion as he spoke.

"Yeah absolutely, I'll be right there." I ended the call and dressed as quickly as possible. I hadn't even bothered to look at the time before answering—it was three o'clock in the morning. Nothing good could be happening at three o'clock in the morning.

Chapter Five

As I pulled into the parking lot at Willowhaven, the first sign something was severely wrong was the wave of blue-and-red flashing lights. The second sign something was severely wrong was the expression on Sebastian's face as a very official looking man in a dress shirt spoke to him. I felt like my body was on autopilot as I exited the car; I approached slowly, not wanting to interrupt their conversation. I met Sebastian's eyes as I closed the distance between us and noticed the muscle in his jaw twitch.

The…officer? Detective? noticed me from the corner of his eye and paused the conversation. "Excuse me, ma'am, you'll have to step away from the area. This is an active crime scene." Recognition flickered in his eyes as he turned to face me. It was Mr. Earl Grey, No Milk.

I heard his words and as my gaze panned across the front of the building, I swallowed hard, unsure what to say. I nodded in acknowledgment, before speaking. "Sebastian asked me to meet him here." I wasn't even sure if my words were loud enough to be heard over the chaos of the scene.

"Detective Fox," he said, touching his chest by way of introduction. "You work at the bakery," he said it as a statement rather than a question.

"I *own* the bakery," I corrected. "Kendall Howard." I wasn't sure if I should extend my hand in greeting, or just leave it at that. I'd never been to a crime scene before. My brain whirled trying to understand what happened here. "Seb, what on Earth is going on?"

"It's Grams, Kendall. Something has happened…and I can't even make sense of it. They called me when they found her, and I called you as soon as I got a chance. She's….she's gone. Grams is gone." The last words came out as barely a whisper. I saw tears gathering in the corners of Sebastian's eyes as he spoke. I wrapped my arms around him, though I was chilled to the bone and I doubted I had much warmth to offer.

I stepped back and turned to the Detective. "Do you know what happened?"

"No, unfortunately. We're still assessing the scene." His breath misted the air as he spoke, and—as if realizing it was after three o'clock in the morning in December for the first time—suggested, "Let's step inside so we can talk." Detective Fox motioned toward the front entrance of Willowhaven, which felt so foreign right now. I stepped over the threshold and there was none of the warmth from earlier in the evening. My steps faltered as I realized that was the last time I saw Prudie alive; Sebastian seemed to notice, and my heart broke as I saw the pain in his eyes. Prudie was his whole world. I tightened my grip around Sebastian's arm as we walked and leaned my head on his shoulder.

The security desk was a hive of activity. An officer sat where the guard normally was, and waved us through as soon as he saw Detective Fox. The three of us made our way toward the residential wing which was bustling with people. Police officers had caution tape wrapped around chairs outside Prudie's door, and two guards stood on either side to limit who could access the scene. As we followed Detective Fox, the reality of the situation hit me like a ton of bricks: he called it a crime scene. I heard his words at the time, but they didn't register. I presumed when Sebastian said she was gone that Prudie had died of natural causes. But now...

Detective Fox stopped short of Prudie's room. The door was open, and I could see people combing every inch of the room... looking for evidence? I let out a shuddering breath, and Sebastian grabbed my hand. He glanced at me, a silent question if it was OK. I squeezed gently to reassure him; he was the one who needed support right now—not me.

"Miss...Howard," Detective Fox started as he flipped through a few pages of his little notebook. "We'll have to get a statement from you; we can do that either here or at the station, it's up to you."

I was more than a little confused—why did they need a statement...from me? I was home asleep! "Uh, sure. I'll have to open the bakery this morning. If we're not busy I can have my assistant watch the shop, otherwise it won't be until after closing."

As if reading my mind—I really should figure out how to keep my facial features from giving myself away—Detective Fox said, "I know you're probably wondering why we need a statement. Rest assured, it's routine procedure and needed to help establish a timeline of events. It's also necessary because there was some evidence found that may need some clarification from you." Fox looked at me, his face a mask.

"Evidence?" I breathed, certain the air was being siphoned out of the building. "What evidence could *I* possibly explain?"

"You provided various desserts earlier in the evening to the staff and residents of Willowhaven Assisted Living, is that correct?"

I froze. Everything around me froze. Time stood still. "Wait....what?"

"Please come down to the station at your earliest convenience today, Miss Howard. I will be there all day." Detective Fox handed me a business card with his contact information on it and I slipped it in my shirt pocket. "Mr. Shaw, I'm very sorry for your loss. I know this is a difficult time, so please let me know if there is anyone I can contact on your behalf." He handed Sebastian a contact card as well. "Please keep yourself available in the event we need additional information." Fox nodded solemnly to us before he turned on his heel and disappeared into the scrum of Willowhaven staff and officers. I stared after the detective, my mind swirling.

Sebastian touched my shoulder lightly and I startled. "Kendall?"

"I...what is going on, Sebastian?" I tried to keep my voice level, but the words cracked at the last syllable of his name. "Why do I have to go in for questioning? Why aren't you allowed to leave? And what does baking pie have to do with giving a statement to the freaking police?" I felt woozy. *Deep breaths, Kendall. Deep breaths.*

Sebastian scrubbed his face with his hand and sighed heavily. "Because of how they found Grams, Kendall. I didn't get a chance to tell you everything before Detective Fox started in. One of the late night staff members was doing a routine walkthrough of the area and noticed Grams's door was ajar which was unusual for her. She liked her room pitch black for sleeping," a faint smile teased at the corner of his mouth, no doubt recalling a memory of Prudie. "They found the maintenance guy knocked out on the floor. Grams was in her bed, seemingly unharmed, but she was already..." Sebastian took a deep breath. "He woke up a bit later but was fuzzy on the details."

My eyes swept the residential wing, searching for what, I didn't know. Certainly not answers. I tilted my head, considering Sebastian's words again. "Wait...the maintenance guy?" Something about that seemed odd to me.

Sebastian nodded in agreement. "Nothing makes sense. If he

really was knocked out, someone else had to have been there, too."
Sebastian's expression was hard to read…was it fear? Concern?
Suspicion?

Elevated voices drew our attention to a corner of the make-shift
command center where the man I'd met in the parking lot was
simultaneously being tended to by nursing staff and questioned by
a police officer.

"It's like I already told you, I was checking the thermostat in
her room. I had a work order last week and I was just checking to
make sure it was still working." His face was a portrait of fury and
I was thankful to not be on the receiving end of that.

The officer scribbled in his pad and continued asking the
agitated man about the events of the evening. "Mr. Kemp—Neil—
what's your normal process when you have a maintenance work
order? Is there a certain timeline you have to follow?" The officer
stared at him, awaiting a response. When none came, he proceeded
to ask, "Do you recall seeing anyone else in the room with you?"

The man winced as one of the nursing staff dabbed the gash on
his temple with something on a gauze pad. "I…I don't remember. I
know the door was cracked open, and I thought I heard a noise
from inside. It was too dark in the room to see much, but when I
grabbed for my flashlight that's when…You know that feeling
when you can tell something is near you? I don't remember
anything after that," he said through gritted teeth. "Look, man, do
we have to do this now? Can I please just go home?"

"Because of the head injury you'll need to be monitored for
signs of a concussion. We can check with the nurses to see if they
can keep you here, or you can go to the hospital if you'd prefer. Is
there anyone I can call for you, Mr. Kemp?"

Neil rolled his shoulders and exhaled sharply, trying to gather
himself before speaking again. "No, there's no one to call. I'll just
go to the hospital." There was a sadness to his words.

The officer nodded and spoke into his radio making arrangements for the ambulance. He handed Neil a card, asking him to please contact the police department if he happens to remember anything.

As he was being helped onto a gurney, Neil looked toward Prudie's room. It was hard to read the expression on his face…was it guilt, or regret? Right before the paramedics wheeled him away, the officer had one more question.

"Being a maintenance man, I suspect you'd have keys to just about every door in this building, is that right?"

"That's right. I have an access badge for certain rooms, but I have keys for others or when emergencies come up."

"Can you show me the keyring you normally carry with you?"

Neil produced a metal ring loaded with several very similar looking keys, each having a different color tag for identification. "Here," he held them up to the officer.

"Are these *all* the keys in your possession, Mr. Kemp?"

Confusion passed over Neil's face. "Uh, yeah, why?"

"Does this key look familiar?" The officer held up a much smaller key that looked nothing like a door key. I was just as confused as Neil looked.

Neil swallowed hard before responding, "I've never seen that key before, sir."

Before we could catch any more of the conversation, another officer approached Sebastian and me, ushering us to the door and reminding us to keep ourselves available. We walked silently to the parking lot. What do you say to someone who just lost one of the people they loved most in the world?

"Seb, do you want to get coffee? Or just talk? Or just…be?" I knew the diner at the edge of town was likely open, and thought a change of scenery might do us both some good.

He squeezed my hand. "I'd like that. I don't think I want to be alone right now."

Chapter Six

IT WAS ALMOST FIVE O'CLOCK IN THE MORNING WHEN I RETURNED to my apartment after spending time with Sebastian. I felt bad leaving him alone, but he insisted he felt better after we talked. We tried to sort out what could have happened to Prudie; it just didn't make sense. If she woke up and found someone in her room, maybe it startled her and she had a heart attack?

I asked Sebastian if Prudie had anything turn up missing from her room recently; he never remembered her mentioning it, but knows Celeste and Issac warned her about keeping certain things in her room. Apparently Prudie was one of the older generations that felt it was safer to keep your money under your mattress rather than in a bank...or in this case, valuable jewelry.

Willowhaven staff urged her to get a safe deposit box: the directors viewed it as an unnecessary liability, and their insurance agency seemed to agree. Prudie insisted it was safe; if anyone tried any funny business, she'd give them what they had coming. Eventually, Sebastian and Prudie's lawyer convinced her; she gave strict instructions on which bank she trusted most, and how much to insure the contents for.

Remembering the key the officer questioned Neil about, I

wondered if that was to the safe deposit box? Could Neil have been searching her room for it? Or, did he catch someone else in the act of searching for it, and that's who knocked him out? My mind was spinning with so many questions, and I was afraid we wouldn't be able to answer them.

I considered calling Cayden to cover the bakery all day, but I needed to keep my mind busy. I needn't have worried though. Setting the emergency brake on the Beetle, I glanced up at the back of the bakery and noticed both Tess and Cayden's cars in the parking lot; I hadn't expected to see either of them so early, but I was very thankful to see my friends. It was unlikely they'd heard about Prudie yet; I definitely needed more coffee for the conversations that would unfold.

As I hung my coat on the hook, I realized the ovens were already warming the kitchen and I smelled coffee brewing. Cayden had the pans out for the scones, and I could have cried from relief. I was very thankful to Past Kendall for leaving pre-made dough in the fridge; batter for the muffins would come together quickly.

"I did not expect to see you here so early! But I am so happy I could hug you!" I held my arms out toward Cayden, who recoiled slightly. "I know, I know...you're not a hugger."

Tess came into the kitchen holding two large coffee mugs. "My hero," I said, taking one that read "I'd rather be baking" across the front.

"The question I have," Tess said, "is why weren't you here when we got here?" Her tone suggested she was expecting some scandalous answer...and for once I was very sorry to disappoint her.

"Actually, I need to talk to you guys about something." I wasn't sure how to even begin, so I just said it. "Prudie died last night. Er, early this morning."

Cayden stared in disbelief. Tess sat her coffee down and rushed to give me a hug. She also was not a hugger, but she knew when the situation warranted violating her rules on personal space. "Oh, Ken. How is Sebastian?" she asked.

"He's…I'm not really sure. He seemed alright when I left him, but I can't begin to imagine what he's going through. I mean, I remember how I felt when Gran died, but this…This just feels… different." I shrugged, not sure how to express my feelings.

"I guess she was more sick than they initially thought, then?" Cayden asked.

I was quiet for a few seconds before answering, and felt a shift in the room. "Oh no," they whispered.

"Back up, Kendall. Tell us everything you know."

And so I did…I launched into the events of the early morning hours: the phone call at three o'clock, the police chaos at Willowhaven. And Prudie, dead.

"So they don't know for sure what happened? As in, it may or may not be natural causes?" Cayden's eyes widened, and I knew their true crime radar was going off. That was another reason I hired them—we bonded over podcasts and murder books.

"Apparently, but I don't really have much information; it was so chaotic! I just know I have to go down to the station and talk with a Detective Fox—"

"Detective Fox?" Tess interrupted.

"Yes, Mr. Earl Grey, No Milk himself," I replied. "I was surprised to see him again so soon."

"Hmm," was all Tess said.

"Who is Mr. Earl Grey? Why are you being so weird?" Cayden asked Tess. I remembered they were in the kitchen the afternoon he came into the bakery and missed the introduction.

Tess blushed. "There's not much to tell," she said. Cayden and I stared, our eyes burning into her soul, willing her to speak. Even though I already knew about Detective Fox, I wondered if Tess had anything new to share. "I met him at the high school when they did CSI Night, and we've talked a few times since then…and he's very nice to look at." Tess waved away the last words as if she were merely talking about the weather or a new sweater. She cleared her throat. "This is not the time to discuss my social life. Kendall, let me drive you to the police station." Tess successfully changed the subject, and that was that.

"Let me go upstairs and freshen up. Cayden, there should be plenty of dough for the scones, which I see you're already working on. Thank you. I owe you! I'm not sure how busy it will be today, though I'm sure people will be looking for gossip if anything gets out. Please don't encourage any busy-bodies." I ran upstairs to splash some water on my face and change into a fresh shirt; when I rushed to meet Sebastian at Willowhaven I barely had time to dress, so I'd thrown on whatever I was wearing yesterday afternoon, coffee stains and all. I reappeared in the bakery's kitchen, grabbed my keys, and motioned for Tess to follow.

As Tess and I reached the police station entrance Celeste opened the doors, almost bowling us over. "Oh! Hi, I sure wasn't expecting to see you here!"

"Hey Celeste. Detective Fox asked me to come down to give a statement," I explained, shrugging. "Is that why you're here, too? Was he mean? Am I going to cry?" I recognized my weaknesses and fully admit that conflict makes me uncomfortable. It was bad enough when a customer was unhappy with their order, I couldn't imagine what this would be like.

Celeste scoffed, "It doesn't make any sense. These big city detectives just don't understand how close-knit communities work! Why would anyone want to hurt Prudie?!" We talked for a bit longer before she left, Celeste reassuring me everything would be fine and that the police would get to the bottom of things in time.

"Well, let's get this show on the road," I muttered. Pushing through the doors to the station, we were immediately met with a very sparsely furnished waiting area and a large reception desk. Seeing as I'd never had a reason to be at the police station the whole time I've lived in Millwood, I'm not sure what I was expecting. The woman behind the desk, who I knew as a customer from the bakery (cherry tart, large black coffee), glanced up, giving us a gentle smile.

"Hi Kendall, how are you doing, hun?" she asked. I immediately regretted living in such a small town. Everyone knew you—and your business.

"Hey Marsha, I'm hanging in there. I'm here to see Detective Fox, please." I kept it short, not wanting to encourage any idle chit-chat. I really wanted to get this over with as soon as humanly possible. My palms were already starting to sweat.

Marsha nodded and pressed a button on her phone; it lit up and she spoke into her headset, "Detective Fox, Ms. Howard is here to see you. Yes, Kendall Howard. I'll send her back." Marsha directed us to a conference room down the hall, offered us coffee, then quietly closed the door behind her. For once in my life, I actually declined the coffee; I didn't think my stomach would be able to handle it. I didn't know how long Tess would be able to wait with me, but I appreciated her presence.

"Well, I hope this isn't as intense as it looks on TV," Tess said.

"I know. I'm sweating through my shirt and I'm not even guilty!" I laughed nervously, wondering how often people experiencing hot flashes were suspected of crimes—I am sure the sweatiness didn't help support my claim of innocence, it just made me look suspicious. A bead of sweat trickled down my back as if in response to this thought.

A gentle knock on the door sounded before slowly opening; Detective Fox stepped in, file folder in one hand, large travel tumbler in the other. The tumbler was a sensible stainless steel, gray and shiny and nondescript. Fitting, I thought, as I studied his features; I didn't get a good look at him when he stopped by the bakery. His sandy hair which I now noticed had flecks of gray was kept short and tidy, as I'd expect from someone in his line of work. A no-nonsense kind of guy. He was still wearing the same button down as when I'd seen him at Willowhaven a mere few hours earlier, albeit a bit more rumpled...good grief, had it really only been a few hours? As he sat the items on the table, I caught sight of a small sticker near the lid—it looked like a potato with googly eyes and an ear of corn. Detective Fox noticed me staring at it and chuckled. "Eyes and Ears..." I felt a little of the anxiety release from my shoulders as he sat down in front of us; I certainly appreciated a good pun.

"Tess, I wasn't expecting to see you here." Detective Fox nodded at her, though he seemed a little surprised to see her.

"Uh, hi. Jor...Detective Fox." Tess smiled, sheepishly. I smiled at how awkward she sounded; Tess was normally cool as a cucumber, but today she seemed zesty as a pickled gherkin.

"Well, I guess this saves me some time. Since you were involved in the preparation of the pies as well as present at the events last night, I'll have another officer take your statement; I'm sure you understand." Detective Fox called for one of the officers to escort Tess to another room down the hall. She offered me a look of solidarity—or maybe it was panic—as she followed behind. I noticed her absence immediately, and a new wave of anxiety washed over me.

"Right. Kendall, we are just going to have a conversation; no charges are being made against you, and you are free to end this discussion at any time. The conversation will be recorded. Do you understand, or have any questions?"

I nodded in understanding, "No questions...well, I *do* have questions, but I know you can't really tell me anything. Something just doesn't seem right with this whole situation, though."

"Thank you for understanding the position I'm in. Your suspicions aren't unfounded—things aren't adding up to a simple case of natural causes. We have a skilled team working to put the pieces together as quickly as we can to give the Shaw family closure and time to grieve."

Detective Fox pressed a button on a recording device between us. "This conversation is going to be recorded, which I am informing you of now. Please speak clearly, and be sure to speak any affirmative or negative reactions rather than nodding your head. Now, suppose you walk me through your day yesterday."

I was generally aware of the types of questions that would be asked, but it didn't make me any less nervous. I became aware of my pulse felt through my fingertips and my mouth grew dry from speaking. I ran through my day as requested, trying to recall anything that might be helpful or relevant for the detective. It also didn't help that I was a chronic over-explainer, so I was making a conscious effort to stay on track.

The line of questioning changed and Detective Fox asked about the bakery and how I came to own it, which seemed a little odd. Even though I told myself to keep things brief, words came spilling out, how Gran supported me throughout the whole process up until she passed away, and how Tess and I share the building.

"Would you say your business is suffering due to lack of income?" the detective asked; the question caught me a bit off guard.

"Suffering? No. Would it be nice to have a little more income and add some more equipment or additional staff? Of course. I'd love to add an extra oven or two and expand my offerings—that's something I'm hoping to do next year, but there's not much money in slinging dough." I chuckled nervously at my own joke, Detective Fox offered me a slight smile; he didn't seem as amused by it. "But, no, I wouldn't say the bakery is suffering." I was trying to connect the dots as to why this would be relevant, but Detective Fox moved on to his next set of questions.

"Do you own the building? That area is the historic district, I imagine the payment for a building like that isn't cheap."

"Actually, Tess and I both own the building. We purchased it a few years ago, and we split the space—I get half the building for the bakery and a few tables for patrons, and she has the rest for her bookshop. And the bakery brings in enough to cover those expenses." I added before Detective Fox could ask. *Was he trying to establish a motive?*

Detective Fox cleared his throat and took a drink, the potato's googly eyes jiggling as he brought it to his mouth. It was very hard to take him seriously with that thing. "Ah, well, I do have to cover all the bases, Ms. Howard. I do have one more question for you, though. How close are you and Sebastian Shaw?"

I paused before answering, though I wasn't sure why; I had nothing to hide. "I've known Seb—uh, Sebastian—for years. Prudie was there when Gran moved into the assisted living complex, and they were best friends, so naturally I got to know Sebastian fairly well. She was practically a second grandmother to me, which makes this all so hard to understand."

"And how long have you and Tess been providing desserts to Willowhaven? This is an annual event, as I understand it?" The abrupt shift of topics threw me off, which I'm sure was the point.

"Right, we started when we were kids as part of a community service project," I said, then went on to explain why we continued. "We've been doing it ever since."

"Have there ever been complaints before? Any illnesses after these communal events?"

"Are you suggesting…?" I couldn't even finish my thought. It's not often I am speechless, but this series of events was proving it to be possible. When I finally found my words, they came out in a whisper, "I…what? No, that's not possible."

I eyed Detective Fox, searching his face for any indication that this was some trick to get me to confess something. His face was as blank as the wall behind him. Just as I was about to say more—something, anything to refute that claim—a sharp rap at the door startled me. The officer who had been with Tess eased open the door and nodded at Detective Fox; he motioned for the officer to fully enter the room. I saw Tess standing in the hallway and she seemed unfazed by things; I wondered if her questioning was similar to mine.

"Sorry for the interruption Detective, but we just received this and I thought you would be interested." The young officer handed Detective Fox a sheet of paper then excused himself from the room. As Detective Fox scanned the document, he struggled to keep his expression neutral.

I could just barely make out the bold, black text at the top of the page: TOXICOLOGY. Detective Fox dialed his phone quickly and he was watching me out of the corner of his eye. I averted my attention, pretending I hadn't been trying to read the paper or to listen to his conversation. He was "calling in a favor" and asking for clarification about some aspect of the report, if there was any way of expediting further testing on those trace substances. *Traces of what?* I pushed my chair back, mostly because I felt like I might burst if I didn't move.

As I stood, Detective Fox looked at me sharply, his eyes questioning. *What do you know, Kendall?* I imagined him thinking. *Nothing, Detective, but I wish I had some answers.*

$Chapter\ Seven$

On the way back to the bakery, Tess and I shared our experiences from the police station; Tess wasn't sure what to make of things—she only knew the officer received some piece of information and cut their time short—but after I explained what I thought the information was, she sucked in a sharp breath.

It felt like the weight of the world was resting on my shoulders as we crossed the parking lot from Tess's car to the back door of the bakery. I tossed my keys in the basket on the counter and grabbed my apron from the hook by the door; Tess mumbled something about unboxing some book orders. When I finished washing and drying my hands, I pushed through the doors to the bakery where I found Cayden wiping down the counter, their head bopping to whatever tunes were coming through their ear buds, hair flopping in their eyes. "Hey, Ken—are you OK?"

"Eh, I've been better. Being questioned in the death of a friend's grandmother was not on my bingo card for this lifetime." I flipped the switch on the coffee machine and drummed my fingers on the counter while waiting for it to finish dispensing the magic bean juice; the aroma curled around me like a warm blanket. "Have things been slow today?" I stirred the creamer in slowly, the dark

47

brown liquid quickly becoming a lighter shade, and my mood lifting the slightest bit. Never underestimate the power of a strong cup of coffee.

Cayden let out a slow breath. "Well, it's certainly been interesting," they said as they pulled a tray of scones from the case. "People are very chatty today." They gave me a pointed look while passing over a blueberry scone. They must have baked another batch because this one was still a little warm.

"I am exhausted, my brain feels like mush, and I have been on the verge of tears all day. If you tell me it was the gossip brigade, I might just have a breakdown right here in the bakery."

"Well, Diane and Natalia were in earlier picking up their usual order of tarts and coffee. A woman, who is apparently Celeste's aunt, came in just as they were leaving and I overheard them chatting about what happened to Prudie. It seems like someone over at Willowhaven has the impression that whatever killed Prudie wasn't just down to poor health. They were so absorbed in their conversation, when I mentioned the discount you have running on the hand pies, they grew very quiet and took a seat in the far corner."

I groaned as I buried my head in my hands. "Ugh. What in the name of coffee beans…is this about the pie?"

Cayden looked dumbstruck. "Did I know about that? Anyway, I was so shocked I almost dropped a perfectly good slice of custard pie in a customer's lap. I tried to pretend I hadn't noticed, hoping they'd keep talking. All I could gather was that Ernest overheard Prudie talking with her lawyer about updating her will. By this point I'd hovered over the customer far longer than is appropriate so I made myself busy cleaning the tables." Cayden finally took a breath, and shook their head after the dizzying replay of events.

"Detective Fox asked me weird questions about how long we've been taking desserts to Willowhaven and if anyone complained about getting sick. Right before we left, he was following up on something he read on the toxicology report. I am not a criminal mastermind, but I certainly wouldn't be dumb enough to implicate myself with my own baked goods."

"That would seem too obvious," Cayden agreed. "I am sure Detective Fox doesn't seriously think you would be involved. He just has to cover all his bases."

I murmured in agreement and was quiet the remainder of the day, turning over all the facts I knew to this point. The problem, I realized, was I didn't actually have many facts at all. I had rumors and whispers...and apparently baked goods in a dead woman's room. Cayden offered to close for me, but it wouldn't be long until then, and I needed the distraction and comfort of being in my bakery. A few regulars came in for their late afternoon treats, and I was grateful no one felt the need to ask questions; either word hadn't spread much, or people weren't foolish enough to believe rumors.

Finally, closing time hit and I was never so happy to be done with my day. After cleaning up the tables and counters and making sure there was enough dough for the morning, I trudged upstairs to my apartment where a very large glass of wine was waiting for me. Sleep took its time to come, so I grabbed a notebook and decided to write down what I knew: who was there that night, who *wasn't* there that night, and who interacted with Prudie. The list was short, but maybe things would start to make sense. I'd make it a point to talk with Tess and Cayden to see if they remembered anything unusual.

※

I WOKE feeling like I slept with cotton in my mouth. That one large glass of wine turned into two...which turned into half the bottle; definitely not one of my better choices in life. Cracking one eye open to check the time, I groaned and buried my head under the duvet. Enjoying just a few more minutes of darkness and the cozy warmth of the bed, the realization that Prudie was gone slammed into my chest. My heart ached for Sebastian. I'd call this morning to check in on him.

Grabbing fresh clothes, I made my way to the bathroom to wash away the sleep. I turned the faucet to the shower and waited for the water to heat, and read my notes from last night; thankfully I finished them before I finished the wine so they were still legible. Prudie looked tired and asked to go back to her room early. Was she really recovered enough from the pneumonia? I scribbled an extra note in the margin to talk with Issac; I'm not above bribing folks with baked goods to get some answers.

Showered, dressed, and freshly caffeinated I headed down the stairs to begin opening the bakery for the day. No doubt the town gossips would be dropping by for a scone and 'the tea' as kids say…

With the ovens preheating, I grabbed my apron and got busy pulling ingredients from the shelves. Anytime something was weighing on my mind or I needed to think, baking always pulled me into the zone. I could focus on specific tangible actions that resulted in something wonderful almost every time. I often felt that was why I was so drawn to baking with Gran Lottie; with ADHD there was no room for guessing or suggestions; sometimes my brain needed very specific measurements or instructions: 3/4 teaspoon of salt, 2-3/4 cup of flour, combine in medium sized bowl, bake for 25 minutes. Sure, you could experiment a bit with flavoring or adjusting certain ingredients, but the foundation of the recipe had to stay the same…otherwise, much like life, things started to crumble.

As I stirred the wet ingredients into the dry, I thought about the pie found in Prudie's room. I recalled she had half a blueberry hand-pie when we were gathered in the dining room; maybe she didn't finish it. Maybe one of the nurses left it in her room. Either way, it was the last thing she ate before she died, and that was a very unsettling feeling.

I turned the dough onto the parchment-lined pan, cut it into wedges, and brushed the tops with some milk before sprinkling cinnamon and sugar on top. I popped the pan into the large freezer to allow the gluten in the flour to relax a bit and chill the fat, a trick Gran taught me that makes for the best scones. While those chilled, I started on the next batch. The bell over the front door to the bakery jingled followed by Cayden calling out a "hello;" I glanced at the clock realizing it was a bit later in the morning than I thought. There was still plenty of time to get things made, especially now that Cayden was here to lend a hand.

"Hey, Cayden." I waved a floury hand. "How's it going this morning?" Cayden looked me up and down slowly. "Uh, do I look that bad?"

"You just look…like you've been through it. Are you holding up OK?" Cayden asked, rubbing their hands together for warmth. "I don't know if I'll ever get used to these Midwest winters. How do y'all tolerate the cold?!" Sometimes I forgot Cayden was from the South until their slight drawl slipped out. Even after living in Millwood for a few years, it did take some adjusting to get used to our climate compared to Georgia.

"It gets easier. Dressing in layers helps…and so does coffee. Want some?" I offered as they washed their hands before grabbing a knife to cut chunks of butter.

"Yes, please. Did you at least get some rest last night?"

"As much as I could have expected, I guess. Thanks to the wine." Cayden made a face at this comment; they knew wine wasn't my favorite, and it must have been a desperate situation if I resorted to that. "I haven't talked to Sebastian since yesterday morning; I wanted to give him some time but I don't want him to think he's alone in this," I paused before continuing, "I feel like there's a fine line between comforting someone and being over-bearing." I tossed my dish towel on the counter in frustration.

Cayden placed a hand on my arm, careful not to leave a buttery grease mark behind, "I am sure he would appreciate your company. Why don't you call him after we open? I can handle the bakery for a bit."

We worked in comfortable silence until all the scones were ready for the display case. Today's specials were the cinnamon sugar scones that I loved with a cup of coffee, and the white chocolate cherry scones that Cayden came up with last fall. They seemed to be popular this time of year, perfect with a cup of hot cocoa or tea. I set one aside for Tess before taking inventory of the tarts and pies left over from the previous day. The tarts were fine to place back in the display case—they could last a couple days as long as they were refrigerated overnight. The pies, though, were really only a single day item, so I repurposed any left over into various crumbles or crisps. Giving the counters one last wipe with a damp cloth removing any stray fingerprints from our efforts, Cayden flipped the open sign over and unlocked the door.

The morning was off to a moderate start; the shops along Mill Street were offering coordinated discounts in the lead up to Christmas, so I decided to join in on the promotions. Admittedly ten percent wasn't a huge discount, but I couldn't really afford to offer much more than that. What I told Detective Fox was true—we were turning a very modest profit, just enough for additional marketing or any emergencies that might come up. The promotion seemed to keep foot traffic steady, though, which helped. Now, though, with the rumors flying around town I wondered how much of a negative impact that would have on the bakery.

A noisy group came in, chittering like excited squirrels and pointing at various items in the display case, trying to decide what to buy as an afternoon sweet treat. I listened in amusement as they debated the qualifications of a pie:

"Like, I'm pretty sure they're all just little pies," a girl with violet hair said.

"Nah, my auntie said it had to be fruit filling to be pie. These have like pudding or something," said a young man, dark curls peeking out from his knit hat. He was eyeing the custard tarts off to the side.

"OK but what about those? They just look like non-greasy pizza puffs," the friend wearing a scarf asked, pointing to some hand pies in the back row. She was so bundled up, I barely saw her mouth move.

"Who cares, they look amazing and I'm getting hangry," Violet Haired Girl said as her annoyance started to set in.

I bit the inside of my cheek to keep from laughing. "If you have questions about anything or want a sample before you decide, just let me know."

"So, like, my friends and I wondered about the pies…I mean, like, aren't these really all pies, just different sizes and stuff?" The Scarf asked, loosening the scarf just enough to un-muffle her words.

"Ah, yes, the age old debate…it's been a point of many arguments in my family but I can clear that up for you," I leaned in for effect. "If it has a lid and a base, it's a pie. If it has a base but no lid, you got yourself a tart. If it only has a lid and no base, well, I can't help you with that because it's probably a mistake. A delicious mistake, but a mistake all the same." They stared back at me as if I'd grown three heads while talking.

"Right, well, I think we'll take the three, uh, tarts in the middle." The young man pointed, avoiding eye contact with me.

"Excellent choice! I'll get those boxed up for you!"

Cayden was cleaning one of the tables when Tess came in through the back of her bookshop. "Well I did not expect it to snow today," she grumped, stomping her feet on the floor to dislodge the snow that followed her in. "I thought it wasn't supposed to start until later tonight!"

"How much are we supposed to get?" Cayden called from the bakery, peering out the large front window. Fat flakes fell to the sidewalk, and I made a mental note to grab the shovel from the storage closet.

"I don't know; last I heard it was a few inches, but you know how quickly that can change."

I liked the snow, especially at this time of year; the warm glow of the Christmas lights seemed to twinkle even more, as if they know it's their time to put on a show. It made the shop windows sparkle and shine. "It's going to be a weird holiday this year," I mused as I rearranged the items in the display case to make up for the morning's purchases.

"Have you heard from him, Ken?" Tess asked gently. She didn't have to say who.

I smiled sadly before replying. "I'm going to call him later this morning. Offer to bring him lunch or something." I continued fidgeting with the display case, lost in thought. "Do you really think they found pie in her room?" I wondered aloud after making sure there were no customers within earshot. "It just makes no sense!"

Tess finished sorting through the latest book delivery, slipping the order sheets for each customer inside their respective books. "The whole thing has been bothering me, but that just seemed extra random." She straightened the stack of new releases to be displayed as she spoke. One with a purple cover featuring a majestic-looking dragon and a fierce woman caught my eye and I made a note to add it to my ever-growing to-be-read list. Having your best friend own a bookstore was a double-edged sword: I had unlimited access to all manner of books, but never enough time to read them.

"Issac and Celeste said Prudie hadn't been feeling well for a little bit—a week or so, right?" I recalled Prudie joking about offering a pie sampler plate at the bakery; it wasn't a bad idea, actually, but I wasn't in the right frame of mind to plan promotions just now. I made a mental note to add a pie flight to the menu. Maybe we could name it after Prudie.

"Right. So why would she have pie sitting in her room? I highly doubt she was jonesing for a midnight snack," Cayden said.

"And what was up with that maintenance guy…Neil?" Tess called from behind the counter of the bookshop. "Someone whacked him in the head? That means he wasn't alone in there!"

"I've been trying to work that out. I know Sebastian said Prudie likes her room pitch dark to sleep, so maybe he didn't see anyone while his eyes were adjusting to the light." I recalled the agitation that radiated from him while he was being questioned at Willowhaven. "He said he was checking on a maintenance issue… but why so late at night?"

"That's kind of creepy if he's sneaking around the residents' rooms," Cayden replied.

"None of this makes any sense at all. Why Prudie, of all people? I wish…I wish it was a horrible, horrible dream."

Chapter Eight

Around lunch time, after I shoveled a path along the sidewalk—the snow hadn't let up since Tess arrived—I called Sebastian. I wasn't sure if he'd cancelled the remaining jobs he had lined up, but knowing him, he'd want to keep his mind busy. I can't say I blamed him at all.

The phone picked up on the third ring, and Sebastian's voice sounded tired.

"Hey you, I just wanted to check in and see how you were doing. I didn't want to bother you but—"

Sebastian cut me off before I could finish the thought. "I am so glad you called, Ken. I needed to take a break."

We talked for a bit, him about the project he was wrapping up for a client, and me about the silly conversation with the teens. We threw in some weather discussion for good measure.

"Seb, do you need me to bring anything to you…dinner or anything?"

He chuckled before replying, "You don't need to bring dinner. You know how folks are around here; I've had a steady stream of casseroles and hot dishes all morning. There's barely any room in my freezer." *Ah, Midwest nice in full force.* "But I'd very much appreciate seeing you," he added.

"I think I can make that happen. Will you be around this evening, around seven o'clock? I can stop over after I close."

We finished making plans before hanging up. Even under the circumstances, I felt butterflies in my stomach at the thought of seeing Sebastian. As I got closer to the bakery, I heard Tess and Cayden talking with someone and froze in my tracks...

"That's absurd, why would she do anything of the sort?" Tess said.

"I have no idea, but I do know I'm questioning if I want to support a potential criminal!" The mystery voice said. It was a woman, but I was too focused on the words to think about who it might be.

"Ma'am, please keep your voice down," Cayden urged. I didn't know if there were other customers in the bakery...I prayed there weren't.

"I'll calm down when whoever killed Prudie Shaw is behind bars!" Shortly after the woman shouted, I heard the bell on the door jingle indicating she left—I hoped.

I took a deep breath before walking into the bakery, steeling myself for whatever waited for me across the threshold. I scanned the room which was thankfully empty. After hearing this person's tirade, though, I wondered if it was just a slow day or if word was spreading around town. Tess looked at me and offered a weak smile.

"Ugh. I knew this would happen. Who was that?" I asked as I massaged my temples. I was normally very good about recognizing customers, but this woman didn't seem familiar at all.

"Mrs. Billings. I'm sure she only came in here to stir the pot; she hasn't been in for months." Cayden said.

"Lovely. I only caught the tail-end of that, did she say anything else?" I cringed, half expecting Tess to tell me the whole town considered me a murder suspect.

"Not really, just that she demanded to have anything blueberry removed from the menus, and was threatening to call the health department to have us thoroughly inspected," Cayden snorted at the absurdity of the situation. I'm glad one of us could see the humor.

My heart rate increased at the thought of being closed down by the health department. "Surely if I were that serious of a suspect, Detective Fox would have been on the bakery's doorstep?" I voiced the thought out loud. Tess and Cayden nodded in agreement.

"I'll be right back" I turned to go upstairs to my apartment. As tempting as a nap sounded, it wasn't the time.

I snatched my notebook from the table where I'd left it the night before, along with a few different colored pens. Whether there was any useful information there or not, I wanted to talk it through with my friends...both Tess and Cayden were far more rational thinkers and would tell me if I was overthinking things. Maybe they noticed something I didn't that night.

Huffing and puffing from racing down the stairs, I slowed to catch my breath; maybe I needed to rethink that gym membership after all. I grabbed a pen from the counter and plopped down on one of the tables. Given how much snow was coming down, I didn't expect many more customers today; it was already close to two o'clock in the afternoon and a couple of the shops along Mill Street closed early due to the snow.

"What are you doing?" Cayden asked, looking curiously at my notebook. It was spiral-bound with a light teal cover and little brown poo emojis floating around the words "Important Sh*t" printed in a silver foil. Definitely high class note taking supplies.

"We are going to start compiling a list of what we know. Well, I already started...you and Tess are going to help me." I looked between the two of them expectantly, hoping they wouldn't think I was off my rocker. They just nodded at me as if they'd expected this. I loved my friends.

"Right. So, I started last night." I pointed to the page where I'd written down everything exactly as I remembered it: the pie social, seeing Prudie being taken back to her room earlier, having coffee with Sebastian after…witnessing the chaos at Willowhaven. "Do either of you remember anything I might have missed?"

I handed each of them a pen so they could make notes; Cayden had green, Tess had blue. While they reviewed my notes, I made us cocoa and grabbed a few tarts from the case. I stood, reading over Tess's shoulder for a few minutes.

"Oh! What about the nurse who lost his badge?" I said, startling Cayden. "Sorry," I apologized. "Do you remember hearing that conversation?"

"Not really, I was across the room playing cards with Harold and Barbara," Cayden said.

"I only heard him say he rarely takes it off; just to go to the gym and home. Maybe he left it in the locker room or something?"

I tapped the pen on my chin, thinking. "I already planned to ask Issac about Prudie being taken to her room early, maybe I'll ask about that badge. If I make his favorite cookies, maybe he'll be willing to talk." I grinned.

The three of us continued to discuss things right up to closing time. When I realized the time, I dashed upstairs and slid my notebook into my bag before making sure I didn't have dough anywhere unpleasant, then made my way to Sebastian's house.

Chapter Nine

"ANY UPDATES FROM DETECTIVE FOX?" I ASKED SEBASTIAN AS WE sat on his couch, some mindless television show in the background. He lived in an older neighborhood across town in a modest bungalow; dark gray siding with white trim made it look more modern than it was. Millwood was generally divided into three sections: the older neighborhoods, the historic district where the Mill Street Shoppes were, and the newer neighborhoods which featured lots of apartments and condominiums, as well as a few single family homes.

"Actually he called me after I talked with you," Seb sipped his beer and I patiently waited for him to explain. "He got the autopsy results back." Sebastian was quiet for a few minutes. I placed my hand over his, and squeezed.

"We don't have to talk about this right now, I'm sorry."

"No, it's fine. I mean…it's not *fine*, but you know what I mean." He offered a slight smile, which I returned. "Originally it looked like it was just a complication from the pneumonia. Obviously not uncommon with someone her age. But when they studied the rest of the report there were traces of odd substances found in her…" he trailed off, uncertain how to say it. Or maybe he didn't want to acknowledge it. I nodded encouragingly.

"They found something in her system that was unexpected. I can't remember what Detective Fox said it was…some kind of sedative." He frowned.

"She was mur—" I clapped a hand over my mouth to stop myself from saying the word. It seemed so harsh. Cold and uncaring. Sebastian realized what I was about to say, and nodded only once.

I debated coming right out and asking him to talk through theories with me. Part of me wanted to show him the notebook and the things Tess, Cayden, and I remembered from that night. But I didn't want to cause him further discomfort. But if Prudie was *murdered*?

"Out with it. You look like you're scheming," Sebastian said.

I bit my lower lip, trying to find the right words. "Well, not really *scheming*. I was thinking," I said. "I know, sometimes that can seem worse than a scheme." I went to the kitchen to refill my glass with water.

"And…?"

"Well. It's just that things seem strange. With Prudie, I mean. Something was bothering me the other night so I decided to just make some notes…things I remembered from the night she—of the pie social." I fished the notebook from my bag and handed it too him. He studied the cover, shook his head and smiled. "Well it *is* important," I said, defensively.

He opened the book, his eyes darting across the page. He flipped through the next two pages, taking in all the chicken scratches, then he sat the book down on the cushion between us. "Well?" I asked.

"Do you have anywhere you need to be?"

I checked the time; it was only eight o'clock. I was a night owl, so I didn't mind late nights at all. "Nope, what's up?"

Sebastian stood, taking my glass and his empty beer bottle to the kitchen sink. Then he tossed me my coat and scarf. "C'mon. We're going to Willowhaven."

WE REGISTERED at the security desk once again, accepting our visitor's badges. This was a new guard I hadn't seen before, and I wondered if they were taking extra measures to keep patients and staff members safe.

The halls were quiet as we made our way to the assisted living complex. The night nurses had just started their shifts, and I wondered when Olivia would be back to her regular schedule. They moved through their routines as though it was just another day. As though one of their residents hadn't died in the last 48 hours. I supposed death was common around here, but this was different. Suspicious. Mysterious.

As we reached the nurses station, I saw Issac and Celeste talking together; their heads bent as though in secret conference. Sebastian tugged on my arm slightly, which I interpreted as a sign to approach with care. We slowed our pace a bit, not wanting to sneak up on them. Issac must have sensed our presence; he glanced up. "Hey, guys. Wasn't expecting to see either of you around here."

"Hey there. I know, it's probably weird to stop by, especially so late. But…" Sebastian paused.

"How are you guys holding up?" I asked, looking from Celeste to Issac, and offering Sebastian a chance to gather his thoughts. I can't lie—the thought crossed my mind to stop by on my own, but with Sebastian here it looked more convincing…less like sticking my nose where it didn't belong.

"Oh, you know, as well as can be expected around here." Celeste offered me a half-smile.

"How are the residents coping? It's got to be so hard for them."

I couldn't imagine losing a friend so tragically. *Did they know the details of Prudie's death?*

"It's been pretty quiet. Barbara and Elenore are taking it the hardest; they're working on the next film club and trying to choose a movie in memory of Prudie." Celeste wiped at the corner of her eyes as she spoke. "Ernest and Harold…well, they're being their usual selves."

"Have you heard…anything about Grams's death?" Sebastian asked. I appreciated his willingness to come right out and ask.

Issac looked to Celeste, who nodded yes. Then he looked to Sebastian and me, tilting his head in the direction of the hallway. "Let's go somewhere to talk," he said quietly.

He waved his badge in front of a card reader, and the door slowly swung open. The words "Authorized Staff Only" were painted in bold red letters on the door. We followed him down the hall; it was so quiet you could hear the material of Issac's scrubs as he walked. Lights popped on as we passed rooms with blinds drawn; name plates on the doors indicating these belonged to higher-level staff members. Issac stopped at one such door, to wave his badge again; the door plate was engraved with his name. The sound of the lock clicking open seemed so loud in the hall it made me flinch.

We entered into a tidy office, containing a desk where a computer sat, and a large chair that looked very comfortable. On the opposite side sat two chairs (not as comfortable looking), and a small table off to the left side. There were several green plants with shiny leaves, and I admired Issac's green thumb; I was barely capable of keeping a cactus alive. A bookshelf displayed a dozen or so medical textbooks, along with a few framed photos of an adorable Shih Tzu.

Issac closed the door behind us and motioned for us to sit. He looked at Sebastian as he situated himself in his cushy chair, the wheels squeaking and cutting through the silence.

"Detective Fox informed us of their findings this morning. This is the first time since I've worked here we've been contacted after a resident's death, but they want to investigate further—you *have* spoken with Detective Fox about this, right?" Issac stopped himself before continuing, not wanting to be the one to deliver such troubling news.

Sebastian nodded. "Yeah, I talked to him this afternoon."

Issac continued, "After reviewing her medical charts, we determined that no one who was authorized to approve medications for Prudie signed off on anything the police reports picked up. Since it's an ongoing investigation, I can't tell you specifics...sort of the puzzle piece that might lead us to who was behind this. Detective Fox asked us not to release the information." Issac looked to Sebastian sympathetically.

"So...there were medications used on my grandmother but no one seems to know where they came from?" Sebastian was trying to keep his voice low and calm, but I could feel the muscles tense in his hand.

"That's why Detective Fox handed over their findings. There will be a full investigation launched into how this may have happened. Please know we will do everything to get to the bottom of this."

There was a call on Issac's work-issued phone, and he excused himself to answer it. Watching his outline through the blinds, I saw him move just out of the window frame. I couldn't hear his voice any longer, so I quickly grabbed the folder off his desk. Sebastian stiffened next to me, unsure how to react.

"What are you doing?" he hissed at me.

"Shh. Trust me, I know what I'm doing!" It was a bluff; I knew what I wanted to do, but I didn't know if I could pull it off. I took out my phone and began snapping pictures of each document, front and back. I winced after the first one; the volume was up on my phone and the fake shutter sound felt like it was ten times louder than normal. I didn't have time to read them, so I wasn't even sure if it was relevant information...but I needed to start somewhere.

"Kendall!" Sebastian hissed again.

"Poke your head out to see if he's coming back!" I jerked my head toward the door. I still couldn't hear Issac, but the ringing in my ears from the adrenaline was pretty loud. Finally I reached the last page, right as a bead of sweat dripped off my forehead and landed on the folder.

"Quick! He's coming!"

I slammed the folder shut and flipped it back around, so it would be facing the same direction as when he left. Unfortunately I couldn't remember if he'd left it opened or closed, so I hoped he wouldn't notice.

Issac entered the room, looking a little perturbed. I tried to discreetly swab my forehead with my sleeve, remembering I had a coat on that was waterproof.

"You alright, Kendall? You look flushed," Issac asked as he studied my face.

"Oh yeah, fine! Just a hot flash." I fanned my face for effect. "Kind of looking forward to getting outside just to cool down!"

Sebastian checked his watch; I wasn't sure if it was performative or if he was really concerned about the time. "Speaking of, we should be going. Issac, thanks for talking with me. I'm sorry if I lashed out," Sebastian offered his hand to Issac, who accepted it and shook it.

"I really am sorry I can't give you more information than that. We all loved Prudie, and we won't rest until we get to the bottom of this," Issac said, and I believed him.

BACK IN THE CAR, Sebastian was quiet; we drove in silence for a while.

"Are you alright?" I asked, hoping I didn't do something that upset him. I had to admit to myself it was impulsive and could likely get me into serious trouble if I got caught. But I needed more information. It's just how my brain worked. And now, knowing Willowhaven was doing their own investigation, I feared red tape would tie things up.

"I just…" he sighed. "There's a part of me that doesn't want to know something bad happened to her," he said. "I don't think I can bring myself to see whatever is in her file. Not right now, anyway."

I squeezed his hand. "You don't have to look at anything if you don't want to," I said. While I knew Detective Fox would make sure this is solved, I had a feeling those wheels of justice would turn as slow as molasses in January, especially if they had to rely on Willowhaven. They're still a business, and I'm sure they didn't want to risk word getting out about this. Prudie deserved to rest in peace. Sebastian deserved to know who did this, and to see them held accountable. *And I don't want to be the center of the rumor mill.*

Back at home, I was too exhausted to even think about anything besides bed. As soon as my head hit the pillow I was sawing logs and didn't wake up until morning.

Chapter Ten

SUNDAY ROLLED AROUND AND I HAD NEVER BEEN SO THANKFUL for a day off in my life. While I'd hoped to sleep in, I was up bright and early—well, as bright as it gets on an early December morning. I shoved my feet into my slippers, smiling at the happy little red pandas staring up at me, and shuffled to the kitchen for some much needed coffee. Rather than mess with the single-serve pods today, I pulled out the multi-cup coffee maker; I had a feeling I was going to need it.

While the coffee was brewing, I grabbed my laptop from my room along with my notebook. As anxious as I was to jump right in, my stomach growled and demanded food. A few pieces of cinnamon-sugar toast seemed to tame the beast within. I popped the last bit of toast into my mouth, brushing the cinnamon and sugar from my hands just as the coffee was ready. I settled at the table, steaming mug of coffee in hand, and waited for the laptop to wake up; I would definitely need the larger screen to see the details on these photos. Once I transferred them over, I opened the first image. The form came up, and I sighed in relief that most of the important bits were in focus or hadn't been cut off.

It was on Willowhaven letterhead and appeared to be documenting the incident with Prudie. The letter described how she was found:

> ...one of the nurses making her rounds noticed the resident's door was partially open, then noticed a man on the floor. After checking his vitals, she checked the resident's and determined there was no pulse. The nurse verified using different pulse points as well as the monitor which had been in place as the resident was recovering from illness. Once confirmed, the nurse noted the date and time of her findings and then proceeded to follow normal protocol.

I shivered; the words on the page reduced Prudie Shaw's death to a mere clinical procedure. It was interesting though, learning how she was discovered. The letter went on to outline how the police were notified and that Willowhaven would be operating in full cooperation with law enforcement, as well as conducting their own investigation.

In my notebook I jotted down a few notes about the nurse finding both Neil and Prudie, along with the official date and time she was declared deceased. I moved on to the next photo, which was slightly off center. This form detailed all of Prudie's medications and dosages, as of her last visit with the physician. My eyes scanned the list for anything that stood out, though I didn't really know what these medications were. The form was dated about a week before her death; the physician did note her heart rate and blood pressure were a bit low, and that Prudie mentioned feeling fatigued. His examination determined she had early stages of pneumonia and prescribed fluids, rest, and an antibiotic. I added some of this to my notes. An hour and a half had gone by and I felt like I didn't have much more information than I did when I started. I had a few more photos to sort through, but I needed a break and a shower.

Feeling refreshed, I plopped down on the couch, unsure what to do with myself. I sent Tess a message asking if she was busy and if she'd want to come over; I could use her as a sounding board. She agreed, and within the hour she was nestled on my couch, one of my fluffy blankets draped around her shoulders and mug of hot cocoa on the table.

"You want a peppermint stick?" I asked from the kitchen.

"Who keeps peppermint sticks on hand?" she teased, knowing full well when it came to holiday treats I was well-stocked.

"Uh, I think you know better than to ask that."

"Yeah, sure, why not," she finally agreed. She was reading through my notebook when I came back into the room. "Is this everything you've found so far?"

"Nope. I have several more photos to go through…" I trailed off as I retrieved my laptop from the kitchen.

She looked at the screen, then looked back at me; she looked bewildered. "Do I want to know where you got these?" she asked, pointing at the screen with the peppermint stick.

"Probably not…but since you asked, Sebastian and I stopped by Willowhaven; he wanted to talk with Issac or Celeste about something that came back from the autopsy findings."

"Suspicious things? Because that letter from Willowhaven made it sound like they aren't handling this like a routine death."

I nodded my head in agreement.

"I am guessing Issac or Celeste didn't just give these to you…" Tess narrowed her eyes at me.

"Issac stepped out of his office to take a phone call; while he was gone I took as many photos as I could of everything in Prudie's folder."

"Impressive," she said, and I wasn't sure if that was a touch of sarcasm or awe in her voice.

We were quiet for a while as Tess looked through the images, making a few notes here and there. She sat back after reaching the last one, and shook her head. "None of this makes any sense."

"Did you see something? I haven't made it through all of them."

"I don't really know what to make of it, but it seems odd that they'd give Prudie a sedative if she was already experiencing low heart rate. I remember when my granddad potentially needed surgery, the doctors were concerned about giving him any anesthesia because his heart wasn't in the greatest shape. He might not have come out of it," Tess explained.

"Issac mentioned no one on her care team who could authorize new medications did," I recalled. "And I didn't see anything noted in her chart, did you?"

Tess shook her head. "No, nothing." She bit her thumbnail as she thought.

I studied the list of suspects from the other night; at the time they didn't seem like suspects, but now…I wasn't even sure where to start.

"Let's start with who had access to Prudie, either as Willowhaven staff, or visitors," Tess suggested.

"Issac and Celeste obviously have access to her, but I can't see either of them doing something so horrible. I mean, pretty much anyone at Willowhaven could be a suspect," I groaned.

"When did Prudie start feeling sick? I think it was in her chart," Tess flipped back to my notes about the medical exam from the physician. "She was already complaining of not feeling well at least a week before she died."

I nodded slowly, the realization setting in that we were dealing with some serious foul play.

"I wonder…"

"I don't know if I want to hear your next words," Tess said.

"When do you go back to restock the book cart?" I asked.

"Not until after Christmas, why?"

I thought about this for a minute, wondering how to make this work in our favor. Christmas was still several days away, and that seemed like too long to wait. I nibbled on my bottom lip as I tried to think of other ways. I could pretend like I was delivering an order for staff...I'd done it in the past, but that was before people were suspicious of my baked goods.

"Earth to Kendall..." Tess waved her hand in front of my face.

"Sorry. I was just trying to think of an excuse to visit Willowhaven. For research purposes. I don't think it'd look good if I just waltzed in with a tray of muffins or cookies when there are already rumors spreading." I stood to pace the room when my phone chimed with a new text message from Sebastian, asking if he could call. I loved it when people asked before calling me; it took some of the anxiety out of the whole experience. I made it easier on him and called him.

"Hey there, what's up?"

"I didn't mean for you to call me, but thanks. I wanted to let you know sooner, but things have been so hectic. Grams's funeral will be on Monday afternoon, at the chapel behind Willowhaven. I realize that's tomorrow, but..." The sadness in Sebastian's voice was heavy, and I wanted to reach through the phone to hug him.

"No worries, I'll make sure to let Tess and Cayden know. Are you doing alright?"

"As well as can be expected, I guess."

We talked a bit more and he apologized for not asking me to make anything for the reception after the funeral, but considering the circumstances, he thought it would be less awkward for everyone if he just had Willowhaven take care of things. I was actually thankful for that. We ended the call, and I informed Tess of the arrangements before texting Cayden.

"Poor Seb, I can't believe he had to deal with all of that on his own."

One thing about being best friends with someone for a majority of your life was something like a sixth-sense that developed over the years. I was quiet for too long, and Tess groaned.

"What are you planning?"

"I'm just saying, we'll already be there. Everyone will be distracted with the funeral activities." I explained my idea to Tess, though I admitted it wasn't fully formed.

"What exactly are you hoping to find? It's not like you have free reign of the building. You still have to go through security." The pitch of Tess's voice rose, and I could tell she was growing frustrated with me.

"I know, I just...I can't sit around and do nothing. It will give me a chance to people-watch; you know, see how they react. Someone has to know something! And I can ask some questions... get an idea of the people who came to pay their respects. It works for Jessica Fletcher," I said, realizing how silly that sounded.

Tess sighed and shook her head. "Jessica Fletcher always seemed to conveniently come across dead bodies before she started investigating."

"You don't even have to be a part of this," I offered. "I'm not trying to rope you into anything. I just want to try to get some answers."

"I am going to pretend I don't know anything if anyone asks what you're up to..." Tess said, sounding resigned to the fact that I would do this whether I had her approval or not. "Besides, who else would bail you out of jail for meddling."

Chapter Eleven

T ESS AND I DECIDED WE NEEDED SOME FRESH AIR SO I SUGGESTED we stop by her place so she could grab whatever she'd need while staying with me. I figured there was no sense in waiting until they actually started work on the plumbing.

Tess lived a few blocks over from Sebastian's neighborhood. In the '90s they remodeled several of the large Victorian-style homes, turning them into duplexes. Most of them still retained their Victorian charm, with elaborate woodwork and colorful exteriors. The house Tess lived in was a tasteful shade somewhere between blue and gray with a berry-colored door to match the accents; the trim was a soft white and contrasted nicely. It was sandwiched between two buildings with a more muted color scheme; I always thought that was the perfect representation of Tess: a woman who stands out on her own in a world of beige and tan. We parked in front of her house, closest to the door. Her unit, thankfully, was on the lower level which made it easy to tote things to the car.

"Holy beans, how much cat stuff are you bringing?" I teased Tess. So far I'd carried an automatic water dispenser, a food dispenser, two cat beds, and one small carry-on sized duffel bag of assorted toys and treats. Tess followed behind me with a cat tree.

"I just want to make sure he has enough familiar stuff so he doesn't wind up destroying everything in sight," she said with a shrug.

"When you put it that way, let's bring everything you have."

Tess made one last trip inside, this time grabbing her own things; I gawked at her when she emerged carrying one small suitcase.

"That's it?"

"It's not like I'll be there very long," she said, as if we hadn't just moved every single possession her cat owned into the car. "Let me just tell my neighbor where I'll be; be right back!" Tess scampered off to climb the stairs to her neighbor's house, and after a few minutes of chit-chat she scampered back down, ready to go.

"Did you remember to actually bring Mittens McGee with you?" I asked, certain I hadn't seen a cat carrier. No sooner than the words left my mouth we were treated to the most ear-piercing yowl I'd ever witnessed. "Guess that answers that question."

"Hush, McGee. You're fine. You're going on an adventure!" Tess said in a sing-song voice to her cat. Tess leaned closer to me and said in a low voice, "I have to say it like that, otherwise he thinks we're going to the V-E-T." She whispered the letters and I just shook my head.

"Well I certainly don't want him to mistake my apartment for the v—"

"V-E-T," Tess interrupted me. "Trust me, you don't want to know what happens when he hears that word." The look on Tess's face made me realize she was right; I didn't want to know.

BACK AT MY APARTMENT, we settled McGee into his new surroundings which seemed to be going better than I anticipated.

Tess stopped in the doorway and stared; McGee was in my lap and purring as loud as the engine in my Beetle.

"Have I been replaced so soon?" she asked.

"Nah, he's only up here because I bribed him." I scratched behind the feline's ear and was rewarded with a contented sigh. It had been ages since I had a pet in the house and I think I was looking forward to this four-legged friendship.

"Sometimes you gotta do whatever it takes. Are you hungry? Because I'm starving after all that." I agreed, and we decided on pizza. She put me in charge of finding a movie to watch and gathering drinks, which unfortunately meant disturbing the cat sleeping on my lap. McGee hopped down, turned his yellow eyes to me with a look I could only describe as disdainful, then disappeared down the hallway.

"So much for that bribe," I mumbled.

I was in the mood for something funny so I settled on Christmas Vacation. Yes, I'd watched it a couple times already, but it was a sure thing to lift my mood and make me laugh. And honestly, who couldn't relate to the feeling of wanting to host a good old fashioned family Christmas only for it to go horribly wrong?

"I knew you'd pick that one," Tess said with a laugh. I handed her a bottle of Aunt Edna's Christmas Sweater—the latest seasonal offering from our local brewery—and it felt like a perfect evening with my best friend. Once the pizza arrived, I hit play on the movie, and we settled in for some laughs.

Once the movie finished, I went downstairs and began preparing some basic offerings for the morning; I planned to close early to attend Prudie's funeral. While I worked, I thought back over the things Tess and I uncovered earlier in the day. It was looking more and more like someone killed Prudie, but why? She was well-loved in the community and I never heard anyone utter an unkind thing about her.

"Oh, Prudie," I whispered, "what secrets did you take with you?"

Chapter Twelve

THE DAY LOOKED FITTING FOR A FUNERAL. STARING OUT THE FRONT window as I drank my coffee, I wondered if we'd get rain or snow. We'd had several days of cold temperatures, but a front moved through and threatened rain. I hoped for Sebastian's sake we'd have snow today; somehow that seemed less somber than rain. I taped the sign to the front door announcing our early closure and my thoughts drifted to how he was handling everything; Sebastian didn't have much in the way of family, and I couldn't decide if that would make things easier for him. At least he had his friends.

It was a slow morning; not many customers came in, and those who did weren't very chatty. It was just as well, I wasn't really in the mood for it. I managed to sell out of the scones I'd made, however, so at least it wasn't a complete waste of time. Tess hadn't bothered opening the bookstore, but came down to check inventory and keep me company. Shortly before closing she ran across the street to pick up lunch for us; I wasn't really hungry, but figured I should try to eat something rather than relying on my morning coffee to keep me going. Finally one o'clock rolled around; I made sure the Closed sign was up, flipped the lights off and the door was locked.

I SIFTED through my closet trying to find something suitable to wear. While black was a staple in my wardrobe, it was mostly limited to t-shirts or other novelty shirts that definitely didn't seem appropriate. Oh, I'm sure Prudie wouldn't have minded; she almost certainly would let out one of her booming laughs that immediately made you want to join in, even if you had no idea what she was laughing about. She'd shake her head and smile, saying something like, "If you'd shown up in anything else, I'd have wondered if you'd been body-snatched." I shoved a few shirts aside, settling on a long-sleeved black dress with silver flecks that I paired with tights and black boots. The tights were purple, a nod to Prudie's favorite color.

I was just giving myself one last look in the mirror when my phone chimed with a new text message: Tess was on her way to pick me up as promised; since she'd been staying with me and had a limited wardrobe, she needed to stop by her house to find something suitable to wear. I grabbed my bag and coat and made my way down to the backdoor of the bakery to wait for Tess, who pulled up and beeped her horn, letting me know she'd arrived; I locked the door behind me and climbed into her passenger seat.

"I didn't know if you wanted the butt warmer on yet, so I didn't preheat your seat."

I was grateful for a heatless seat for the moment. "As much as I like the idea, I think I'd spontaneously combust right now," I laughed.

The non-denominational chapel was in the back of the Willowhaven property, which explains why I never realized it was there. Sebastian explained it was built to give residents a chance to pay their respects without having to travel; some families used this as an affordable alternative to a regular funeral service, but Prudie actually requested any services be held here. Sebastian asked several times if she was sure, reassuring her she had the means, but she insisted on Willowhaven.

We parked at the entrance closest to the chapel. It was an octagonal building with beautiful stained glass windows that took up about two thirds of each wall, each scene featured abstract arrangements of colors that seemed to evoke feelings of calm and peace. Inside, there was a short hallway from the entryway to the chapel doors lined with floral arrangements and other memorials from folks in the community; it looked like a jungle started to sprout from the floor. Gorgeous wreaths and huge bouquets of white and purple flowers were tucked in every available space it seemed. I spotted the planter of purple irises Tess, Cayden, and I ordered.

I knew we were early; there weren't a lot of cars in the parking lot and I didn't see a lot of people milling around, mostly staff members signing the guest book or looking over the photos that Sebastian and some of the residents provided. I was not looking forward to seeing those photos because I knew I'd be a sobbing mess...good thing I wore the waterproof mascara today and restocked the package of tissues in my bag. If crying was a superpower, I'd be the most powerful woman in the world.

"Should we try to find Sebastian and see if there's anything else we can do to help?" Tess nudged me from my thoughts.

"That's a good idea. Though if he's in the middle of talking with people, I don't want to bother him." I didn't see him as my eyes moved around the room. *And I can get a look at who's here already.* Given Tess's reaction when I suggested we could people watch, I did not voice this thought out loud.

Sebastian was seated with a small group of people talking in low voices with the occasional laugh sneaking out. I know people felt there was a certain sense of reverence to be maintained at a funeral, but Prudie would have wanted people to laugh and cry as they felt moved to. He glanced up and his gaze locked onto mine, a smile forming. I offered a slight wave, not wanting to pull his attention from the group he was visiting with. I didn't need to worry, though, because he excused himself before walking to Tess and me. He greeted me with a hug and a kiss on the cheek. Tess stepped toward him for an awkward side-hug.

"Sorry, we didn't mean to interrupt." I nodded toward the group he'd just left.

"No, it's fine. We were just catching up. They were neighbors of Grams's before she moved to Willowhaven. I hadn't seen some of them for a few years so it was nice to talk a bit."

"We just wanted to see if there was anything else that needed to be done, but it looks like everything's been taken care of," Tess observed.

"Yeah, the chapel staff—which I didn't even know was a thing —has done an amazing job with everything." Sebastian said with a relieved sigh.

"Oh, Cayden apologizes for not being able to make it, but wanted you to know they were thinking of you." I relayed the text I'd received last night from Cayden; a family emergency meant a trip to the city to sit with their brother at the hospital. An adventurous niece decided to leap from playground equipment, resulting in a severely broken arm requiring surgery.

We talked a bit longer until an official looking woman approached. Her face was soft and welcoming, and her voice matched her appearance. She wore a sensible pantsuit in blue so dark it appeared black, which contrasted nicely with her silver cropped hair. She looked to be in her late fifties. "Sebastian, sorry to interrupt. I just wanted to let you know that we'll begin in about 15 minutes." She patted him on the arm before walking away.

"Grams used to babysit for her," he chuckled. "It just seemed appropriate to have Sarah officiate."

"I guess we should find our seats," I said looking around the room realizing it had filled in quite a bit since we'd been talking. I surveyed the faces, a mix of sadness and grief, but no one seemed out of place. Turning my head back toward the front, I saw Neil sitting near the back. His head still sported a bandage, and he had some impressive bruising around his eye. He nodded in acknowledgement but quickly looked away.

"Please, sit with me." Sebastian all but pulled us with him as he picked up his suit jacket that had been draped across some chairs. We took our places—Tess first, then me, and Sebastian on the end —and waited for Sarah to begin. There was a slight commotion toward the back of the chapel as a late-comer tried to find a seat near the front. *Should have gotten here sooner, buddy.*

"Friends, on behalf of the Shaw family, I would like to say welcome and thank you for coming to this celebration of an extraordinary woman, Prudie Shaw," Sarah began. Her words were measured, her voice calm. Prudie wasn't what I'd consider religious, but she was a woman of faith and aspects of that were present in Sarah's eulogy. Messages of love and kindness, of generosity, of friendship. She invited Sebastian to say a few words, and he did so, eloquently.

"Thank you all for coming to help celebrate the life of my grandmother. She had a special way of touching peoples' lives, and even if you only met her once for a few minutes, she would make you feel like you'd been friends for years. I don't think Grams truly knew a stranger." The sound of a sharp cough echoed through the chapel, cutting Sebastian off. I swiveled in my seat; my eyes landed on the man who arrived late, his face hard, lips pursed as if he'd just eaten a lemon.

Sebastian continued. "She was the most generous person in my life, and I will forever be grateful to her for all the life lessons she taught me. Even the ones that didn't make a lick of sense at the time." A few sniffles and quiet rumbles of laughter scattered across the audience and Sebastian smiled at the sound. "She would rather have us laughing about good memories than crying, so let's honor her wishes: remember the good times, learn from the bad. And never leave the house without clean underwear because you never know when you'll be in an accident." Sebastian returned to his seat as the crowd responded with laughter, and his hand found mine. I squeezed it before leaning into him and whispering how proud I was of him.

Sarah welcomed anyone who wanted to share any memories about Prudie to do so before closing out the celebration. Neighbors spoke of Prudie's ability to sense when people needed a helping hand, and how she always seemed to know the perfect things to say and when to say them. The residents were having a rough time keeping themselves composed and opted to have Issac relay their message. When I turned to watch Issac approach the lectern, I noticed Neil was gone.

"Prudie was a beloved friend to the residents and staff alike here at Willowhaven, and though she will be with us all in spirit—likely keeping a watchful eye on us so we don't cause too much trouble—we will miss her physical presence greatly. She was joy personified." As Issac walked back toward the group, I noticed Barbara and Elenore wiping tears from their faces, but smiling all the same. The tender moment was punctuated by a loud *hhooonnk* as Ernest blew his nose into his handkerchief. Sarah closed out the memorial by reading the lyrics from Prudie's favorite Beatles song, 'In My Life.' I had to tune out most of this part because I knew I'd be ugly-crying within minutes.

Guests started drifting out into the hall where a few tables were set up with the cookies and some other refreshments. Hugs, tears, and laughter echoed through the chapel, and I knew that's exactly what Prudie would have wanted. Trying not to look like I was in a rush, I excused myself as needing to use the restroom; in reality, I was putting my plan into action. When Tess heard me, she gave me a look that I interpreted as "be careful, you're my best friend," but was more likely, "remember who has to bail your butt out if you get in trouble."

I grabbed some water from the refreshments table and made my way around the hall, pretending to take great interest in the floral arrangements. I could sidle up close to people, overhear some conversation, and move on to the next. And hopefully gather some useful information.

The first group, the neighbors Sebastian had been talking with when we arrived, were chatting about Prudie's legendary canasta games. Apparently she was quite the card shark. I moved to admire the wreath of yellow and white roses near another group of folks chatting away; their conversation didn't seem to relate to Prudie, but at least I was up to date on the status of their colonoscopy results.

A small group of five were huddled by a very large peace lily; I tried to artfully hide behind the plant, casually inspecting the leaves. I was thankful most of the people so far had been from out of town and didn't recognize me from the bakery; I didn't know how long that luck would hold out. One of the five mentioned the plant, and in unison they turned to look at it. I was startled to find all eyes were on me, and almost knocked the stand over. Bits of dirt spilled onto the carpet, and I tried to brush them away with my foot.

"Beautiful peace lily," I said, turning my attention back to a leaf that looked a bit wilted. "Been a while since I've seen one this nice."

"It's browning already," a nasally-sounding woman said. "We paid good money for that plant, and it's already wilting and brown."

"Ah, so it is. I didn't see that side of it. What a shame," I tut-tutted as I slowly wandered away, hoping no one witnessed the exchange. I turned my head to glance back, the group resumed talking as if I hadn't even been there. I exhaled, turned around, and ran into a large man. *I really need to stop doing that.*

"So sorry, miss…" the man said, pausing as though waiting for me to introduce myself; I realized then it was the man who arrived late. He looked at me expectantly, waiting for my name. His eyes were a similar shade of green as Sebastian's, but more squinty. His hair was wavy, and a mousy color. Come to think of it, his facial features when taken in all at once were quite rodent-like.

"Uh, Howard. Miss Howard. And I don't believe I know your name," I said, fishing for information.

"Just call me Jay." The man said with a smile, but it didn't reach his eyes. He offered his hand to shake, and I reluctantly accepted it. It was rough and calloused, like wrinkled sandpaper.

"Are you from out of town? Did you know Prudie well?" I asked, trying to make the most of this awkward meeting.

"As a matter of fact, I am. I drove in from Cincinnati," he said. "I knew of Prudie; I think I was too young to get to know her well. I hope I didn't disrupt the service too much with my late arrival, traffic was a killer." His smile was creepy and I wanted out of this conversation as soon as humanly possible.

I felt a hand on my lower back and yelped. Sebastian wrapped his arm around my waist to steady me. "Hey, it's just me. I wondered where you ran off to." He smiled and my unease started to fade. Until the strange man—Jay—decided to speak again.

"Ah, Sebastian. You're Prudie's grandson?" Jay asked, offering Sebastian his hand, just as he had with me.

Sebastian, clearly unsure how this man knew who he was, shook his hand. He nodded, thanked the man for coming, and ushered me away before the conversation grew any more awkward.

"Who was that?" I hissed.

"I have no idea, I've never seen him before in my life."

"How did he know your name?" I asked, but realized that was a dumb question, since the obituary mentioned it, and the officiant introduced Sebastian during the memorial service. "Why would a stranger show up to a funeral? This isn't some new, twisted form of wedding crashing, is it?"

Sebastian snorted a laugh, "I doubt it. Did he say who he was?"

"He said his name was Jay and he drove in from Cincinnati, and that he knew of Prudie," I replied.

"I think Grams lived in Cincinnati for a while when she was younger; probably the son of someone she knew."

Chapter Thirteen

I INVITED SEBASTIAN TO JOIN TESS AND I BACK AT MY APARTMENT for an early dinner and to unwind a bit. We ordered Chinese food before we left Willowhaven and picked it up on our way; Sebastian made sure nothing else was needed from him at the chapel before he stopped home to change into more casual clothes. The food was so fresh, Tess's car windows were steaming up. Right on cue, my stomach growled.

Once inside the apartment, I placed the takeout containers into the oven to help keep them warm while we changed clothes. I didn't actually know if it *did* keep it warm, but my brain thought it did and sometimes that's all that matters. Tess was getting the plates, glasses, and napkins out when I emerged from my room, back in my comfortable clothes.

"Nice footwear." Tess teased, looking at my red panda slippers.

"Hey, I've seen your slippers that look just like McGee, so I don't think you have any room to judge." Tess's slippers looked like they were exact replicas of her fur baby, and I wondered how confused it made the cat. There was clearly some kind of mutual respect there because Mittens McGee hadn't managed to destroy them…yet.

Sebastian let me know he was on his way and within minutes, the three of us were camped out on my couch with delicious lo mein and egg rolls. We decided we needed dumb humor tonight, so we settled on Dumb & Dumber, and took turns reciting lines from the movie.

"Sorry it took me a while to get over here; there was a message from the estate lawyer. He wants to finalize the estate before Christmas."

"I guess there's really no good time to do that," Tess said, wrinkling her nose.

"Probably just wants to wrap things up so you have one less thing to deal with," I suggested.

"Will you come with me, Kendall? It'll be tomorrow evening. I can pick you up." Sebastian smiled, and I found it impossible to say no.

"Of course," I replied.

"Not to change the subject, but you sure were gone a while when you went to the bathroom after the funeral," Tess gave me a pointed look.

"I uh…it must have been something I ate," I lied.

"Bathroom? You were hiding behind a plant when I found you," Sebastian said, confused.

Tess burst out laughing, and I hit her with a decorative pillow. "Oh, so this was your reconnaissance mission," she managed to say between catching her breath. Sebastian looked even more confused.

"I was just mingling, trying to see if I could gather anything interesting."

"From the plant?" Sebastian asked, which threw Tess into another fit of laughter.

"I wanted to see if anyone was acting suspicious," I said. "You know, like they attended out of guilt, or because they're a weirdo and wanted to be there."

"You listen to too many true crime podcasts," Sebastian said. He had a point. "So, did you find anything interesting?"

"There was that man named Jay; seemed weird to attend the funeral of someone you didn't really know," I said. "I did see Neil, still bandaged up. Whoever hit him must have really whacked him hard. He left early, before Issac spoke."

"Who's Jay?" Tess asked.

I explained how I literally bumped into him after the funeral. "He didn't say much, but he just seemed...creepy." I turned to Sebastian, trying to figure out a tactful way to ask my question. "You mentioned Prudie lived in Cincinnati growing up...do you know much about that time in her life?"

Sebastian looked puzzled. "Grams didn't talk much about her childhood. My mom said she had a hard life, but never explained what that meant. I always figured her father wasn't the nicest man. I never met him; he died several years before I was born. He never looked happy in photos," he recalled. "Why do you ask?"

"That man—Jay—said he was from Cincinnati. When I asked how he knew Prudie, he said he only knew of her through family."

"It could have been someone she used to babysit," Sebastian said. "A few folks I talked to were kids who grew up under her care."

We were all quiet for a few seconds before Tess said, "We looked at those documents she snapped pictures of," she stopped, uncertain if she should continue. "We can talk about something else, this doesn't feel like the right time." I hadn't mentioned to her Sebastian's reluctance to look at the information, and I cringed.

"It doesn't, but I don't know if there ever will be a right time." Sebastian flipped open my notebook on the table, and drew in a breath as he read the latest notes we added yesterday. "You really think she was murdered?" His voice was quiet as he asked the question.

"Nothing else makes sense to me." I said, trying to keep myself from launching into a litany of theories or suspicions. *Maybe I did need more wholesome hobbies.*

"This is nuts. Who…who would even want to hurt Grams?" Sebastian asked.

I gathered the dishes and began to rinse them in the sink; I wanted to give Sebastian a chance to let things soak in—though I didn't think this was the kind of thing you could easily absorb. When I came back into the room, Sebastian was looking through the photos I'd taken at Willowhaven.

"So the physician said she had pneumonia. Were other residents sick, too?"

"I remember Celeste mentioning that a couple other residents weren't feeling well around that time," Tess confirmed.

He nodded slowly, mulling something over. "So it could have really been pneumonia…but the other residents are fine; no one else got worse, right?"

"I'm not sure; I was so worried about Prudie being well enough to enjoy the pie social I didn't think to ask who else had been sick, though I'm not sure she would have told me." I was sure that would have been some violation of patient privacy…but the other residents might be willing to share.

We continued discussing theories late into the night. I had no idea what time it was, but I woke up in the darkened living room with a blanket draped over me. Sebastian was gone, and Tess must have gone back to her room. I wondered how long I'd been asleep and hoped I didn't spoil anyone's evening. Or snore too loudly. I stretched a bit before shuffling to my room to go back to sleep.

Chapter Fourteen

It was December 15th and the bakery was swarming with customers. There had been an update published in the Millwood Courier that officially cleared me of any suspicion, and I was looking forward to getting at least that aspect of my life back to normal. Did that account for the uptick in customers, I wondered?

Linda (cinnamon chip scone, coffee with sugar) came in to pick up a pie she ordered at the last minute.

"Hi Kendall. How are things going?" I recalled that Linda was often the origin of information that made its way through Millwood; was she here to see if I had bounced back from the rumors?

"Good morning, Linda. Here to pick up your pie order?" I smiled brightly.

"Figured you'd like to get it out of your hair. I'll just take a coffee today, too." She was practically vibrating already, and I wasn't sure if it was in her best interest to have more coffee...not that I was one to judge.

"Perfect! I'll get that ready for you." I motioned for Cayden to follow me to the kitchen. "I sense there is something bubbling under the surface. Can you try to fish it out of her?"

Cayden nodded as they walked back to the counter to engage in the not-so-subtle art of being nosy. Business school didn't prepare me for how much of a busy-body I'd become when owning a shop in a small town; it reminded me of the beauty shop from Murder, She Wrote. Last month I overheard one customer discussing how she convinced her daughter-in-law to use a steam bath of garlic, pickle juice, and apple cider vinegar to induce labor.

It took a few minutes, but Cayden finally cracked the nut. Olivia hadn't been to work in several days claiming she was sick, and there were talks they might hire a temporary nurse in her absence.

"The bit about hiring temporary staff was new," I said, wondering how that might hinder getting to the bottom of Prudie's death.

The snow began falling in the early afternoon. By about two o'clock, there was a decent amount covering the sidewalks. I checked the weather app to see how much we were supposed to get; the predictions were anywhere from one to four inches.

As the day wore on, there were two things that I couldn't stop wondering: Did Olivia pick up the pneumonia that was being passed around Willowhaven? She wasn't at Prudie's funeral, but if she were still sick, that would be a reasonable explanation; apparently that's what everyone thought. And how was Jay connected to Prudie? If he'd said she was his babysitter, I could see attending the funeral...but only knowing "of someone" through family seemed odd. A couple hours before closing, I asked Cayden to cover the bakery while I retreated to the kitchen to do some thinking.

I grabbed ingredients from the pantry, thinking we all could use a good pick-me-up; what better way than Gran Lottie's famous chewy peanut bars. It was one of the first recipes she taught me to make on my own, after catching me licking the spoon one too many times. I'd also make up a batch of cookies to use for persuasion tactics. It had been a while since I stopped by Willowhaven and just maybe I could convince Issac to share some info if I made his favorite cookies.

What would you say about all this, Gran? I figured Gran would be pragmatic; not worrying about a thing unless you knew for certain you were responsible. I wish I inherited *that* trait from Gran. I cleaned up my mess—I never was a tidy baker, something Gran had always teased me about—and slid the pan of peanut chews in the fridge. I checked the time and realized I didn't have enough to make the cookies if I wanted to decompress a bit before Sebastian arrived; maybe I could convince him to bake with me if we got back early enough.

I poked my head into the bakery from the kitchen; foot traffic slowed with the increasing snow and I decided to close early, which meant I also had enough time for a nice soak in the tub—my second favorite place to do some thinking. Cayden locked up, and I headed straight for the bathtub. Tess made plans to meet her cousin Finnley in the city to finish Christmas shopping and would likely stay overnight, so I didn't have to worry about what time I'd be back.

I made the mistake of sitting down on the couch when I got upstairs. My eyes were beginning to grow heavy as gentle sounds of Christmas music drifted from my phone. Half an hour later, I was awakened by the sound of purring in my ear; I turned my head and was nose-to-nose with Mittens McGee. "Well, hello, sir."

McGee purred louder before his little paws went into biscuit-making action. "I never understood why they call it biscuit making...you don't knead biscuits," I mused. I felt for my phone on the table to check the time, though the waning light outside told me it was after four thirty already. Sighing, I scratched McGee between his ears, his eyes going to slits as the biscuit-making slowed.

"Ah, no; you are welcome to sleep but not on me—I need to get up!" McGee merely peered at me through one yellow eye. I picked him up and redeposited him in the puddle of blankets I left behind.

I looked forward to a good soak in the tub…and maybe a face mask. I fished one of the masks from my drawer—coffee infused with peppermint—while I waited for the tub to fill. Sinking into the deliciously hot water, I sighed happily as I unwrapped the face mask and arranged it on my face, leaning my head back and closing my eyes to relax. After a few minutes I heard the bathroom door creak open and peeked through one eye to see McGee sauntering into the bathroom. "Uh, this is a party of one, if you don't mind."

McGee hopped onto the toilet, which was right behind my head; if I leaned back far enough I could see he was watching intently. What happened next was instantaneous yet everything moved in slow motion: I felt a gentle paw-tap on my forehead, followed by an additional paw on the top of my head. Before I could move, there was white-and-black fur in my face, a *kersploosh* into the bathwater, and the warbling cries of one very unhappy feline. In my panic to hoist McGee up over the edge of the tub, I lost my grip on the tub and slid under the water, sputtering as it went up my nose and in my mouth. Managing to get my hand under Mittens McGee, I was able to lift him up out of the water while I tried to feel for the edge to pull myself to a seated position. Finally upright and with enough water out of my eyes, I could see enough to grab a towel in which I promptly wrapped McGee so he could start to dry. The look he alternated between me and the bathtub was one of pure disdain and distrust, as if he couldn't believe I would betray him in such a way. "Don't blame me, friend, you did this to yourself."

Once I was out of the tub and wrapped in my robe, I fished out my face mask and unplugged the drain; McGee stared in satisfaction, watching his mortal enemy swirl away. I glanced at the poor little dude still huddled in the towel and couldn't help but laugh. I scooped him up and sat him on the counter to make sure at least his ears were dried to avoid any infection. Before I could reach for the cotton swabs he jumped and made a run for it down the hallway.

After mostly-drying my hair, I dressed and made sure there were no puddles left on the bathroom floor. I had a lot of sensory quirks, but by far the worst was stepping in something wet when wearing socks. If there was ever a form of punishment that might get me to spill my deepest, darkest secrets, wet socks would definitely do it. I also made sure to follow McGee's trail to the bedroom to make sure his little wet paw prints were sopped up, though he ran so fast I'm not sure his feet touched the floor.

Satisfied that things were as in order as they could be I grabbed my notebook and threw it in my purse; I needed someone to bounce ideas off of, and as much as I love Tess and Cayden, they're often quick to agree with me. I want someone who isn't afraid to challenge my line of thinking, and Sebastian can see through my nonsense. As if summoned by my thoughts, my phone chirped with a message that he was on his way. *That man really is a keeper*, I could hear Gran Lottie saying in my head. *He sure is, Gran. He sure is.*

Chapter Fifteen

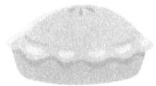

THE LAWYER'S OFFICE WAS IN A BUSINESS COMPLEX AT THE EDGE of town. In the main lobby, there was an intercom with a list of all the businesses in the building; Sebastian pressed a button and informed the voice on the other end he was here to finalize his grandmother's estate. I slipped my hand into his and squeezed lightly. We were met by a man wearing a dark gray three-piece suit who I could only presume was the lawyer.

"Mr. Shaw," the man said, extending his hand toward Sebastian. "Thank you for coming by. I apologize if it was short notice, but I wanted to make sure we had things settled before the holidays. One less thing for you to worry about," he said.

"Please, call me Sebastian." He shook the man's hand and then turned toward me. "This is Kendall Howard," Sebastian introduced me. Looking more closely at the man's face, I realized I'd served him in the bakery a few times. "Mr. Knox has been so helpful through all of this."

"Ah yes, you own the bakery in town. Delicious pies, my wife orders one every year for Thanksgiving." He smiled warmly, shaking my hand.

"Thank you, it's nice to meet you, Mr. Knox," I replied.

We were shown to a room that looked much fancier than any conference room I'd ever seen. There was a leather sofa and loveseat, leather armchairs, shelves of books lining the walls, an electric fireplace, and soothing warm light washing over everything. Mr. Knox motioned toward one of the sofas and told us to make ourselves comfortable. There was a cart with carafes of both cold and hot water, tea bags, slices of lemon, and a small plate of cookies—shortbread, it looked like.

"We'll get started in just a minute, I have a few additional copies to make." Mr. Knox left the room, leaving us alone.

"Wow, this is some room," I said, gawking at the solid oak fireplace, admiring how realistic the flames looked.

"He's a nice guy; I've done some computer work for him before. Grams was adamant he handle her affairs," Sebastian explained.

The lawyer returned to the room, a thick folder in one hand and a pad of paper and a couple pens in the other. He sat in one of the armchairs, glasses perched on his nose. "Normally this is all done behind the scenes and there's no need to meet, but your grandmother had a couple specific items listed in her will I just wanted to review with you.

"These first few documents don't require anything from you, they're more informational, acknowledging the will was filed and probate has started. Again, nothing for you to do." Mr. Knox flipped the pages over to the other side of the folder.

"This is a final copy of Prudie's will, as it was filed with the court." He handed Sebastian the copy to review. The document identified Sebastian as the sole beneficiary of her assets, which was not surprising. As far as I knew, the Shaw family consisted of Prudie and Sebastian; he was an only child, as was his mother.

"As we discussed the other day, the assets are held in a trust which you are free to draw on at any time. There are no restrictions on what those funds could be used for," Mr. Knox explained. Sebastian acknowledged this with a nod.

"Willowhaven provided me with an amended final bill, if you can sign here acknowledging the payment will be made from her trust, I can get that taken care of. Other than that, Prudie had no outstanding debts; as you well know her home was paid off, she had no credit cards. That's really all there is to it. Prudie made this extremely easy for everyone involved." Mr. Knox gathered the pages neatly and placed them back in the folder.

"Grams had a safety deposit box...what happens with that?" Sebastian asked.

"Ah, right. Typically, the bank will require a copy of the death certificate before they'll distribute the contents. Did Prudie leave you a key?"

"As far as I know, Grams only had one key for it and she kept it on a chain around her neck. I don't know if there was a spare." Sebastian shrugged.

Mr. Knox looked through the papers in his folder, frowning. He scrubbed his face in thought as he read through the paperwork a second time.

"I don't see a key listed in the inventory of her room," he replied. "Did anyone at Willowhaven mention it to you?"

Sebastian shook his head no. "No one from Willowhaven has given me any information on her personal items; I figured because of the investigation, they were holding those items." There was a hint of frustration in his voice, and I couldn't blame him.

"Maybe that's what Detective Fox called about; we've been playing phone-tag all day it seems. I will reach out to him first thing in the morning and be in touch."

We made idle conversation for a few minutes: Mr. Knox asking how the bakery was doing, Sebastian asking if Mr. Knox was having any more network issues throughout the office. I tried my best to keep my yawn contained but was embarrassingly unsuccessful.

"I think that's our cue to head out," Sebastian said, standing.

"Thank you again, Sebastian, for stopping over. Prudie was a remarkable woman and will be greatly missed. If you have any further questions, or need anything at all, please don't hesitate to call me." Mr. Knox stood to escort us out of the office.

"Seb, do you think…" I hesitated, not sure how to even word my question in a way that didn't make me sound like I needed a tin foil hat.

"Out with it…you're thinking about something, I can tell."

"Well, it's just the comment about that safety deposit box. You said Prudie had one key that you knew of, right? And she kept it on her?" I nibbled on my finger while I tried to fit the pieces together. "Do you think it's possible whoever was in her room took the key? I mean, they found one on Neil, right?" I recalled the officer holding it up for him to identify, and Neil saying he had no idea what it was. Was it an act?

Sebastian was silent as we climbed into the car. I could tell he was mulling this over by the way he pulled gently at his top lip; it was his concentration fidget I'd come to recognize. After a few minutes he sighed heavily. "I don't even know how Neil would have known about the key. Issac and Celeste knew, but that's it." He paused as something clicked for him.

"We were trying to talk Grams into not keeping anything too valuable in her room, and Olivia walked in. Grams had just finished explaining what was in that box and how much it was worth; I was surprised to see her come in because it was earlier than normal, but you mentioned she was taking earlier shifts?"

"Yeah. I heard her on the phone the other day saying something about it being weird to be there in the daytime," I said.

The snow started back up while we were inside with Mr. Knox, so the drive back to my apartment was slow-going. The alley was cleared, but the parking area looked like it needed some attention. Before climbing out of the car, I turned to look at Sebastian—really look at him. Sure, there was the zing of attraction as my eyes skimmed over his lips and the warmth of familiarity as I recalled how long we'd been friends. But most of all, there was the comfort of safety I couldn't remember feeling around anyone else. I felt like I could be my true self with him, and it made all the difference in the world.

Sebastian, realizing I was still sitting there, glanced my way; he smirked as he caught my gaze *and* blush, my reaction to turn away not fast enough. "Something on your mind?" he asked, amused by my flustered state.

"I…" I started to reply, but hesitated. Should I be honest with him? Hearing Gran Lottie's voice echoing through my head, I silently repeated the words to myself: *Peach, you only have this one life; don't hide away from those who care.* I swallowed before continuing, "I was just looking at you. And I was realizing how safe I feel with you." Before he could interrupt (and before I lost my resolve), I continued, "I feel like I can be myself around you and you won't judge me, or take advantage of my quirks." I used air quotes around the word; past partners had called them quirks, but had also exploited them sometimes. They knew how to push my buttons to get their way, and years of that made me feel broken. But with Sebastian…

Sebastian was quiet for a few minutes before he moved to open the car door. I felt a split second of panic—had I said the wrong thing? Was that too much, too soon? *Aw, hell,* I thought, *this is why I stick to sourdough and books.* I turned to face forward, and stared out the windshield contemplating my next move; I was startled by a tap on the window.

I unfastened my seatbelt and opened the door, realizing we were parked on an icy patch. Thankfully Sebastian parked close enough to the Beetle I could use it for support as well. I looked up into his green eyes and studied his expression…which was not easy when there was almost a foot height difference between us.

Shifting my feet to avoid the ice, I managed to find the ice anyway; I spun to grab the open car door. One foot slid left, the other slid back before bumping against the edge of the Beetle's running board; I swore as pain shot up my calf muscle. Sebastian's arm wrapped around me pulling me closer to him; I assumed it was to keep me from falling further, accident prone as I was. I opened my mouth to speak—apologize—but before I could utter a word, his mouth found mine. The kiss was gentle and soft, calming and exciting all at once.

I risked releasing my grip on the door frame as my hands found the back of his neck, pulling him closer. My fingers toyed with the short hairs on the back of his head. Forgetting we were standing over a precarious patch of ice, I rose to my tip toes and immediately regretted the decision: down I went with a squawk, my butt smacking those darned running boards before settling on the solid cold pavement. Sebastian somehow managed to stay relatively upright; he still held on to my hand, but it wasn't enough to rescue my bruised ego.

Scrabbling to move as far from the ice as I could, I crawled to my knees before hoisting myself up using the Beetle's ample fender. I patted Betty's rear quarter thankfully before turning my attention to Sebastian, who was trying to control his amusement; it was no use—as soon as I saw him wiping a tear from the corner of his eye, I was consumed in a fit of giggles.

Taking a few deep breaths to calm himself, Sebastian chuckled, "Well, that went as well as I could have hoped for an official first kiss." He winked, and I immediately felt my insides jiggle like one of those questionable desserts from Gran Lottie's vintage cookbooks.

"We'll just have to try that again…maybe when it's *not* icy. Or cold. Or in a parking lot." I shivered as I looked around, glaring at the ice. Another yawn escaped me, clouding the air with my breath.

Sebastian took a step toward me, chuckling before planting another kiss on my lips. "Time flies when you're having fun." He winked before turning to walk to his car.

Chapter Sixteen

FLOATING ON CLOUD NINE THE NEXT MORNING, I RISKED KNEADING the dough for the last batch of scones into oblivion. While details of Prudie's death took up a lot of space in my head, the kiss with Sebastian occupied my thoughts this morning. His soft lips. The way his strong arms held me as I…flailed and fell on my butt. I had to laugh—it was exactly what I'd wanted, and I couldn't imagine our first kiss being any other way.

The scones finally escaped my distracted abuse and I hoped they wouldn't end up too tough. After I popped them into the oven, I began work on a batch of hand pies and tarts.

"I see you're in good spirits this morning." Tess said, startling me, as she waited for the ancient relic that served as the point-of-sale computer to come to life.

"I swear you're as bad as your cat at sneaking up on people. I didn't even hear you come home."

"Speaking of my cat, is there a reason he sprints down the hall and avoids following me into the bathroom? Not that I'm complaining; for once I finally have a little privacy in there."

"Uh, yeah. About that…" I went on to explain McGee's adventure in the tub. "I tried to dry his ears but he darted away and hid in your room before I could." I grimaced.

"Well that explains why the rug in front of the bed was damp this morning," Tess said.

"I felt bad for him...I mean, it was hilarious, but I don't want him to be traumatized by it." I did feel a little bad for Mittens McGee.

"It's his own fault." Tess shrugged.

"That's exactly what *I* told him!"

"Now, back to this good mood you're in…" Tess tried to resume our previous conversation.

"Hmmm? Oh, that." I waved a hand in the air, dismissively. I busied myself with the coffee maker. "You want one?" I asked Tess, pointing to a mug.

"Nope, we're not avoiding it! You were smiling like a fool and you look like you've actually slept for the first time in days. Spill. It."

"Fine. If you *must* know…Seb and I kissed. And I fell down. And it was magical." The words rushed out of me and I grinned like a child who had bamboozled their parent into a second dessert.

"I knew it!" Tess cried with a triumphant fist pump.

The bell over the bakery door jingled announcing Cayden's presence; I lost track of time and noticed it was already time to open.

"Hey, y'all. What's shakin' this morning?" Cayden asked.

"Kendall was just telling me about her date with Sebastian… and their FIRST KISS!" Tess squealed at Cayden.

"First of all, it was not a date. We went to the lawyer's office to finalize Prudie's estate." I said.

"Geez, who knew estate planning was so hot," Cayden joked, as they grabbed an apron from the hook behind the counter, put some gloves on and began filling the display case. "How was it?"

"It was fine, I guess. As far as that kind of thing goes. More straight forward than Gran Lottie's, that's for sure."

Cayden interrupted me before I could finish her thought. "Uh, no, not the lawyer's office. The smooch. Was it good? Sloppy? He doesn't seem like he'd be a sloppy kisser..." Now they were just trying to get a rise out of me.

I narrowed my eyes at Cayden. "It was lovely. He was a perfect gentleman, his lips were very soft and warm. And before you ask, no tongue."

"That might have happened if you didn't fall on your butt, though." Tess said.

"You...fell...you know what, that doesn't surprise me. But, yay! I'm so glad you two finally came to your senses!" Cayden said.

"Not to change the subject, but Issac messaged me asking if I could drop off some books about grieving for their book cart, but I have a delivery coming in and I don't want to miss it," Tess called from her office. Again, she moved with cat-like speed I didn't even know she wasn't at the counter.

"If Cayden is willing to watch the bakery, I can drop them off for you," I volunteered. I was looking for an excuse to get back to Willowhaven; this would be a perfect reason.

We finished getting the display cases stocked and flipped the sign to Open. The roads were pretty clear and the sun was shining, so I was hoping for a good day. Gentle holiday music played through the overhead speakers, and warm cinnamon and brown sugar scented the air thanks to the apple-cinnamon tarts just coming out of the oven. They turned out to be my best seller this season, followed closely by the cranberry-orange scones. The pomegranate wasn't as popular, so I made a note for next year.

"Are these all the books you pulled?" I looked through the stack. Titles like "How To Process Your Grief," and "Coping With Loss" were mixed in with books about self-care and low-stress holidays. I loved that Tess treated her bookstore like a library; most of the books she added to the book cart were used, sometimes bought from the sales when the actual library would clear out the older or less popular books from their inventory.

"Yep. I let Issac know you'd be bringing them," Tess said.

After making sure Cayden had everything they needed, I loaded the books in the Beetle along with the little wagon Tess normally used to transport them, and set out for Willowhaven. I forgot about my bribery methods, and ran back in to fill a container with some of the peanut chews I made yesterday.

A different guard was at the security desk today, and after checking in and getting my visitor's badge (name spelled correctly this time), I wondered what kind of cookie he liked. He looked like an oatmeal raisin kind of guy; like he'd read the handbook and follow the rules to a T, only bending them for very rare occasions. I wondered how he'd respond to a baked good bribe.

Issac was sitting at the desk sorting through some paperwork as I approached.

"Hey, Issac! Tess said you needed some books for the cart," I said, nodding toward the wagon trailing behind me.

"Excellent, thank you!" He came around the desk and looked through the collection. "These will be perfect." His eyes landed on the container nestled next to a book titled "Live, Laugh, Love." Issac picked it up and opened the lid. "I thought that's what was in there," he said.

"It's been a rough few days, I thought it might cheer folks up," I said. "Go ahead and take some!"

Issac took a couple of the peanut bars from the container, setting them next to whatever he was working on. I tried to get a look, but couldn't see well enough from where I was standing.

"Well, I won't keep you. Looks like you're busy," I said, trying a new tactic.

He gestured as if shooing a bug away. "Just the schedule. We had to do some rearranging with O—" Issac stopped short. "We've had some absences."

Ah-ha! "Oh, hopefully it's nothing serious." I fidgeted with the cup of pens sitting on the counter, almost knocking them over.

"You are so terrible at this, Kendall." Issac shook his head. I touched my hand to my chest, as if to say 'who, me?'; I'm not sure I'd ever heard anyone guffaw before, but that's definitely how I would categorize the sound Issac made.

"I just saw the listing in the paper for temporary staffing. I didn't think anything of it, but someone mentioned it at the bakery this morning, not even ten minutes after I read it!"

"Gotta love the Millwood rumor mill," Issac muttered.

"Olivia didn't get sick with pneumonia, did she? I remembered her missing out on the pie social."

"I can't really say anything because of privacy laws, but finding some additional coverage was necessary."

What did that mean? Was she really sick, or did something else come up? I willed Issac to give me just a morsel of something more to go from.

I tried to think of a very tasty carrot to dangle in front of Issac, seeing if he'd take the bait. "I just hope she's alright, and can bounce back from whatever is going on. Oh, hey, do you still love monster cookies? I was going to do some recreational baking... thought I'd get everyone's favorites."

Issac stared blankly at me, the muscle in his cheek twitching. I thought for sure he'd tell me to kick rocks and send me on my way. Instead, he checked his watch, then pressed a button on the desk phone. "Hey Debbie? Can you come up front for a few minutes, it's time for my break. Thanks!" He gave me a look that was hard to read; something between 'I'm going to kill you for this,' and 'I can't *wait* to spill the tea!'

Debbie came up and we chatted a bit while Issac signed out of the terminal for his break. He motioned for me to join him outside in the courtyard, nestled in the middle of the main buildings of Willowhaven. Benches were scattered around for seating among decorative landscaping; large planters filled with seasonal greenery created an alcove-like feeling. It was cold outside, but I was buzzing with anticipation and I didn't notice much.

Issac took a deep breath before speaking. "I really shouldn't be saying anything about this, but with everything that's happened in the last few days…" he trailed off.

I nodded encouraging him to continue.

"Everything was normal, up until a few weeks ago. Olivia kept offering to cover shifts during the day, which wouldn't be a big deal but she always made such a production about how she preferred the night shift…and honestly, given her attitude and demeanor, it was best for everyone if she had minimal contact with the visitors."

"Did she do well during the day shifts?" I thought it'd be very difficult to change between two very different working schedules.

"For the most part, yeah. She lucked out because a lot of the residents had activities or therapy sessions scheduled during her shift, so they had minimal contact with her."

"I wonder if that's how she got sick," I said, assuming she really was sick. Issac hadn't confirmed this, and I wondered if he'd notice.

"Could be; she was around the residents who were diagnosed with pneumonia, so it would make sense. Hospitals and nursing facilities are hot beds for that kind of thing." *Ah, so she was sick!* At least that was one bit of information confirmed.

I tried to think back to the notebook, and any other things Issac might be able to help me with before he had to get back from his break.

"Maybe she could use some cookies or something to speed up the recovery," I said. As the words left my mouth, a plan started to form. "Her last name is Bench, right?"

"Birch." It was a single word answer, and I felt Issac's eyes on me. "She really was sick, you know," he said, as if trying to dissuade me. It wouldn't work so easily.

I smiled and nodded. "Maybe I'll just send her flowers instead." That seemed to satisfy him, though he still peered at me with skeptical blue eyes.

Issac returned to work while I stacked the books on the cart. I offered him another peanut chew before I left, which he greedily accepted. As I was wheeling the cart back to the reading corner, Debbie returned to her office through the staff-only doors. As they swung open, I caught sight of a nurse I didn't recognize, at least from this distance; their long blonde hair was tied back into a messy ponytail and her uniform seemed a little wrinkled. Maybe this was one of the temporary nurses Issac mentioned, but would they have an office? Just as the doors were closing, the nurse waved her badge and disappeared from sight.

Tugging the little wagon behind me, now empty of books, I walked toward the security desk to return my visitor badge and sign out. I was close to the break area for the rehabilitation nurses and my ears caught a few words that grabbed my attention. I slowed, trying to think of a way to hover just outside the room. Thankfully there weren't many people around, so I settled for the oldest trick in the book: tying my shoelaces.

I made sure I was out of the main pathway, angled the wagon just enough to obscure my movements—which probably made it more obvious—and knelt down to check my shoe. It was hard to maneuver around a bulky winter coat, so I unzipped it. My scarf dangled down, which I thought might help hide the fake shoe-tying.

"…he just got the bandages off…"

"…still doesn't know…"

"I wonder who…"

"I heard they think someone…"

Realizing I likely wouldn't get too much information this way, I started to stand. My foot shifted and I was yanked back down toward the floor; I was standing on my scarf. I heard footsteps approaching from behind, and tried to play it cool. I moved my foot again, making sure the scarf was out of the way, and as soon as I stood, I smacked into something. No, someone.

"Kendall?" A familiar voice said my name, and my cheeks warmed. Issac stood behind me, a hand on my shoulder to steady me from toppling over.

"Uh, hi! I was just on my way to return this and noticed my shoe was untied." I held up the badge. "Figured I'd take care of that before I..." *Tripped and fell? Caused an accident? Got caught eavesdropping?* Before I could finish my sentence, the nurses from the break area stepped out, startled to see someone.

"Oh!" A nurse with red hair yelped, her hand flying to her chest. "Uh, hi Issac," she said. She looked at me, confused.

"Sorry, just needed to tie my shoe," I said, wiggling my foot and rolling my eyes internally at myself. I wanted to ask about their conversation, but that would imply I was listening in. I needn't have worried, though; Neil came around the corner, whistling and reading over a list.

"Neil! We were just talking about you!" the red-headed nurse said. "How is your head feeling?" Her words sounded syrupy, dripping with concern.

"Oh, it's alright. A bit sore to the touch, but nothing a little ice and ibuprofen won't take care of." He gingerly tapped the side of his head; there was an epic bruise there, and I thought I saw faint stitch lines.

"Did you need stitches?" I asked before I could stop myself. All eyes turned to me at once while I floundered with how to make up for my awkwardness. "Uh, I saw you that night...when they were asking you questions. It looked like a pretty wicked bump."

"Pie Lady," he said, then apologized. "I'm sorry, I can't recall your name. Things have been kind of spotty for me since...well, you know." He lowered his head, sadness in his voice. I wondered if that meant he still didn't know much about what happened in Prudie's room that night.

"This is Kendall," Issac introduced me to everyone, who nodded in greeting. "She was just leaving. Weren't you?" He grabbed the handle of my little wagon, ushered me to the security desk to return my badge, then walked me to my car. *Drat him!*

"Hey! What's this all about?" I protested.

"Kendall, I've known you long enough to know you're up to something." He looked at me, and I wondered if he was expecting a response.

"I don't know what you mean," I said, trying to sound offended he'd hint at such a thing.

"Just…be careful. And stop eavesdropping on people."

I huffed in annoyance before I climbed into my car. I needed some time to think, so I called to let Tess and Cayden know I was making a pit stop at the grocery store.

Chapter Seventeen

THE GROCERY WAS JAMMED PACKED. I LUCKED OUT AND FOUND A parking spot close enough to the entrance that it didn't feel like an expedition. People were, for the most part, in good moods; it could have been the festive music drifting through the overhead speakers, but more likely it was because of all the free samples. Cheese of all kinds, fancy crackers with spreads, chocolate truffles…it may not have been a great idea to come here before lunch. Following the lead of those around me, though, I wandered station to station, collecting little toothpicks-full of yummy snacks.

Having just snatched an extra meatball when the store clerk turned to refill the sample tray, I was looking in the display case for the variety I just sampled. Instead of grabbing the bag, I grabbed an unknown hand by mistake.

"Ope! I'm so sorry!" I apologized as I yanked my hand back.

"No, it's fine! I—" the human attached to said hand started to speak, but stopped short. I glanced up to see what was wrong, and the human—a woman—looked startled to see me.

I couldn't figure out what startled her; she looked vaguely familiar, but it's likely just someone who came into the bakery a few times. I smiled at her before she turned and walked away.

Weird...I'm pretty sure I put deodorant on this morning. I tried to sniff inconspicuously, but it was no help. Shaking it off as just another strange encounter for the day, I grabbed my meatballs and a few extra items before heading to the registers.

The checkout line is where I always reevaluated my life choices...or in this case, my meatball needs. I only had a few items, so the cashier at the service counter offered to ring me up. I made sure I wasn't going to plow into anyone before moving to the new line, and as I turned my head my eyes met the woman from the freezer section. I smiled, she frowned; I was starting to take this personally. There were several lanes separating us, and after taking in her wrinkled uniform and the blonde tied-back hair, it dawned on me why she seemed familiar: the nurse at Willowhaven. Still, though, why was she acting so strangely?

I placed my items on the counter and greeting the clerk when I heard a commotion. People with raised voices saying "Hey," or "watch it!" along with the sound of carts dragging across the floor. The cashier looked around me and shook her head.

"I really hate it when people change their minds when it's this busy," she said with a sigh. "They never think about the perishable items in their carts after abandoning them. That will be $28.79," she said.

I turned just in time to see the blonde woman walking briskly out the door, the cart abandoned in the middle of the checkout line. I quickly scanned my card to pay for my groceries, grabbed my bags and high-tailed it out of the store. It was at this point I *should* have returned to City of Pies; what I actually did was drive around the parking lot until I spotted the woman pulling onto Main Street. I had no plan, and no idea where I was going. I thought about calling Tess, but what would I tell her? *I'm following a nurse who works at Willowhaven and I have no idea why?*

Keeping several car lengths between us—much more difficult than it looks in the movies, especially during holiday traffic—I followed the dark red compact car across town, ending up near an older apartment complex. This woman drove with purpose, barely stopping at the intersection and narrowly missing a man on a bicycle. Traffic had thinned greatly by now, so I had to keep even more of a gap between us. She pulled into the complex's parking lot; I didn't want to risk being seen, so I circled the perimeter trying to keep her in my sight.

The car came to a stop and backed under a carport. From my view, I couldn't really see much. My palms were sweaty as I waited for the woman to exit, but she never came out. I waited several minutes before giving up, keeping one eye on the carport and one eye on my notebook as I added a few notes from the day: *Who is the blonde nurse? Why did she leave the store after seeing me? Can we find out when she started at Willowhaven?*

I made a U-turn in the road and decided to head back to the bakery. I looked to the rearview mirror just in time to see someone exiting the carport, but the blonde woman never did.

<hr>

"You *WHAT?*" Tess and Cayden exclaimed in tandem.

"I don't see what the big deal is; how was it any different than taking a drive?" I asked, defensively.

On the way back to the bakery, I debated telling them about my adventure; not only was I certain they'd scold me (they did), I was positive they would think I was trying too hard to connect dots that weren't there. I suppose it was dumb to go alone, but it wasn't like I planned on confronting the woman.

"I was just curious where she went. She left the store in such a hurry; she left her cart in the middle of the checkout lane, and almost ran someone over at an intersection!"

"Which is probably why you shouldn't have followed her," Cayden said.

"Why did she seem worth following?" Tess asked.

"Tell me you wouldn't find it suspicious if, after making eye contact with a woman you've never met, they felt the need to flee. What was I supposed to think?"

But was that what really prompted me to follow her? I honestly couldn't say for sure. It was an instinct that felt like it'd eat me alive if I didn't listen to it.

"Something just felt...off," I shrugged. "It's not a great answer, but it's my answer. Anyway, Issac said thanks for the books. He also indirectly confirmed that Olivia is out on leave due to illness..."

"My, someone had a busy day," Tess teased.

"Neil's head is better too, though his memories are still spotty about the night Prudie died," I added.

"Anything else you want to share?" Cayden asked.

I pretended to give it some thought, tilting my head side to side as if rolling the idea around. "Nope, I think that's about it."

"Don't you think it's weird, though?" I asked as I wiped down the counters. The rest of the day went by in a flash, and closing time was right around the corner.

"Yeah, it is. But I still don't understand why you followed her." Tess's muffled voice called from her office.

"Her behavior just seemed off. I suppose with everything that's happened, I'm a little suspicious. Like, why did Olivia really take a leave of absence? I don't believe she's sick."

"Maybe Prudie's death was traumatic," Cayden offered.

"She wasn't there that night, remember? She called out sick."

"Oh, right. I even talked to Celeste about that; between the nurse who lost his badge and the missing stuff, she chalked it up to just another bit of chaos." Tess said.

Just as I was going to ask about the missing stuff, the bell above the door jingled.

"Welcome to City of Pies! I'm afraid we're just about to close for the day, so our selection is a little slim." I looked up to greet the customer and was surprised to see the man from Prudie's funeral...what did he say his name was? Jay?

"Oh, no problem. I'll just come back tomorrow morning." Jay turned to check our hours. "Guess I'll see you at seven," he said, his thin lips spreading into a grin. He left as quickly as he arrived, and a chill ran through me.

I briskly walked to the front door, flipped the sign to Closed, and locked the door.

"Was that the guy from Prudie's funeral?" Tess asked.

"Yeah. Can confirm, he's still creepy."

After sending Cayden home with the four remaining scones from the day, Tess and I double-checked the locks and went upstairs.

⬡

"WHAT DO YOU WANT FOR DINNER?" Tess called, head buried in the fridge.

"I don't even know what's in there. I did get stuff when I went to the grocery, but I was going to save that for our Christmas dinner." I replied. I'd been looking at recipes for the meatballs and found one that used a Korean barbecue glaze; as much as I loved a traditional Christmas meal of turkey and all the trimmings, I could not be trusted to roast the bird without it coming out like the one in Christmas Vacation.

"Wanna go grab something?"

I startled, not realizing Tess had removed herself from the fridge and was standing next to me. "Uh, sure. I really do need to put a bell around your neck. Even your cat isn't as stealthy as you."

"Sorry," she said. "Now come on, I'm starving."

I opted to drive, much to Tess's dismay; it was cold out and she wanted instant warmth. I needed to put gas in the Beetle and was the quickest to get to the car.

"Don't they make remote starts for these things?" Tess asked through chattering teeth.

"The car is older than I am, Tess. It's a manual transmission...how would that even work?"

"This is why I drive normal, modern cars."

The Beetle sputtered a bit, as if responding to the insult. "Watch it, she might get cranky," I joked. "So, where to?"

I pulled out of the parking lot behind the bakery; the streets were quiet even though it wasn't that late.

"What sounds good?" Tess asked.

"Oh no, we're not playing this game. Just pick a place; I'm fine with anything." Since I didn't have a destination yet, I drove to the gas station. A couple minutes later I was back in the car. willing the Beetle to warm up quickly. "So..." I asked, hoping Tess had something in mind.

"I want..." she trailed off, clearly torn between choices. I pulled away from the gas station and just started driving.

"Where are you going?"

"Nowhere until you pick someplace to eat," I said. She harrumphed in response to that.

I continued driving, no destination in mind. After several minutes I realized I was back in the neighborhood where I'd followed the blonde woman from the grocery store. I hesitated at the intersection before making a decision to pull into the complex parking lot.

I looped around the first building, identified as the management and leasing office, trying to remember how far back the red car drove before parking under the carport. There were three buildings altogether, and on a whim I turned at the second set of mailboxes.

"Where are..." Tess started to ask, then stopped. "Really?" she quirked an eyebrow at me.

"Betty brought us here, I'm just following her lead," I said motioning to the steering wheel.

"I suppose I deserve that," Tess sighed.

I remembered seeing the carport clearly from the road, so I figured it must have been further down the row. The last parking spot was approaching and I held my breath. It was empty.

"Rats!"

Tess craned her head around to look at the building. "You don't even know who that person was," she said. "What were you going to do, go door to door until you found her?"

Tess was right and I said as much. "OK, what's for dinner?" I asked. I pulled into the carport to turn around; as I turned my head to check behind me, something on the ground caught my eye. I put the car in park and climbed out to retrieve it, my eyes widening when I saw it. I grabbed it quickly and got back into the car, handing it to Tess.

"What's this?" she asked before looking at it. "Oh. OH!" she practically shouted. "I guess we have another pitstop to make," she said with a hint of disappointment.

"Yeah, but you might not like this idea…"

Chapter Eighteen

"WHAT ARE YOU DOING, KENDALL?" TESS WHISPERED.

"Just…hush. I'm just curious…"

"Yes, I know, that's what I'm afraid of." Tess sighed as I parked on the far side of Willowhaven, close to the courtyard where Issac and I chatted.

"It's too cold to be out here!"

"Well, with much luck, we won't be out here long," I said, holding up the badge. Tess groaned. Honestly, that was probably a fair reaction. I really had no idea what I was doing, and didn't even want to think about what would happen if I got caught.

"Are you really—" Tess was cut off by the sound of the badge unlocking the door. "Yep, you are."

Warmth from the building welcomed us, even though I was chilled to the bone. I felt badly for making Tess come with me.

"Why don't you wait in the hall; you can be my lookout. Text me if you see someone coming!" I turned the ringer off on my phone, and nodded toward the main hall. "Then you won't get yourself into trouble if I get caught."

Tess rolled her eyes, but nodded and started walking toward the hall. I turned to go the opposite direction. My goal was to stay as far away from the busier parts of the building as possible. I glanced at the arrows on the wall: right led to the rehabilitation unit, left led to the administrative offices. *Bingo!*

Walking at a normal pace, and trying to keep my shoes from making too much noise, I gripped my phone so tightly my knuckles were white. I could feel sweat beading up on the small of my back; now was not a good time for a hot flash to strike. I slowed when I approached a corner, barely breathing in an attempt to hear what might be ahead; I crept forward, peeking around the corner. I recognized a set of double doors just like the ones Issac brought Sebastian and I through the other night. There was a card reader on the door, the little light shining red. *Moment of truth, Kendall.*

I pulled the badge from my pocket and held my breath as I waved it in front of the card reader. At first, nothing happened and my shoulders dropped—partially in relief, partially in disappointment. I tried it again, this time repositioning the badge in my hand so it was fully facing the reader. The red light flickered before turning green, and the lock on the door released. I did a victorious fist pump before making sure no one was in the hall.

The coast was clear, for now, so I scurried through the doors as they slowly started to close. Once on the other side, I tried to remember how far down I saw the blonde nurse when she entered one of these rooms. My eyes darted from side to side, looking for both door plates and people; I hoped because it was late enough, there wouldn't be many people to encounter.

About half way down the hall, I noticed another room with a badge reader. There was a large window in the door and bright white light spilled out into the hall. Walls of automated shelving units lined two of the walls; the other wall featured refrigerated units and a counter with various scales, counting machines, and a computer.

I glanced at my phone and silently swore; I had no signal back here. If Tess tried to message me in warning, I wouldn't see it in time. I swallowed hard, took a deep breath, and placed the badge against the card reader. Once again, the little light flickered and turned green. I was in.

I stepped inside and looked around, searching for signs of life. No one seemed to be in here, and I exhaled. Just as the door was closing I thought I heard voices coming down the hall. This time I swore out loud. I rounded a row of tables in the middle of the room, not taking time to see what papers were there. I presumed they were request forms for medications, but I wasn't exactly sure how things worked here. Reaching the back of the room I heard a click by the door; I ducked back into the shadows, praying whoever it was couldn't see me.

Two nurses made a beeline for the computer on the counter. One scanned their badge and began typing a request, while the other waited for the automated shelving to rotate into the correct position. I felt very vulnerable in the position I was in and tried to push further into the shadows, but I was pinned against a filing cabinet. I crouched down feeling that making myself smaller would be beneficial, even though I'd lose my line of sight on the nurses. At this point I was sweating so heavily I didn't much care.

The nurses talked about their holiday plans while they worked; one complaining about the potential for more snow, the other complaining about having to take the train into the city to see her sister-in-law. Their conversation seemed mundane until I heard one of them mention Olivia's name.

"It has kind of been nice without Olivia around."

"That girl is so weird."

"And who was that new guy she was with?"

"Which one…"

My ears perked up at this, and I was hoping to get a little more information, but their voices started to fade as they made their way to the door. Right before they stepped through, a harsh vibrating sound echoed through the room. *No. No no no no…*

"Did you hear that?" One of the nurses stopped and turned to look into the room.

I squished myself against the wall as much as I could, realizing it was my phone vibrating against the filing cabinet, the denim of my jeans doing little to muffle the sound. It picked a wonderful time to pick up the signal. I heard footsteps into the room, stopping in the middle.

"One of the newbies probably left their phone in here again," the other nurse said. "I found one the other day. They had really bad taste in music." The sound of her laughter faded as the door clicked closed behind them. I breathed a heavy sigh and willed my hands to stop shaking before sliding my phone from my pocket.

> Nurses, headed down the admin hall! Not
> sure where you are!

I eased out from behind the cabinet, my scarf getting caught on one of the corners. As I untangled the fringe, I noticed there were strands of hair sticking out of one of the other cabinets. I quickly looked around for something to stick them in; since it was a pharmacy there was no shortage of gloves and bottles and plastic baggies. I secured the strands in a baggie and after making sure the coast was clear, I hastily escaped the pharmacy, down the admin hall, not slowing until I passed through the doors where I began this wild adventure.

"Where. Have. You. Been?" Tess hissed at me; if she kept this up she'd be a snake before Christmas.

"I was, uh, exploring," I said with a smile.

"Did you get my text?"

"I did, yes. Right as the two nurses were leaving the room where I was hiding. Would have been perfect, too, if the signal hadn't decided to pick that moment to reconnect while I was cozied up to a filing cabinet." I grinned.

Tess smacked her forehead and sighed. "Did they see you?"

"No, I think I was hidden well enough…they don't miss Olivia, though. And apparently she was seen with some new guy." I offered the tidbits I learned, though I admit it really wasn't much.

"I hope you felt it was worth it," Tess said in a tone that would have made Gran Lottie proud.

I patted the baggie in my coat pocket. "That remains to be seen, I think. Now, let's return this badge before I decide to do something even stupid."

"WHERE DID YOU FIND THIS?" Celeste asked.

I fidgeted with the fringe of my scarf; I didn't want to tell her the whole story…I'd sound like a weirdo.

"I saw it in a parking lot," I said. *Not a complete fib.*

She flipped the badge over in her hands, as though inspecting the front and back, shaking her head. "Well, Roberto will be glad to have this back. Was it in the gym parking lot?"

I had to stop myself from barking out a laugh…me? at the gym?

"Uh, no. I stopped for gas over near Forrest Avenue and saw it on the ground. At first I thought it was a piece of glass or something, it was hard to tell with the glare of the lights. When I noticed it was from Willowhaven…" I gestured to the badge in her hand. "I figured you'd like it back quickly."

Celeste paged Roberto to the nurses station; what would I say if he asked where it was? I didn't even know who the blonde woman was, but it couldn't have been a coincidence finding it in that carport.

"What's up, Celeste?" Roberto approached the station carrying a backpack and his coat. He was tall with broad shoulders, dark, wavy hair, and brown eyes. Thinking back to the blonde woman, maybe they were seeing each other; they both were attractive enough.

Celeste held up his badge, "Kendall found your access badge."

His eye widened, "Where was it? I've driven all over looking for it!" Something in the way he said it made me believe him.

"Uh, it was in a parking lot near Forrest Avenue. I noticed it when I was getting gas." I shrugged, not really sure what else to say.

"Forrest Avenue? That's the opposite side of town from where I live. And the gym...and the grocery store...I never go over there."

"Celeste...is there any way to see what times it's been used?" I asked. It was absolutely none of my business, but I had a hunch.

"Well, yeah. We can access the log records to see any time it was used. I actually had them pull a report already, just in case." Celeste unlocked one of the filing cabinets near the nurses station and pulled out a folder.

I breathed a sigh of relief, realizing the report was pulled before I used the badge; my card swipes wouldn't show up for her!

Celeste thumbed through some pages before finding what she was looking for. "Here we go..." She ran a finger down the page, looking at all the timestamps.

"What are these?" I asked, pointing to an alphanumeric code next to it.

"The location the badge was used. This one is the staff lounge," she said pointing to a code that read SL02. "Each department has their own, and this one is the rehab staff lounge."

My eyes scanned the report for other examples. "Is anything identified with '02' located in the rehabilitation unit?" I asked.

"Yes. 01 is maintenance, 02 rehab, 03 assisted living, etc. Roberto," she asked, "how long have you been without this badge?"

"It's been about a week, I think. I was off for a couple days and when I returned to work is when I noticed it was missing, after my meal break."

Celeste looked through the report, finding that date range. "I see where we initiated a deactivation that night; it was the pie social, wasn't it?"

"Right," Roberto agreed.

"Hmm. This can't be right…" Celeste signed into the terminal and arrowed through a few screens. "Well it looks like someone cancelled my request to deactivate the badge. I'll have to talk with security to officially have it deactivated and issue a new one for you."

Roberto gathered his things to leave as Celeste called security to alert them of the situation. She sighed as she hung up the phone and began massaging her temples.

"Security said someone told them I'd cancelled the request because they already returned the badge and Roberto was in the middle of a shift," she said. "What a day."

"You make it sound like this isn't the first issue to come up," Tess said.

Celeste laughed. "Not in the least. Personnel issues, more missing stuff, and now this badge." She tossed the offending badge on the desk.

"Missing stuff? You mean from the residents' rooms again?" I asked.

"No, that hasn't happened for a few days, now that you mention it." Celeste looked conflicted about saying more. I wondered if my guessing would make things easier for her, but Tess beat me to it.

"More discrepancies with medications?" She asked, quietly. "You mentioned it last week."

"I just don't know what's going on around here." Celeste shook her head in disbelief.

I chewed my bottom lip, wondering how to ask about the blonde nurse I saw without making Celeste's blood pressure spike; there really didn't seem to be a way around it.

"Are you still using temporary nurses to help through the holidays?"

"We have to, otherwise there wouldn't be enough coverage. Why?"

"It's probably nothing…but I was just curious who the blonde nurse was. I saw her here the other day, and didn't recognize her."

Celeste looked thoughtful, likely trying to run through the list of staff in her head. "I'm coming up blank, but that doesn't mean anything; we've had a revolving door the last few days. Hence my frustration over one more thing happening," she explained. "You can't tell me any more about her?"

"Unfortunately, no. I only saw her earlier this afternoon. She had a long blonde ponytail. Her uniform was wrinkled, too. Not a huge deal, I just remembered thinking it was odd; everyone else always looks so put-together." I tried to think of any other identifying features I noticed. "I only saw her from a distance…well, here anyway…"

"Stop being so cryptic, and just tell her!" Tess hissed.

"Fine. I saw her this afternoon when I was dropping off books to Issac," I went on to explain seeing her in the hallway, the incident at the grocery store, and finally my ridiculous decision to follow her. "She pulled into the apartment complex on Forrest Avenue," I said.

"That's where you found Roberto's badge, isn't it?" Celeste guessed. I nodded in confirmation.

"Thank you for that; when I talk with security I'll have them pull records for her badge too. If I can narrow down the employees, do you think you'd recognize her again?"

"I'd recognize that stringy blonde hair anywhere."

⬤

By THE TIME we left Willowhaven, most drive-thru restaurants were closed.

"Well, guess it's a bowl of cereal for dinner," Tess said.

"I'm sorry, I didn't mean for that to take so long."

"None of this makes sense, does it? Why does this blonde lady keep popping up?" she asked.

When I stopped at an intersection, I fished around in my pocket. I held up the baggie to Tess.

"What is that?" Tess took the baggie and held it up in the street light. Fortunately it was winter and we were both wearing gloves; I'm sure Detective Fox would have a field day with our fingerprints being all over it.

"I found that when I was getting up close and personal with the filing cabinet," I replied. "Blonde strands of hair that got caught in one of the drawers…I need to find some way to get this to Detective Fox." I turned to Tess and batted my eyelashes at her.

"Ugh. Fine, I'll give it to him," Tess said. "I don't know what to tell him when he asks about it, though."

"I'm sure you can distract him long enough to slip it into his pocket," I said with a wink. Tess just rolled her eyes, but didn't dispute the idea.

Finally, we pulled into the bakery parking lot. I set the emergency brake, and we hustled inside to get warm. Mittens McGee greeted us with a pathetic cry; he could see the bottom of his food bowl.

"You get to eat after I get to eat," Tess said. He turned, tail up, and sauntered away.

"Apple-cinnamon O's, or Toasty Cinnamon Squares?" I asked, holding a box in each hand. "Or peanut butter toast?"

"I think peanut butter toast," Tess said.

I retrieved the peanut butter from the pantry, while Tess grabbed the jam. We ate in silence, the occasional crunching sounds coming from McGee.

"Ah, that's why he was cranky; he ate all the chewy bits already."

"I, too, would be cranky about that," I said. I pulled the notebook from my bag and added the information we discovered tonight. "We're still nowhere close to this making sense," I complained.

"Maybe Celeste will have something tomorrow," Tess suggested.

I yawned, the excitement of the day catching up with me. Tess and I cleaned up our breakfast-for-dinner plates, and said good night. I checked the time, trying to decide if it was too late to text Sebastian. It was just after eleven o'clock so I thought I'd risk it.

> Hey, Seb! Sorry for the late text, just wanted to see how you were doing. Talk to you tomorrow. xx

I didn't even wait for a reply from him before falling asleep.

Chapter Nineteen

My alarm screeched to wake me up from an unsettled sleep. I didn't recall any strange dreams, so it was probably just from eating too late. I checked my phone for a reply from Sebastian:

> Hey, you! Sorry I missed your message. I was thinking of stopping by the bakery later today. Hope you're not too busy for me! ;)

Smiling, I grabbed my jeans and the new shirt one of my regular customers gifted me for the holidays, featuring a chubby cat wearing a Santa hat baking cookies with text that reads 'Baking spirits bright,' and headed for the shower to try and wake up. Unfortunately the shower only made me want to curl back up and sleep under a warm blanket.

As I waited for the coffee to brew, I peeked out the living room window; it was still dark, but in the reflection of streetlights I could see a coating of fresh snow on the ground. Excitement filled me; I never quite lost that childlike anticipation. Fresh snow, I felt, was like a blank canvas; a chance to see things around you from a new perspective. Sure, this feeling would quickly dissipate as I was forced to deal with slippery sidewalks and bad drivers who somehow forgot from one year to the next how snow works...but tucked away in my apartment or in the bakery, I could pretend I was in a snow globe. The sputtering from the coffee maker snapped me back into reality—the one where I forgot to actually put coffee in the machine. *It's going to be a long day.*

As soon as my feet hit the bottom step of the stairs, I knew something was wrong. The floor was cold and I could feel a draft. Reaching for the light switch, I surveyed the kitchen; everything seemed fine: the freezer and refrigerators were closed and running, the backdoor was still locked. I paused to think of what might be wrong when I heard voices coming from the bakery.

Panic filled me; did someone break in? Were they still here? I looked around for something heavy to wield as a weapon just in case. I slid my phone from my back pocket and sent a series of frantic texts to Tess:

> Are you awake?
>
> Please tell me that's you and Detective Earl Grey in the bakery?
>
> Tess!!

The three dots bounced on my screen.

> Sorry to disappoint, just got out of the shower. Why?

I didn't know how to respond so I sent a brief response of

> IDK, if you come down, be quiet and stay in the kitchen.

Soon my apartment door was opening.

"Ken? What is going on?" Tess whispered loudly.

"Shh. I hear voices in the bakery."

"Why is it so cold?!" Tess said, louder than I would have liked.

"Hello? Kendall? Is that you?" a voice from the bakery called out. It sounded familiar, but I was too anxious to identify it quickly.

"Um, yes?" It came out as more of a question than an answer. I peeked my head through the doorway into the bakery and all the breath in my lungs wooshed out. Splotches formed in my vision, and I thought I was going to pass out. I felt arms around me before I could hit the floor.

"What the…" It was Tess, but I had no idea what she was saying. My vision was still a little blurry and I was trying to take deep breaths. What was wrong with me? Cold hands tapped my cheeks, and that was enough to snap me out of it.

"No," I groaned. "No, no, no," I repeated. "This can't be for real. I'm dreaming right?" I looked to Tess, who was talking to the mystery voice from earlier. Nova, the woman who owned Golden Hour Vintage was standing in the bakery, shaking her head. I started to stand, but Tess grabbed my arm.

"Stop. There's broken glass everywhere," she warned me. I heard the words, and I saw the scene in front of me—the beautiful front window of my bakery, shattered—but I couldn't believe what I was looking at.

"How…why…?" I couldn't even form complete thoughts, I was so shocked.

"We called the police, dear," Nova said. "They should be here soon."

My eyes searched the bakery, trying to make sense of the scene: Glass strewn everywhere across the floor. One of the evergreen trees and a deer toppled over. Tess was distracted talking to Nova, so I rose to my feet. Even my best attempt at sidestepping the shards resulted in crunching glass beneath my feet. Thank goodness I'd worn actual shoes this morning and not my slippers.

Tears stung my eyes as red and blue flashing lights illuminated Mill Street; the tires of the police cars screeching to a halt. An officer was trying to clear the sidewalk of people, most obliged, but some were too busy talking to notice him. Once he started stringing yellow police tape across the front of the building, their chatter died down and folks started to disperse. Despite my efforts to contain it, a sob escaped as Detective Fox approached, his little notebook in hand.

"Are you OK?" he asked.

I nodded, unable to speak for the moment.

"Can you walk me through what you found this morning?"

I took a deep breath and tried to calm myself.

"Take your time, it's OK." Detective Fox placed a hand on my shoulder in an act of comfort.

"I came downstairs like I normally do, to preheat the ovens in the kitchen," I said as I gestured toward the kitchen with my thumb. "When I got to the bottom step something didn't seem right. It felt colder than normal…then I heard voices." I explained everything that happened up until he arrived.

"Do you have any idea who could have done this?"

I knew it was a routine question, but it frustrated me all the same. "I have no idea."

"We're going to have a look around, see if we can find anything. Sit tight, alright?" Detective Fox turned his attention to the mess at hand.

I walked toward one of the shelves with some of Gran's baking dishes, relieved to see them unharmed. I stepped to the side to move out of the way of an officer when pain shot up my ankle as I my foot landed on something large and uneven.

At my feet was a large rock, about the size of a grapefruit. I bent down and reached for it but stopped short, realizing it was evidence.

"Detective? You might find this interesting," I said, not-so-gracefully collapsing on one of the chairs.

Detective Fox and the officer came over to where I was sitting, leg propped up on the chair next to me. With my other foot, I pointed toward the rock. "I think I found the cause of this mess." I shifted in my seat, but searing pain stopped me. "Tess? Can you get me some ice?" I called out. I wasn't sure where she was at; hopefully still down here. Within a few seconds she handed me a bundle of ice wrapped in a towel. I winced as I placed it on my ankle.

"Is that...a note?" The officer asked before pulling on a glove to pick it up.

"I thought they only did that kind of thing on TV," I mused.

The officer removed the rubber band, stretched so thin it was transparent in places, dropping it in the evidence bag Detective Fox was holding open for him. He unfolded the note. The writing was in black marker, with bold yet shaky lettering. A chill coursed down my spine as I read the words again and again: MIND UR OWN BUSINESS.

"What the..." I whispered.

Detective Fox looked at me pointedly, like a parent expecting their child to confess to some petty offense. "This wouldn't have anything to do with Ms. Shaw's death, would it?"

I thought back to the previous days...the blonde nurse I followed, asking questions about Olivia, the strange run-in with Jay...heck, even the disgruntled customer. I swallowed hard before responding. "I have no idea, Detective." It was a little fib, but I felt it was in the interest of self-preservation.

He didn't seem convinced, but said nothing further about it. "We're going to continue investigating this; you'll need to close the bakery until we give you the all-clear," the detective said.

My heart sank. "Close the bakery? This close to Christmas?" I wasn't sure I could afford to be closed that long. Hopefully this would be covered by insurance.

"I'm sorry; we'll move as quickly as we can. In the meantime, you may want to consider installing some security cameras." Detective Fox handed me a list of some of the options Mr. Larsen kept in stock at the hardware store. "Bob should be able to help you out with these," he said.

Tess came to sit with me, patting me on the back.

"Oh! Can you run upstairs and get the…thing…that I found last night at Willowhaven? He's already disappointed in me, may as well make it worth his time."

While I waited for Tess, I called Cayden; they were quick to volunteer to make a small mural to hang over the opening that used to be my window. It was a lovely gesture and I appreciated their help. Tess came back into the bakery, but went straight to Detective Fox. *Ugh, don't put yourself in the middle of this!*

"There!" she said, far more chipper than I would have guessed, after handing over potential evidence found by a nosy best friend.

"Tess, you didn't have to do that. You don't need to get in the middle of all this," I said, gesturing around the bakery.

"Pfft. It's fine. Besides, I think he'll have an easier time forgiving me, than he will you." She gave me a sly look, and I decided I didn't want to know any more.

Even though I figured the police tape would do it's job of letting people know we were closed, I taped a sign to the front door of the bakery. Reading the words "Closed until further notice," hurt my heart. Realizing there was nothing I could do, I retreated to my apartment, hobbling up the stairs.

I sent Sebastian a message, letting him know what happened. He said he'd be over as soon as he was finished with his appointment, and if I was feeling up to it we could go to Larsen's hardware together to get the security cameras. Tess came up a few minutes later, after making sure Detective Fox and the other officer didn't need anything further. She refilled the plastic baggie with ice for me, and brought me a mug of hot cocoa, complete with peppermint stick.

"How did this happen, Tess?" I didn't actually expect an answer, which was good because I didn't get one. "Do you think…"

"I don't know what to think, Ken. It could be related, or it could be random. Nova said she had someone vandalize her dumpster last week, and the man who was walking his dog said they've had a few car break-ins on their street; they're a couple blocks over." I knew Tess was trying her best to comfort me, but it wasn't working.

"Yeah, but I bet those creeps didn't leave a note with their destruction," I huffed.

SEBASTIAN ARRIVED as promised and Tess let him in through the back door of the kitchen. My ankle felt well enough that I could put a little bit of weight on it to walk; as long as I had something— or someone—to lean on, I'd be fine.

"Are you OK?" Sebastian asked when he noticed my slight limp.

I waved my hand dismissively. "Yeah, I'm fine. Just tripped on the rock that destroyed my window," I grumbled.

"You feel up to hobbling down to the hardware store?" he asked.

"Sure. I think we need to talk, too...it's been an eventful couple of days."

Sebastian looked at me with a question in his eyes, but didn't say anything.

Chapter Twenty

MR. LARSEN GREETED SEBASTIAN AND ME AS WE PULLED OPEN THE door to Mill Street Hardware, and we followed the sound of his voice to the service counter. The store had been in the Larsen family for a century, and Bob Larsen operated it now with the help of his kids. The Larsens also own the Mill Street Hobby Shop next door; the town council just honored the store's 75th anniversary of providing Millwood with a variety of activities and skills. Bob's wife, Louise, held all manner of classes taught by folks in the community; the sewing classes were the most popular and often had waitlists—Gran even took a few of them when she was newly married, which is when she made many of her aprons.

"Kendall! Sebastian! To what do I owe the pleasure of this visit?" Bob asked cheerily.

I produced the information Detective Fox gave me about the security cameras. "Mr. Larsen—" I started, but Bob interrupted me before I could continue.

"Please, call me Bob. I'd make a dumb joke about 'Mr. Larsen being my father,' but my kids tell me it's 'cringe' and roll their eyes…" he joked.

I smiled and continued, "Alright then, Bob. Detective Fox gave me this list of possible options for a security camera for the bakery." I noticed a wary look as he accepted the paper from me. "Before you get too concerned, any nonsense seems to be targeted to yours truly, though I was planning to talk to the other shops along our side of the street to see if they've noticed anything. No one has mentioned it, so I presume it's just the bakery...lucky me."

"Ah, yes, let's see what we have here." Bob turned to his computer to search through what he had in inventory. "Do you have a preference in features? Some of these can get quite pricey when you factor in all the bells and whistles," he asked, looking at me over the top of his glasses.

"I admit I am not as knowledgeable with the techie doo-dads as Sebastian, so I defer to him for guidance. My only requirement is nothing that will break the bank...since I now have a window to replace." I frowned.

"Doo-dads?" Sebastian asked. He sounded like this was an insult to tech gadgets.

"Eh, you know what I mean. You're the smarty pants and tech whiz, I trust you." I smiled sweetly at Sebastian which seemed to reduce his indignation.

After explaining what was going on, Bob pulled two options for us to look at more closely. With Sebastian's help I chose a set that wasn't going to put too much of a financial strain on me, but would provide enough security that it made the price tag feel worth it. I paid for the cameras and any hardware needed for Sebastian to install them for me.

We returned to the apartment and Sebastian spread all the equipment on the table.

"Before you get too involved, do you want lunch?" Tess asked.

"I've never been one to turn down food," I said. "I'm feeling soupish today, so maybe we can stop by O'Devlin's, they have the best potato and leek soup."

Sebastian waved his hand in acknowledgement as he unfolded the instruction manual, deep in thought. Tess scribbled down our orders before calling them in. It was a touch early for lunch, but with all the commotion from the morning I never had a chance to grab breakfast. I was really looking forward to my soup and Scotch Eggs.

O'Devlin's Irish Pub has been a staple in Millwood for ages; in fact, the current owners—Austin and Robin—were 4th generation O'Devlins and still operated the restaurant the same way Austin's great-great-grandfather did. I loved the idea of a place where people can gather and share their life experiences being a fixture across generations, and I hoped I could foster that same kind of thing with City of Pies.

"Ken, you OK? You look a million miles away." Sebastian nudged me gently with his elbow, and I realized I was staring off into space.

"Oh, I'm fine. Just thinking about how much history our little town has with these businesses and families, and how they each offer something of value to the community," I sighed before adding, "and hoping the bakery will be a place people look back on with fond memories." I smiled at Sebastian before adding, "Without the broken window, obviously."

"Kendall, you know your bakery—and you—are something special, and you're helping families make their memories with delicious baked goods. Think of all the special occasions you've helped people celebrate with your pies!" He smiled back, and my knees wobbled just a bit at the sight of his dimples.

Arms laden with takeout bags, Tess returned and delicious smells filled the apartment; Mittens McGee came racing from his hideout.

"Oh, well, I guess we can share, McGee," I said, scratching behind his ears; his tail twitched as if to say he found that barely acceptable.

"He does have food, though I am sure he finds it to be of the peasantry." Tess rolled her eyes.

"I didn't realize you guys were staying here," Sebastian said. As soon as the words left his mouth, McGee pounced on his foot, attacking his shoelaces with a ferocity rivaled only by a lion in the wild. "Tess, it's kind of weird your cat knows when he's being talked about."

"I swear he understands English and Spanish. I don't speak a lick of it, but any time one of those telenovelas is on, he stares at the TV, enraptured by whatever's happening," Tess said. "It's his comfort show," she explained as if it were completely normal for a cat to have a favorite TV show.

"Anyway, they're replacing some pipes at my duplex, and the water will be turned off for a few days. Kendall made me stay with her," Tess said.

"You were going to stay in a hotel with a lumpy bed and crummy room service. That sounds dreadful," I said. "Besides, look how much excitement you'd be missing!"

We continued eating our respective lunches, a comfortable silence broken by the occasional crunch of chips or the slurp of soup; I tried not to, but it was too good to be polite.

I CLEARED AWAY the trash once we had mostly finished, completely satisfied if not a little overly full. Sebastian started installing the cameras, so I decided I'd pay our business neighbors a visit to let them know about the new devices and ask if they'd happen to notice anything odd in the last few days. I presumed Detective Fox or one of his officers already did, but I was curious to know myself.

"I'll be right back," I announced. "I don't want to be in your way while you're working," I said to Sebastian. "I'm just going next door to talk with Nova." I felt the look Sebastian was giving me, and knew he thought I might be up to something.

Golden Hour Vintage was an adorable vintage resale shop and I tried to limit how often I visited. Nova Blackwood, the owner, did an outstanding job of curating the most eclectic collection of vintage clothing, furniture, and bric-a-brac I'd ever seen. Most of the items in my apartment were from Golden Hour; I was a sucker for some good Mid-Century Modern pieces, which were getting harder to find thanks to those trendy home decorating shows and influencers. Nova and I were friendly, though, and she often set aside items she thought I might be interested in. It was almost eerie how well she could judge things like that, and sometimes I wondered if there was more to Nova than she was willing to let on.

A doorbell chime sounded as I stepped into the shop; it was warm and welcoming and made me smile as soon as I crossed the threshold. Nova was behind the counter, sorting through a recent haul, likely from an estate sale; her head was down and she was in the zone. "Hi, Kendall! How are you holding up, love?" she asked without even looking up. *How does she do that?!*

"Oh, as well as can be expected, I guess. How are you?" I asked, my eyes glancing around the shop to see if anything needed to come home with me.

"Busy! I got boxes of stuff from an estate sale a couple towns over; stuff they weren't able to sell and weren't sure what to do with. You know me, I'm like a beacon for the wayward muumuus and costume jewelry. Oh! That reminds me…I have a couple things I set aside for you to look at!" Nova scurried off to the back and returned a minute later with a medium-sized box; my eyes nearly popped when I saw the four peach lustre pie dishes, along with a set of four peach lustre coffee cups and saucers, and a set of cheeky little pie birds, all in pristine condition.

"These are so amazing!" I exclaimed, longing to pick them up, but I was so afraid I'd break something before I found out how much she was asking for them.

"You can touch them, you know, they won't break easily…" Nova said with a smile.

"I know, but the way things are going lately, I just don't want to tempt the universe. They're gorgeous! How much are you asking for everything?" I knew full well I didn't need these lovely items, but the heart wants what the heart wants…and mine was pining for these beautiful vintage pieces.

"Let's call it…$50 for the whole set."

I stared blankly. "I'm sorry…$50? For the whole set?" I was certain I was not hearing her correctly. Those cups and saucers alone usually sold for that much in mediocre condition; these looked almost pristine.

Nova smiled. "Yes, for the whole box of goodies. I know it doesn't seem like much, but truth be told, I picked them just for you; you're the only person I know who would appreciate them!"

"Nova, you are a bright, shiny gem, you know that?" I beamed at her, truly touched she thought of me enough to pull these aside for me. "I'll have to come back later to pay you for them. I didn't come with the intention of shopping…though given my track record, I should know better than that!"

"Well, I know where to find you, so settle up whenever you can. Now, about that window of yours…"

"Ugh, I know. It's horrible. I wanted to give you a heads-up that I'm having security cameras installed at Detective Fox's recommendation; they'll cover part of your shop, too. I also wondered if you've noticed anything unusual lately?"

"I haven't seen anything, per se…" Nova trailed off, looking at me as if judging how much to say.

"Did you…*sense* anything?" I asked, taking a guess. Maybe we'd be having that talk sooner rather than later. Nova smiled.

"Perceptive, Kendall. Very perceptive. I have sensed things, but

I don't know how to explain it. I know, it probably sounds all very woo-woo to you…" she waved the thought away.

"I was actually just thinking I'd like to have a more in-depth conversation with you about that kind of thing, so, I guess that makes me woo-woo adjacent. Anyway, I was just curious. Detective Fox hasn't mentioned if he'd spoken with other shop owners, so I was…"

"Investigating?"

"Um, more like…curiosity." At least she didn't call it snooping…which is what I felt like I'd been doing.

"Well like I said, I've sensed *something* but it hasn't become clear just yet. I can…look into it further…if you'd like and let you know?" Nova gave me a knowing look.

"If it's not too much trouble; I figured it'd benefit all of us, not just me or the bakery. No rush…with whatever." I wasn't sure what to call it…Investigating? Meditating? Scrying? *Ooh, could she teach me how to do that?*

Realizing I trailed off, I spoke again before turning to leave, "Well, I appreciate it again." I tapped the box of glassware, "I'll be back over to pay for these."

"You can go ahead and take them. Like I said, I know where to find you." She grinned, then faltered, "Though with what you've told me, maybe that's not such a good thing."

I laughed and hefted the box into my arms, careful not to allow the glass to clank together. Some of these would go in a display case in the bakery, some would go upstairs for display, but the rest of the items were getting used because life is too short to put pretty things on a shelf.

"Oh, Kendall? Be careful. Some things aren't what they seem." Nova turned and disappeared down the back hall.

Chapter Twenty-One

AFTER MY VISIT WITH NOVA, I WENT TO THE BAKERY TO SEE HOW Sebastian was coming along with installing the cameras. I needn't have worried, he was almost done with the second camera at the front of the store.

"Tess said she had some errands to run and wasn't sure when she'd be back. She said Mittens McGee has been fed, and shouldn't be a bother," Sebastian relayed her message. "Did you have a nice chat with Nova?" Sebastian asked as he climbed down the ladder. He eyed the box of treasures in my arms.

"I did! She said she'd keep her eyes peeled for anything that seemed unusual, and hadn't noticed anything so far. Well, notice wasn't the right word...she said 'sensed' wasn't quite right, whatever that means." I hesitated, unsure how far into the woo Sebastian was willing to venture.

"I always figured there was something...different...about her."

Sebastian's response surprised me; he was so logical and scientific about things, I figured he'd dismiss 'sensing something' as simply having indigestion.

"I'm not sure what she meant exactly, but you're right—I've always felt like Nova maybe had some sixth sense." I tested the waters, seeing if there was any reaction. Sebastian ignored me, focusing instead on putting his tools away.

"Now that you're back, we can get the cameras set up on your network and connect the backup drive. There are notifications you can set up, so we can figure that out too." Sebastian paused, checking the time. "Do you need me to come back later for that? I know you've had a rough day."

Did he want to leave already? I tried not to overthink it…but, it was not working. Shocker. "I don't have any plans, so you're welcome to stay as long as you want."

He glanced at me, "How late do you want me to stay?"

Heat flushed my cheeks, and I was certain Sebastian could see me blushing. "I, uh…" *Was he messing with me?*

"You're cute when you're flustered. Let's get this started, and if it gets too late we can order pizza or something."

And so we did. We set up the feed for the camera so that it would save directly to an external hard drive and I would receive a notification any time something showed up.

"I don't suppose there's a way to tell it only human—or vaguely human—shapes?" I asked, even though I knew how ridiculous that sounded.

Sebastian laughed, "Uh, no, I don't think so. Why, are you expecting non-human shaped things?" He looked at me quizzically.

"I think there's a family of raccoons living in the storm drain across the alley. I just didn't want a hundred notifications when their little family decides they need a midnight snack at the dumpster."

"You certainly lead a colorful life here at City of Pies, don't you?"

I nodded in agreement. "Gotta keep things interesting, I guess."

While he worked, I debated how to broach the topic of following the blonde nurse and finding that badge.

"You're quiet," he said.

"Well, we haven't really had a chance to talk about—" I wasn't sure what to call it.

"Your sleuthing?" Sebastian asked, grinning.

I was going to protest, but realized there was no point; that's exactly what it was. "Tess and I have discovered some things," I said. "But we can talk about this when you're done, I don't want to interfere with your work."

"You would never interfere with my work, Kendall." The way he said my name made me want to melt.

Without really thinking about it, I kissed him on the temple. It was such an uncharacteristic move, yet it felt so natural. Sebastian snaked an arm around my waist and gave me a squeeze. No words said, just a comfortable interaction of affection. That moment of warmth and comfort was broken by a grouchy-sounding yowl from the back of the apartment.

"Uh, maybe I should check on McGee." I followed the mews to the guest room where I found the cat sprawled on the floor looking like he was completely strung out.

"I see we found the catnip." I laughed as I spotted the upturned canister, and he just stared at me with glazed eyes. I double-checked the room to make sure there was nothing he could destroy or that could harm him. Satisfied McGee was blissed out for the evening, I left the door cracked open enough for a feline body to sneak through should he feel the need to adventure and returned to the kitchen and Sebastian.

"Everything OK? He sounded..." Sebastian searched for the right word, but I filled it in for him.

"High. He managed to knock over the tin of catnip that Tess brought. Little dude looked like he was having one heck of a trip."

Sebastian shook his head. "That cat is something else."

After clicking a few more buttons, he pushed back from the table and announced he was finished. "I'm going to pop outside the back and front of the bakery; hopefully it triggers a notification for you," he said as he put his coat on.

The camera feed was displayed on my laptop and I could see a black-and-white image of someone coming out the back door of the bakery. Sure enough, my phone chimed with a notification and a still image of the feed. Sebastian approached the dumpster only to come to an abrupt stop; he looked like he was playing a game of freeze tag with someone. He took a tentative step toward the dumpster, only to have the lid bounce open. Sebastian jumped.

The dumpster lid slowly crept open and out came a very round, very shaggy raccoon. It struggled to get a foot…er, paw-hold on the bin, but eventually it found purchase and disappeared over the side. The lid popped open again, and this time a raccoon started chucking items out of the dumpster for the first raccoon to catch: bread crusts, stale scones, some scraps of fruit. Once they were both back on solid ground, they gathered their treasures and waddled back to the storm drain.

The feed changed, and another notification chimed on my phone, this time from the front of the bakery. I could make out the police tape fluttering in the breeze, and saw Sebastian approach the door. He gave a slight wave before disappearing around the back of the bakery, which gave me another notification. "Well, I guess it's working," I said to no one in particular.

Footsteps on the stairs told me Sebastian was back inside.

"I see what you mean about the raccoons," he said. "Clever little guys, aren't they?"

"The notifications worked perfectly," I said, and thanked him.

"Now, why don't you catch me up on everything…" He nodded toward the notebook on the table.

"Can I get you anything? Soda? Beer? Popcorn?" I offered, cringing at myself for sounding like an over-eager hostess. I wasn't trying to be 'Susie Homemaker' but I got the sense Sebastian could use an evening to relax just as much as I could.

"Nah, I'm good." He smiled

We situated ourselves on the couch, which of course I over-thought. *Should I let Sebastian choose where to sit first, or should I just take my usual seat. Ah, thank you ADHD Brain for making even the most mundane tasks complicated and overwhelming.* My legs propelled me to my usual right-side cushion (probably perma-nently indented with my butt-print) and Sebastian settled in next to me. I presumed he'd take the opposite end, but he plopped himself down with a sigh.

"So...an odd thing happened the other day..." I went on to explain everything, including finding the access badge and returning it to Willowhaven.

Sebastian looked thoughtful, his hand propped under his chin; I've noticed he did that when he was thinking. "So, Celeste didn't know who the blonde nurse was?"

"No; since they've had additional coverage, she wasn't sure if it was a temporary nurse, or one of the regulars. She was going to pull some of the files with their badge photos."

"And this Roberto claims he doesn't go to that side of town?"

I shook my head no. "Things are getting more strange the longer this goes on. Why did she freak out at the store? I've liter-ally never seen her before." I've thought this through a dozen different ways and nothing made sense.

I became suddenly aware just how close Sebastian was. The subtle scent of his cologne. The warmth from his thigh touching mine sent a ripple of heat through me. *It's a thigh, get yourself together.* Sebastian shifted, now the full length of his leg was against mine.

"You OK?" he asked.

I gulped loudly, almost choking on my spit. "Yep, great, actual-ly," I replied, realizing how dumb that sounded. He just smirked at me, as he settled in closer.

"Do you mind if I put my feet up?"

"Not at all; do you need a blanket or anything? Sometimes it can get a little drafty in here." I half-stood, ready to grab a blanket from the closet when Sebastian caught my hand.

He pulled me back down to the couch, and I landed with a very unattractive 'oof.' I tried to reposition myself so I wasn't slumped against him, but he still held my hand which made it a little difficult to maneuver. He leaned his shoulder into mine, as if telling me to stop wiggling around. Ready to apologize for practically sitting on him, I turned slowly to look at him realizing we were nose-to-nose when I did so. Sebastian leaned his forehead to mine and we just sat there for a few seconds, quiet, content. I debated ignoring the urge to kiss him—his lips were right there, after all—but some part of my brain acted before logic and reason could talk me out of it. My lips landed on his, almost missing and landing on his chin.

Sebastian released my hand, and for a brief moment I thought maybe it was to end the kiss and move away from me. Look, when you've lived most of your life with rejection sensitivity and difficulty regulating your emotions, you tend to misread a LOT of signs. You also feel like everything is your fault and apologize a lot, which was something my therapist and I were working on, but old habits and all that jazz. As disappointment started to seep in when I felt his hand move away from mine, I started to pull away, only to feel resistance. He pulled me closer to him our lips touching again and his fingers tangled in the strands of hair that escaped my messy bun.

At this point I was in a bit of a pickle: I tried to discretely free my leg from under me—it was starting to tingle from lack of circulation—but when I leaned forward, our teeth conked together; I jerked my head back in a panic, only to bite my lip in the process. Not only was I ready to apologize for bonking our heads together, I was ready to crawl into the hall closet and hide until next Christmas. I dropped my head into my hands to hide my embarrassment. *Am I really that big of a klutz? Am I a danger to myself and others? I think we know the answer.*

Sebastian was oddly quiet but I felt movement from him, which I soon realized was laughter. Hysterical, tears-in-the-eyes laughter. Peeking through my fingers at him, his eyes were tightly closed, tears squeezing out of the corners and rolling down his cheeks. He was wheezing—that silent laugh with the occasional gasp for air— and I couldn't help but giggle along with him.

"Seb—"

He placed a finger to my mouth to 'shush' me, the laughter subsiding. "Don't. You did nothing to apologize for." He sighed heavily, that tiredness you feel after a hearty laugh settling in. He glanced at his watch and groaned. "I should probably let you get some sleep." I wanted to protest—to tell him not to leave, and that he could stay if he wanted. That I didn't need to sleep that badly, and that I'd rather just sit here next to him, even if we never uttered a word to each other. But I simply nodded in agreement, trying to stifle the yawn that was threatening to come out at the mention of sleep.

We both stood and after a couple seconds passed, Sebastian enveloped me in a hug; his arms comfortably tight around me. I could feel his heart beating a steady, gentle rhythm that threatened to lull me to sleep.

"A girl sure could get used to this," I said, and felt his chest rumble with a chuckle, and I realized I said the words aloud. Normally I would shrivel up with mortification; for too long I had been made to feel like I was inconveniencing people by having my own feelings, but I was tired of that. Tired of being cautious, of walking on egg shells; tired of guarding my emotions. And that thought was both terrifying and exhilarating.

Sebastian kissed the top of my head and gave me one last

squeeze before releasing me. He winked before turning to grab his coat from the back of the chair in the kitchen.

"Promise me you'll be careful."

I nodded in agreement.

Chapter Twenty-Two

I woke to the smell of coffee and bacon, and my stomach growled. As I tied my robe and shuffled to the kitchen, I found Tess scrambling eggs. "Are you the source of the wonderful smells that woke me up?"

"Oh, sorry. I didn't want to wake you, but thought you could use a good breakfast after yesterday." Tess set plates of fluffy scrambled eggs, crispy bacon, and a few slices of toast on the table, along with some strawberry jam, peanut butter, honey, and cinnamon. She slid my favorite bottle of hot sauce to me.

I doused my eggs with the zingy red sauce and took a big bite. "Thank you," I said after swallowing. I glanced through my phone notifications, thankful there were none from the security camera.

"You know, I'm really surprised you don't have your tree up yet. Though I guess you have been a little preoccupied."

"Yes, investigating a murder does tend to tie up one's social schedule," I joked. "I was hoping to pick up a small tree today. I know Christmas is right around the corner, but I have to have a tree!"

"That sounds good, actually. I feel like I've done nothing festive." Tess held up her hands before I could say anything. "Yes,

I know, I am not usually a festive type…but something just feels kind of different this year." She shrugged. "Besides, we can't really reopen until we get the all clear from Jord—Detective Fox." Tess closing the bookstore was a point of argument; she had a perfectly good door on her side of the building, but she insisted on closing in solidarity. She used the excuse that the building was the crime scene, not just the bakery; I suspected it was to make me feel better about the whole situation.

I smiled at the slip in saying his name. "You can say his name, you know," I teased. She just rolled her eyes at me.

"Alright, that settles it…we'll have a festive day out tree shopping…and maybe even a Christmas movie to *wrap* things up." I wiggled my eyebrows at her. "See what I did there…wrap…like presents…" Tess threw her wadded up napkin at me before pushing back from the table. "I'll see if Cayden wants to tag along too."

We cleared the dishes from the table and got ready for our holiday adventure. I texted Cayden who responded almost immediately that they'd love to join us and would meet us at the apartment; I promised I would not drive Betty and we could all avoid needing a spinal adjustment later. Showered and festively dressed —yet another cheesy holiday shirt, this time from Tess that was a stack of books draped with Christmas lights and said 'All booked for the holidays' on it—and I was ready to go. Tess came out wearing the most hideous sweater I'd ever seen, and it took every ounce of my being not to gasp in horror. "That's…"

"Ugly as sin? Yes, I know, that's the point." Tess said, pleased with the effect the offending sweater had on me. "This was one of my errands yesterday; Mom sent it to me. I plan to take pictures everywhere we go today to let her know I'm wearing it and haven't stashed it away in the back of the closet." Tess's parents were retired and spent most of their time traveling; they were currently enjoying the sun-drenched beaches of the Amalfi Coast, and this sweater apparently was a nod to their well-known production of limoncello: happy, robust lemons sporting jaunty Santa hats and strings of Christmas lights.

"That can't be a real sweater. Like, I can't imagine any respectable Italian would have sold that to someone in good faith. It has to be a tourist prank." I marveled at the vibrant lemons which seemed to dance across the front.

"Isn't that kind of the point of most touristy things, though?" Tess had a point, I couldn't argue that.

ONCE CAYDEN ARRIVED, we trudged out to Tess's car. I shivered as I waited for Tess to unlock the doors, bouncing from foot to foot to generate some warmth. Once inside, I cranked on the butt warmer —I really could see the appeal of heated seats—and snuggled down into my coat. It wouldn't be long before a hot flash attacked my sense of peace and comfort, but I'd enjoy this moment of toastiness while I could.

"Frasier's Tree Farm?" Tess asked. She really didn't need to; the Frasiers owned the largest tree farm in the county and we'd gone there ever since we were kids to pick out our trees.

"Yep! I just want a small tree for the apartment."

"Didn't their daughter just come back from…where was she? Portland? Why would she come back here?" Cayden asked.

"Hey, we're a charming midwestern community, thankyouvery-much," I replied. "I'm sure her parents appreciate the extra help." I often wondered what it would be like to have a seasonal business… I'm not sure I could handle that kind of stress. The bakery was hard enough to keep up with around major holidays, but at least people still wanted pies other times of the year.

The winding drive gave way to the crowded parking lot; clearly I was not the only one who procrastinated putting up a tree this year. Families milled around, hauling huge trees behind them, one of the farmhands following close behind to help secure the tree to the top of the car. One family was struggling with a tree three times the size of their car, the helper exasperated and trying to talk them into having it delivered. Tess found a spot, and as soon as I exited the car the scent of pine and fresh cut boughs washed over me.

A large area was sectioned off for the pre-cut trees up front. String lights criss-crossed overhead like a tent, and some of the scrap greenery was draped artfully along the fence posts. The trees were arranged by size—smallest trees no more than a couple feet tall in the front, and the largest trees towering upwards of twenty feet in the back. I couldn't imagine having a room with tall enough ceilings to accommodate a tree that size…let alone trying to decorate it!

I strolled down an aisle and didn't really see anything that caught my eye. They were all nice, but nothing gave me that warm Christmas vibe. Then, as if the universe knew exactly what I was looking for, when I rounded the corner I saw it: about three feet tall and very rotund with branches that stuck out kind of erratically, as if frazzled by all the holiday cheer. I let out a whoop, clapping my hands excitedly, which Tess and Cayden must have heard because they peeked around the corner after me. "I'll grab someone to bundle it for you," Cayden said and trailed off to find help.

"Kendall! Oh my gosh I haven't seen you in ages!" Noelle came jogging down the aisle and gave me a hug. "I'm so glad you guys stopped by today!"

"Hi, Noelle! How long have you been back?"

"It's been about 7 months now. I don't know—most days it doesn't even feel like I've left." Noelle laughed softly, and I could tell she was happy to be home, even if she didn't want to admit it. "When I was laid off, it seemed like a no-brainer to come home to help out."

"Well, it's so great to see you. You should stop by the bakery sometime, if you can manage to get away! Well, once I open back up," I said, realizing no one would be stopping at the bakery any time soon.

"Oh no, did something happen?" she asked. I didn't want to go into too much detail, so I just explained it away as unexpected repairs.

"I am very happy to have found the tree of my dreams this afternoon," I said, smiling and pointing to the chubby little tree. "He'll be perfect in my apartment!"

"Great! I'll get that wrapped in twine for you and hold it at the register." Noelle motioned for us to follow after she hefted the little tree over her shoulder; I kept my distance behind her, afraid I'd get a snoot-full of fir needles. She hustled over to the register and the growing line. In some types of business you could expect to see grumpy customers who were made to wait more than a few minutes, but I don't think I've ever seen anyone cranky at a Christmas tree farm.

I queued up in line behind the last person who was humming "We Wish You A Merry Christmas," and soon I found myself joining in. Tess and Cayden joined me—in line, not humming—and we finally made it to the register.

After I paid and we said our good-byes, we carted the tree to the car where I nestled it in the backseat. Cayden was not pleased with this decision, and fought to wedge themself in among the branches, grumbling and huffing in frustration.

"Sorry," I said. "It would have been squished in the trunk." Cayden just sniffed, pushing away a branch that kept lodging itself under their nose.

Since the register was under the protection of a roof, I hadn't realized it started snowing. A little thrill danced through me and I felt giddy; I must have had a goofy grin on my face, because Tess just shook her head and said, "C'mon Jingle Bells, let's get in the car where it's warm."

We got back to the apartment around five-thirty; Cayden went home, still grumbling about picking pine needles out of their hair. The wind had also picked up, making for some questionable driving conditions.

It had been a chaotic couple of days and I had a lot on my mind, but I was looking forward to relaxing with some holiday tunes and cozy lights.

"I wonder how much snow we're supposed to get tonight?" I asked as Tess and I tromped up the stairs.

"Last I saw it was another three to five inches, but you never know. Those clouds certainly looked like they'd dump it down, though!" Tess called as she unlocked the apartment door. We were greeted by a very unhappy cat perched by his food bowl.

After changing into flannel PJs and my silly panda slippers, Tess fed McGee while I put my favorite Christmas album on the turntable; Bing Crosby started crooning carols to us in no time. I pulled out the storage container of decorations that I kept in the hall closet; these were the things that were too meaningful to risk being in the bakery. I placed my little tree in the stand and added water before doing anything else.

Tess was on light duty, checking to make sure the strands all illuminated. I loved the old vintage-style lights, but didn't trust the vintage electrical wires, plus I liked to leave them on for as long as possible. I was delighted when a company released some retro inspired lights that were LED and snapped up several boxes. Gran would have had a cow with how much I paid for them, but I will not be deprived of my Christmas lights! Tess plugged in a strand and began winding it through the branches, the apartment taking on the soft glow of Christmas.

I added silver beads to the tree, draping them off the branches like a bejeweled lady all dressed up to go out on the town. Then added the vintage Jewel Brite ornaments that used to be Gran's, in all kinds of retro shapes and colors. I always loved looking at their wonky little vignettes nestled inside the plastic; my favorite featured pink transparent plastic with a chunky Santa who had seen better days, and a pair of deer with some trees and snow. The paint on the figurines was chipped and fading, and the mirror-like finish was peeling off, but they still meant the world to me.

Tess had moved on to a much more pressing task for tree decorating: snacks. I heard the pop-pop-pop from the kitchen and soon the smell of butter followed. While some folks felt it was a tradition to string the popcorn into a garland for the tree, we preferred to eat the popcorn.

"Do you want salt on yours?" Tess called as I heard the timer on the microwave go off.

"Actually, there's some taco seasoning in the spice rack—that would be fantastic. I'm not even sure what I have to drink in the fridge, though," I replied.

"Taco seasoning, eh? Aren't we fancy? No worries on the drinks, I found some Prosecco…I hope that's alright? That won't clash with your taco seasoning, will it?" Tess asked, teasingly.

"Prosecco goes with everything!"

Tess brought out one of my vintage serving trays, two tacky-looking retro Christmas glasses bubbling away, and two red-and-green bowls heaped with popcorn. I flipped the main lighting off so we could relax in the gentle glow of the tree's lights, and turned on the electric fireplace. We sat for a few minutes with only the sound of our popcorn crunching and the fizz popping from our drinks before Tess spoke.

"So…who do you really think is behind busting out the window?" Tess asked.

"It's truly uncanny how you can read my mind, Tess. I was just thinking about that."

"I feel like the blonde woman is behind this somehow, but

why? She wasn't even there when Prudie died, was she?" Tess asked.

"I don't think so; I'd never seen her before the other day. I really wish Celeste would get back to me soon with those badge photos," I said, frustrated.

"I wish Neil could remember something…anything…from that night. Jordan let it slip the other afternoon that they'd questioned him again," Tess offered.

"And nothing?"

"Nope. He said he had recurring nightmares about that night, and the only thing that happens in the dream is someone trying to choke him, a prick on the arm, and then getting conked on the head."

"Wait. He felt a poke? Was that for real, or just part of his dream?" This was a new piece of information that might prove useful.

Tess shrugged. "Jordan realized he was babbling and clammed up," she grinned. "He's a lightweight when it comes to wine."

"I don't suppose he let anything slip about those strands of hair?" I knew better than to get my hopes up.

Tess shook her head no. "I'll ask him the next time I see him."

I leaned my head back against the couch, trying to piece this together. If Neil was stabbed with something and didn't realize it until later, it wouldn't have been a severe injury. I didn't recall anyone mentioning it that night—he certainly didn't mention it to the officer.

"You look like you're scheming again," Tess warned. "I told Seb I'd keep an eye on you, and I believe you promised to be careful."

"I was just thinking it might be time to do some bribery baking." I smiled innocently.

Chapter Twenty-Three

THE STORM PREDICTIONS WEREN'T FAR OFF ON THEIR OVERNIGHT accumulations; it looked like a winter wonderland outside, and snow was still falling at a moderate rate. My sleep was fraught with weird dreams: Olivia showing up at the bakery, arms laden with designer bags and glittering jewelry, trying to convince my patrons to buy her wares. I had no idea where that idea came from, and chalked it up to the meager dinner of popcorn and Prosecco.

Lost in thought I barely heard Tess come out of her room. "You're either daydreaming about Seb or you had an epiphany about Prudie's case," she guessed.

"Actually, I was thinking about what kind of Christmas ghost I'd be if I were to haunt you."

"You're so weird. But that's why I love you." Tess laughed as she made a beeline for the coffee maker.

"Want some breakfast?" I offered, holding up some slightly burnt toast. Tess made a face and grabbed a box of cereal instead.

As I chewed, I formulated a new plan to get some more information. I guess that was one upside to the bakery being closed: it gave me more time to poke around.

"Alright," I said, "here's what I'm thinking. I need to go over to

Willowhaven and talk to Celeste. I figured I'd bake a few dozen cookies to bring along; no one can resist the temptation of a fresh chocolate chip cookie. While I'm there I can see if Neil is working." Even though it was a Saturday, I had a feeling he might be catching up on some work.

"Did you actually get any sleep last night?" Tess asked.

"Eh, a little. Weird dreams."

After cleaning up from breakfast and pulling any missing ingredients from the kitchen downstairs, I showered and dressed and Tess and I got to work.

A couple hours later, the kitchen table was stacked with cooling racks, each with rows of perfectly baked cookies.

"We make a pretty great team," I said to Tess who was eating leftover dough.

"Let's just hope this is enough to convince people I'm not there with ulterior motives."

"You mean snooping," Tess offered helpfully. I shot her a look, pretending to be offended.

"Want to come along?"

"Well, I did tell Seb I'd keep an eye on you," Tess said with a sigh. "Give me ten minutes."

Twenty minutes later—Mittens demanded treats when he realized we were leaving him—we were in Tess's car on our way to Willowhaven. It was late enough in the morning that the roads had been mostly cleared, and the sun was trying to peek through the clouds.

Tess parked the car and we used the little wagon again to cart the cookies along with us. The guard at the security desk looked tired…the kind of tired that a delicious homemade cookie might fix. Tess and I signed in, and I rested my elbow on the counter, chin propped on my fist.

"You look like you could use a treat," I said, studying him.

"Uh, a treat, ma'am?" The guard seemed wary. Rightfully so.

I produced a bakery box from the wagon, the smell of butter and sugar creeping out as I opened the lid. "Fresh baked cookie?" I tilted the box toward him.

He looked in the box and like a hound in search for its prize, his nostrils twitched with a sniff. "Cookies?"

"Mmhmm. Made them this morning!" I held the box closer to his reach.

His hand hesitated, clearly debating if this was against some rule in his Security Guard 101 handbook. Finally he picked one up, grinning like a kid. "Thank you, ma'am." He nodded at me before taking a bite; the slightly-warm cookie was crisp on the outside, but the chocolate was still a bit gooey. He closed his eyes as he chewed and sighed.

"Have a good day!" I called over my shoulder as Tess and I made our way down the hallway.

"I never knew a cookie could have that kind of impact on a person," Tess said with awe.

"It's the splash of vanilla bourbon mixed with the brown sugar. Works every time." I grinned.

We found Celeste sitting at the desk, phone cradled between her shoulder and ear. The common area was free of residents and visitors which would make it easier to talk; with any luck, she was able to pull those badge photos and I'd know who this blonde nurse was. Celeste looked up, motioned us toward the desk, and rolled her eyes; after a few minutes she hung up the receiver with a sigh.

"Rough morning?" I asked, eyebrows raised.

"Just going in circles with this staffing agency. I can't wait until the holidays are over so we can get back to normal around here," Celeste huffed.

"Speaking of..." I started to ask about the photos.

"I pulled the badge photos," she said in a low voice, extending a folder toward me. "Hopefully you'll find what you're looking for." She checked her watch for the time. "The residents won't be back for another half-hour or so, so you should have time to look through them. I just ask that you don't take this off the property; I could be in serious trouble if word got out."

I nodded, gripping the folder with both hands, as though it were some invaluable treasure map. I started to walk away before remembering the cookies.

"No good deed goes unnoticed," I said, opening the box with a grin. Once again, the intoxicating aroma of chocolate and sugar wafted out, taunting anyone within smelling distance.

"These smell amazing," Celeste said as she took a couple cookies. "Thank you!"

Tess and I moseyed to one of the more secluded corners of the room, just in case residents started returning from the various activities; Celeste was risking a lot getting these to us to look over, and the last thing we needed was Harold or Ernest looking over our shoulders. We sat side-by-side at a table, the folder between us. Once opened, rows of nurses stared back at us, some smiling, some straight-faced; their first names and assigned units were listed, but no there were no last names.

My eyes scanned the grid of images, hoping to recognize the blonde nurse. A few familiar faces stuck out—the red-headed nurse from the lounge, one of the nurses I saw in the med supply room. After a couple of pages, all their faces started to blur together. Olivia, Issac, Celeste…they were all in there. Neil was even in there. But I saw no sign of the blonde nurse. I groaned in frustration as we flipped to the last page.

"This is only making me realize how terrible I'd be if I had to pick a suspect from a line-up," Tess said.

"She's not in here," I said quietly. I thumbed back to the first pages and reviewed them again. "The blonde nurse isn't in here."

"What does that mean?" Tess asked.

"It means…I don't know. I'm not making it up; I've seen her with my own two eyes. Multiple times."

"Maybe Celeste missed one," Tess offered, trying to be helpful. I was too frustrated to hear her. "Let's ask her before we make any other conclusions," she said. I sat in my seat, unable to move. *How could she not be there?* Tess talked with Celeste and I took one last look through the folder, inspiration striking. *If I can't take the folder with me, I'll take the next best thing.* I quickly snapped a few pictures of all the badge photos, finishing just as Tess returned to the table.

"Celeste said it'd have to be there if she were working here; there have been no terminations logged in the system in the last week." Tess shrugged, looked as defeated as I felt. We left the file with Celeste, thanking her profusely.

I was determined to leave Willowhaven with at least some bit of information that might prove helpful. I still had a box and a half of cookies, after all; someone was bound to need a late morning snack.

The nurses lounge was deserted when I poked my head inside; a T.V. was on in the corner, the volume off. Neatly stacked dishes dried on the counter near the sink. I grabbed one of the boxes of cookies and made a quick note listing what kind they were; I may as well leave one behind. Just as I turned to leave, the red-headed nurse I saw the other day walked into the room. She eyed me suspiciously, then noticed the box of cookies. Her face softened a bit.

"You're that pie lady, right?" she asked, pointing a finger at me.

"Guilty," I said. "Though, today, I'm the cookie lady. I was just dropping this off." I motioned to the box of cookies on the counter. I glanced at the nurse's uniform, which was neatly pressed, reminding me once again how out of place that blonde nurse's uniform seemed. My eyes glimpsed a name tag on the nurse—Sarah—and I decided to shoot my shot.

"Sarah, right?" I asked. She seemed taken aback that I knew her name. "Do you happen to know the blonde-haired nurse that's been working the last few weeks? Long hair, usually in a pony tail?" I motioned with my hand the length of her hair.

"Uh…" Sarah hesitated. She was either unsure she should respond, or she had no idea who I was talking about.

Tess piped up a few seconds later in an attempt to help me out. "She stopped by the bookstore the other day asking about a new release; it was so hectic in there I completely forgot to get her name." Tess smacked her forehead lightly, clearly trying to play up this charade. I mouthed the words *thank you* to her as Sarah turned to face her. "Sorry, Tess O'Connor. I own Pack Up The Books, next door to Kendall's bakery."

"Oh! Right, the bookstore," Sarah still seemed uncertain about something. "You said it was a blonde woman? And she works here?"

"Yep, I saw her the other day, actually…well, about three days ago. I presumed she was one of the temps filling in for someone," I explained. "Long blonde hair, about Tess's height and build," I debated mentioning the state of her uniform. "She seemed….rumpled," I added.

"Huh. I haven't seen anyone around here like that," Sarah replied. "We've had a lot of new faces, but I can't think of anyone off the top of my head who matches that description. Sorry," Sarah shrugged before grabbing a cookie and sitting down by the television.

"Thanks anyway," I said.

"That was a good plan," Tess said as we left the lounge. "Wonder if anyone else is around we could ask?"

"It's like you're in my head," I responded, looking to Tess. "Stop that, it's creepy."

"Hey, we're not best friends for nothing."

We walked a bit further down the hall, passed the authorized entrance. I kicked myself for returning that badge so soon, not that it would do me much good if I was chasing a phantom nurse around Willowhaven. The sound of jangling keys centered my attention back on the present moment, right before Neil came around the corner. For once, I didn't run into him.

"Hi Neil," Tess greeted him.

"Neil! I was actually going to look for you!" I clapped my hands. He looked equally confused and concerned, and honestly, I couldn't blame the guy. "Don't worry, it's nothing bad!" I grabbed the box of cookies and opened the lid. Neil's eyes darted to them.

"Cookies?" he asked.

"Yep, I made some for the staff; figured you guys could use a pick-me-up with everything going on," I said with a shrug.

"Oh, well thanks. It's definitely been weird around here," he said as he picked up a couple cookies.

"I can't even imagine." My eyes traveled to the scar on his head that still looked a bit angry. "How are you healing?" I asked.

Instinctively his hand went to the spot; he winced as his fingers grazed where the stitches had been. "Still a little sore. Not as bad since they removed the stitches. Things are still a little unclear with what happened, though; I get, like, flashes of scenes, but I can't be sure if they're real or just from what people have been talking about." His tone was sad, and I really felt bad for him.

"No luck remembering anything at all?" I asked, quietly. I didn't want to push him too hard for information, but if he could tell me even the smallest detail about that night, it might help.

"It's like I told the detective," he replied. "I remember walking by the room and noticing the door was kind of open. I went to close it, but heard something inside—whispering maybe, but I can't be sure. When I stepped into the room, it was pitch black...couldn't even see my own hand in front of my face. Then I felt someone near me...you know that feeling?" Neil asked, and I nodded in agreement.

"Anyway, that's the last thing I really remember before everything went black." He shrugged his shoulders.

I shivered. I couldn't imagine the feeling of knowing someone was near you and then just going blank. "I'm so sorry you went through that, Neil."

"When I was talking to that detective, he mentioned they found a stick mark in my arm...like from a needle. I don't remember getting stuck by anything, but they think that might be why I've been having trouble remembering what happened." Neil's eyebrows shot up as if he said something wrong. "I...I, uh, don't think I was supposed to tell anyone that." He looked scared. "I've just...it's been eating at me, ya know? I don't really have anyone to talk to."

"I promise we won't say a word, Neil. Anything to help catch who did this...to you *and* to Prudie." I offered him a weak smile. He seemed so frightened and sad; I wondered what his story was. Did I really think this was a person capable of killing an elderly woman while she slept? I was starting to doubt that theory.

Chapter Twenty-Four

IT FELT LIKE WE WERE MENTALLY SPINNING OUR WHEELS, STUCK IN a snowy ditch and waiting for someone to pull us out. Before Tess and I left Willowhaven, I'd asked Neil if anyone heard from Olivia lately. He said no one's seen or heard from her since she went out on leave. Tess thought to ask about the blonde nurse, and he—like all the others—did not remember seeing her. I was starting to wonder if she was a figment of my imagination.

Tess and I were mostly quiet on the way back to the apartment, both of us lost in our thoughts. That silence was broken, however, with the ringing of my phone. I thought about letting it go to voice-mail, but I realized it was my insurance agent and was quick to answer.

"Hello?"

"Ms. Howard? This is Stephanie Carlson from Millwood Mutual Insurance, is this a good time to talk?"

"As long as you have good news for me, yes," I replied with a chuckle.

"Actually, I do have some news I think you'll be happy to hear! Your claim has been approved and you should be receiving a deposit to cover the damages within the next day. If you haven't already, you may go ahead and have your window replaced using one of the contractors we discussed in our initial review."

Tears threatened to spill from my eyes; this was the best news I'd had in a while! "Oh, Stephanie! How in the heck did you get it approved this close to Christmas?" I highly suspected she might be one of Santa's elves in disguise. She explained how she stressed to the underwriters that having the bakery closed was hurting my business—not a lie in the least—and pushed to get things resolved. I was thankful for that, because I'd already signed a deposit with a contractor to have the window installed; Detective Fox let me know I could move forward, which unfortunately meant they hadn't found anything to indicate who may have broken the window in the first place.

I thanked her a dozen times or more before hanging up and sighed, thankful for at least one good thing happening.

"What was all that about?" Tess asked as she pulled into the parking spot behind the bakery.

"My insurance claim was approved and I should be getting the funds in the next day or two! I might even be able to open before Christmas!"

While the bakery storefront had been closed, I still accepted orders for pies and things; the ovens still worked, and I needed something to keep the income flowing, no matter how little it might have been. We set up a makeshift curtain between the bakery and the bookstore so Tess could remain open; her shop assistants had been very helpful in making sure people didn't wander into a temporary crime scene until Detective Fox cleared it.

I sent Sebastian a text message letting him know the good news. I also mentioned Tess and I talked with Neil who had some interesting things to say. Seb said he'd stop by later this afternoon; Detective Fox actually called him to come into the station for an update. My heart skipped a beat at the potential for news on Prudie's death...maybe they were closer than we were to figuring this thing out. Sebastian said he'd be by around two o'clock this afternoon, which meant I had time to write out my notes from my earlier meeting with Neil.

TESS WAS WORKING in the bookstore taking care of some special orders, so I had the apartment to myself...well, Mittens McGee was there, too, but after our last encounter with the bathtub I sensed he was avoiding me at all costs.

Little did he know I was the Giver of Treats today; I shook the package of stinky tuna and liver snacks and heard his little paws hit the floor running. Throwing caution to the wind and forgetting his grudge against me, McGee curled his body around my ankles and lovingly nudged my leg with his head. I chuckled, which was a mistake—I inhaled the fishy fragrance of his treats and promptly began to gag.

"How on Earth do you eat these things, McGee?" I choked the words out, trying to regain composure. He just stared at me intently, head tilted and waiting for me to stop yapping and feed him. I plucked two smaller treats out of the package, trying to limit contact with them; they left their scent on anything they came into contact with. I crouched down to McGee's level and extended my olive branch in the form of smelly snacks. He sniffed my fingers before chomping down, narrowly missing my thumb. Three bites and an audible gulp, the treats vanished and McGee turned his back to me to leave. As I stood to put the treats back and wash my hands, I heard a 'mrrp' and when I turned to look at him, McGee almost seemed to bow his head in thanks. I dried my hands and gave him a couple scratches between his ears, which he deemed satisfactory before trotting back to the bedroom.

Once Sebastian arrived, we grabbed some non-smelly snacks

and settled in. I was anxious to hear what his meeting with Detective Fox was about, so I let him go first.

"Well, it wasn't much," he said with a tinge of disappointment.

"No news at all?" I asked.

"Not really. He said they're following a couple leads but wouldn't release any details. He barely mentioned anything about the safety deposit box or the inventory from Grams's room when I asked, so I'm not sure if that was a dead end or another thing they're keeping close to the vest," Sebastian said.

"He also asked me some odd questions about Grams's early life, which sadly I didn't know much about. She was always pretty quiet about her life before she was married."

"Was he asking general questions, or did he have something specific he was chasing?" I asked.

"He didn't really say," Sebastian answered. "He did mention that those blonde hairs you found were synthetic. He also told me to tell you to leave things to him." Sebastian gave me a pointed look. I couldn't remember telling him about the hair I found at Willowhaven, so I suspect Detective Fox ratted me out.

"You know how hard that is for me," I said.

"I know. But I do wish you'd be careful. How did you get those hairs, anyway?" Sebastian asked.

"Well, it's kind of a funny story…" I explained how I found myself wedged between the wall and a filing cabinet locked in the room with two nurses. Sebastian's face was difficult to read, no emotion displayed. I fidgeted with the fringe on one of the blankets waiting for him to say something…scold me for sneaking around, or chide me for eavesdropping.

"Detective Fox said if you decide to take another career path besides baking, you'd make a good investigator. But for now, he wants you to leave it alone."

I harrumphed. Things didn't seem to be moving fast enough for my liking, and I felt I had the upper hand; I was around people in this community every day. It seemed easier for me to get information as the baker-next-door rather than an intimidating police detective.

"Tess and I talked to Neil," I said. I held up a hand quickly in protest before Sebastian could say anything. "That happened *before* Detective Fox told me to keep my nose out of things...so I don't feel like it counts. I only asked how he was feeling, if his head was doing any better. It's not my fault he started talking about needle marks and being stung by something," I said as a shrugged.

"Roll that back for me," Sebastian said. "Needle marks?"

I explained what Neil told us. "He seemed really shaken up by it," I said. "He looked a little relieved to have someone to talk to."

"Detective Fox didn't mention anything about that to me...but that might be something they're keeping out of the public." Sebastian massaged his temples. "I hope you're the only person he's told."

That was something I didn't know, and said as much. Judging by Neil's reaction, he seemed genuinely concerned he let the information slip. But was it an act? I didn't know him that well—it didn't seem like many people did—so he could be feeding us whatever we wanted to hear.

I added bits of our conversation to the notebook. I still felt stuck, and sighed in frustration. There had to be something here to connect everything...what were we missing?

Chapter Twenty-Five

SEBASTIAN COULD ONLY STAY FOR AN HOUR OR SO, AND ONCE HE left I settled onto the couch with a fresh coffee and a cozy blanket. Sifting through the streaming selections for holiday movies, I settled on "Elf" even though I've watched it so often I had it memorized. I snuggled down into the blanket, my mind still trying to process everything. Neil being stabbed with a needle and realizing Olivia was the woman in the blonde wig just left more questions…questions I wasn't supposed to concern myself with. Did Detective Fox realize how difficult it was to drop this? I decided as long as I kept my thoughts to myself—any maybe shared with Sebastian—it wouldn't technically be investigating. More like… pondering.

Half-watching the movie, and reciting a line every now and then, I retrieved my notebook and looked over my notes; it felt like my list of suspects was mocking me. I wrote a large question mark next to Olivia's name, still uncertain how she fit into this whole scheme.

I willed the words on the page to make sense, to rearrange themselves in the right order or to give me a sign—silly, I know, but I was just ready for this to all be over with. Just as I tossed the notebook aside, I got a notification on my phone from the security app. I presumed it was that pesky raccoon again, so I didn't think much of it. But I could use a good chuckle, so I tapped the screen and navigated to the live stream. I just about dropped the phone when I saw a person—no, a man— walking slowly to the dumpster, glancing around occasionally as if worried someone would see him. I double-tapped the screen to zoom in, the picture not super clear but clear enough I could see the person's general frame: tall, bulky, and strangely familiar. I watched for a few seconds as he paced near the dumpster before turning toward the building, completely unaware he was being watched. I gasped loudly when the man's face came into view…it was Neil.

Tess was still downstairs in the bookstore, so I threw some slippers on and trotted down the stairs. I popped my head into her office and explained what I saw on the security footage, and even showed her the live feed of Neil still pacing by the dumpsters.

"I'm going to talk to him," I said. I wasn't sure if I was hoping she'd stop me, which she didn't. Sebastian's words echoed in my head "stay out of it, let Detective Fox do his job," but I'd just talked to Neil…what could be the harm? *Only the fact he's lurking by your dumpster in the cold…doesn't that seem odd?* Ignoring my own thoughts, I pulled the sweater tighter around me.

I kept an eye on the security feed while I unlocked the door; at the sound of it opening, Neil looked like a deer in headlights… almost feral. I hesitated closing the door behind me; it was still unlocked, but keeping it open might make for an easier escape route, if needed.

"Neil? Is that you?" I asked, as I slipped my feet into a pair of ratty boots I kept by the back door for shoveling. I kept a bit of distance between us and my voice friendly.

He was still pacing, avoiding eye contact. The longer he stayed silent, the more worried I became. Should I go back inside? Should I call for backup? I snorted quietly at the last thought—who would I call? I wasn't the A-Team…heck, I wasn't even the B- or C-Team. Tess knew I was out here, though, and hopefully could hear if I started shouting for help.

"Neil, is everything alright?" I stopped a few feet in front of the dumpster; he still hadn't stopped pacing. "Can I help you with something?"

"I shouldn't have told you that earlier," he said. "About that night." His words were clipped, and I couldn't tell if he was angry, frightened, or both.

"Hey, it's OK! I'll pretend you never said a word about it," I offered. "Tess, too. I'll make sure she forgets the whole thing." As soon as those words left my mouth, Neil turned on me. There was a look in his eyes I couldn't quite make out, but it was as if I'd said something that triggered his fight or flight response. This certainly seemed like he was in fight-mode.

"It was a lie, " he said. This caught my attention. What exactly was the lie, I wondered. I was afraid if I came out and asked him, he'd clam up or run away from me.

"That's OK. I'm nobody, Neil. I'm just trying to help my friend figure out what happened to his grandmother," I said.

"You talk to that detective."

"I try to avoid that detective," I said. "He's no friend of mine." Not entirely true, but Neil didn't need to know that. I didn't know if that tactic would encourage him to keep talking.

"I lied," he repeated. I wondered if I could keep him talking, if he'd finally share what he lied about.

"It's OK, we all lie sometimes, especially if we think it's for the best."

"I meant to be in her room that night. I needed to find some-thing." Neil's pacing slowed, and I hoped maybe I could get some more information from him. I prayed Tess stayed in the bookstore and didn't interrupt us.

"What were you looking for?"

"She said it'd be there. Or at least, that's what I heard. She said it was in her room somewhere, and it was worth a lot of money," Neil was wringing his hands as he spoke.

My mind raced with ideas of what he might have been trying to find. Or who "she" was.

"Did you find it?" I asked.

"Do you think I'd be here talking to you if I did? She lied about it. She set me up," he spat the words. "She wasn't supposed to be there that night, but she was. Her and that man."

"Who, Neil? Who was it that set you up?"

"Your blonde nurse."

So he *did* see the blonde nurse. "Did you tell the police this? Or at least Celeste and Issac?"

Neil looked at me like I had snails crawling on my head. "Are you serious? That'd be the end of me."

"Not if you didn't do anything wrong," I said. "It seems like you were just looking, right? You didn't take anything, you didn't hurt anyone, right?"

"They found the key, though." His voice was sad.

Ah, the key. The small key the officer asked Neil about the night of Prudie's death. The one they supposedly found on him. "They can't prove that you took it, though, right? I mean, you were knocked out...how would you have managed that?"

He paused at this, clearly not having thought it all the way through.

"Tell me what happened...what you remember. I want to help you, Neil," I pleaded with him for more information.

"I overheard them talking one day...the blonde woman and a man. I'd never seen either of them before, but the woman's face felt familiar. Anyway, they were talking about some of the residents that had valuable items in their rooms, and I overheard them mention Prudie. The man was hard to hear, but the woman's voice was a bit louder; she said she'd already looked for it but wasn't able to find it. He insisted it was there, he even overheard Prudie arguing with staff and some man in a suit about it; that she needed to take it off-site. It was too much of a liability, they told her." He swallowed hard; I didn't know if I should invite him inside since it was so cold, but I still wasn't sure what his motive was for coming here.

"So you went to look for it? That night, I mean."

He nodded. "Eventually they said it was jewelry in some kind of lock box. They made it sound like it was kept in her room somewhere, so I figured I could go in and look around. Maybe I'd get lucky and find it, and have no more worries..." he trailed off, his voice thick with emotion.

I wish I had my notebook so I could write all this down; hopefully the security camera was picking up some of the conversation. I wondered if I could activate the recording feature on my phone without Neil noticing. As soon as I moved my arm a fraction, his head shot up and he glared at me.

"I'm not doing anything, just putting my phone in my pocket." I slid it into the pocket of my sweater, and held my hands up showing they were empty. I latched onto something Neil said: the conversation with staff and a man in a suit...would that be the conversation with her lawyer about the safety deposit box?

"I didn't do anything, you know," Neil said. "I was going to, but I didn't."

My teeth started to chatter from the cold. Do I risk going inside with this man? "Come inside to get warm, I'll make some coffee or tea, or whatever you'd like." I nodded toward the bakery. He looked like he was debating it. "I'll make sure no one interrupts us."

I took a backward step toward the door, hoping he'd follow.

Hoping he didn't lunge for me or make a run for it. He matched my movements, slowly walking to the door.

"I'm going to send a text message to Tess, she's in the bookstore. I'll ask her to stay there," I said, tapping out a message and holding my phone out to show him I wasn't trying anything funny. He seemed appeased by this, and nodded once. I hit send, hoping Tess wouldn't be stubborn about it and come to check on me.

Once inside, I pulled a couple chairs over to the counter and grabbed two mugs from the shelf. "Coffee? Tea?"

"Coffee, please." Neil sniffed.

Once our coffee was ready I sat across from him, waiting for him to tell his story.

"I had a maintenance issue to check on near her room. I used that as a reason to go back to work," he said. "No one was there, just the night staff, and the residents were all sleeping. When I got to Prudie's room I noticed the door was kind of open, which is unusual; the nurses weren't supposed to make their rounds for another hour or so. When I got closer, I heard whispering voices—too quiet to make out who they belonged to. I pushed open the door to see what was going on, but that's when I was attacked. The next thing I knew, I was waking up with a nurse hovering over me, and Prudie was dead." Neil took a long drink from his mug, and I wished I had some whiskey or something to spike it; he looked like he could use it.

I remained quiet, allowing this information to sink in. At least this confirmed Neil didn't kill Prudie. But who was in that room with him?

"I'm so sorry you went through that," I finally said after a couple of seconds. "That had to be so terrifying, waking up not knowing what was happening!"

"I felt horrible trying to answer all their questions; I didn't know anything! At least not until a few days ago when bits of memories started surfacing. I started getting threatening phone calls," he said. "At first they'd just hang up when I answered, but eventually they began to warn me about going to the police. If I said a word about anything that happened, they'd make me regret it." His eyes looked wet, and I was worried if he started crying, I might start too.

There seemed to be more he wanted to say. Neil shifted uneasily in his seat, and I waited for him to continue. I'd sit here all day if it meant getting more information.

"How often did you get those calls?"

"Almost daily. I felt like I was losing my mind! It was like they knew I'd started getting flashes of memories, but I have no idea how they'd know that."

"I remember you saying that you felt like something stung you. Did the hospital or Detective Fox ever mention if you were injected with anything?" I could feel my inner Jessica Fletcher coming to life as a thought dawned on me.

"Um, yeah, but I can't remember the name of it. But they did say it's used for sedation. Like, when you have a procedure done and they don't want you to remember what happened," Neil explained. "There's something else I need to tell you, Kendall... about your window," he frowned and stared into his mug of coffee. I swallowed hard.

"Sure, what is it?" I asked, even though I had a feeling I knew what he was going to say.

"When I started getting those calls, they never really said what they had on me. I have a sketchy past, and I wasn't willing to let that come back to haunt me. I'd lost too much already because of it, so I said I'd do what they wanted to keep quiet."

"Ah," I said, realization settling in.

"They said you were asking too many questions and you needed to mind your own business."

The note taped around the rock came to mind. "So breaking my window was a way to slow me down?" I guessed. This all seemed too much to process. Who were these people? What information did they have on Neil? "What if...what if I go with you to the police station? We can talk to Detective Fox. Tess actually is dating him, so he's not all that bad," I half-smiled, trying to ease the tension in the room.

"I...I don't know if I can. I don't want to be in trouble," he said. He seemed like a little kid, afraid of telling their dad they got into a fight at school.

"I think if you come forward it will be a lot easier on you rather than hiding it, or it coming out later," I suggested. "I can even see if he'll come over here, so it's less intimidating. And as for breaking my window, I'm not blaming you for that."

Neil seemed to be seriously considering this, and I hoped against hope he'd go along with it. This might be information that could break open the case!

Finally Neil nodded once in agreement and I resisted the urge to do a victorious fist pump. "See if he'll come here," he said.

I found Detective Fox's contact information and the call connected almost immediately. He didn't seem surprised to hear from me, and I wondered if Tess gave him a heads-up. She kept true to her word and stayed out of sight, though I had a feeling she was listening in from the counter in the bakery.

"He'll be here in a few minutes. Can I get you anything else, more coffee? A cookie? Scone?" All this excitement made me hungry.

"More coffee, thanks. And thank you, for being kind. I was so worried about coming forward. But you seemed like I could trust you," he offered a crooked smile that didn't reach his eyes.

"Thank you for trusting me, Neil."

Within minutes, Detective Fox was seated at the table in my place, and I wandered out to the bakery to give them privacy. Neil said he was fine with me leaving, but I said I'd be just a shout away if he needed anything.

Tess was standing in the doorway to her office, mug of tea in hand. The look on her face was hard to read.

"Well, that was certainly not what I expected," I murmured.

"Did he confess?" she asked. I wondered if I should tell her, or leave it be. Neil trusted me, and I felt bad if I broke that trust.

"To killing Prudie? No. But he did have some information that I think Detective Fox might find useful…and has renewed my resolve to figure out who the heck this woman with the blonde wig is."

Tess looked at me, clearly missing something.

"Did I forget to tell you that? They determined the hairs I found were synthetic…it was from a blonde wig."

Now Tess looked like the one who's brain would combust from overthinking, clearly trying to piece this together. She snapped her fingers and asked, "Do you have those images on your phone still?"

"The badge photos? Yes." I pulled them up and showed them to her.

"Can you send them to me?"

I did as she asked, and she made a beeline to her computer. "Now that we know the hair wasn't real blonde hair…" She trailed off as she worked, transferring the images to her computer and waiting for the photo editing program to open. She searched online for an image of a blonde wig and saved it. Once the program was ready, Tess opened the badge photos and the blonde wig photo, cropping and resizing it to fit. I made an ah-ha sound as I realized what she was doing. She copied and pasted the image multiple times, positioning the blonde hair on each one of the badge photos. When she reached the last row of photos, she clapped her hand over her mouth, eyes wide with surprise.

"What is it? Did you find her?" I asked.

Tess pointed to her computer screen; the woman with a half-smirk looking back at us. I never would have guessed it before, but seeing her with the blonde hair made me freeze in my tracks.

"Who does that look like to you?" Tess asked, toggling between the blonde wig being on and off of the photo.

"The one and only: Olivia Birch."

Chapter Twenty-Six

WE WAITED AS PATIENTLY AS WE COULD FOR DETECTIVE FOX TO finish his conversation with Neil. We also tried our very hardest not to listen in. Fortunately, the revelation of identifying the blonde nurse did a great job stunning Tess and me into silence.

Their voices grew louder as Neil and Detective Fox approached the bakery storefront. Neil emerged first, looking slightly better than he did when I spoke with him, though he still seemed harried after his time with Detective Fox.

"Well, I think that wraps things up for us," Detective Fox said, slipping his notebook into his shirt pocket. I wondered how many of those he went through in a year…maybe they'd make a good Christmas gift.

Neil nodded and thanked me; I wasn't sure if he meant that. Detective Fox wasn't leading him out in handcuffs, so I had to presume he wasn't in any serious trouble. If his story was the same, it didn't appear he was guilty of anything more than being in the wrong place at the wrong time.

"Can I offer you anything before you leave? A coffee to go?" I offered.

"No, thank you. I think I'll be going now." Neil waved in our general direction and I stood to walk him to the back. I couldn't wait for them to finish with the window installation so I could regain the use of my front door!

"Thank you again," Neil said. "I'm sorry if I freaked you out... it was just eating at me, you know?"

"You're fine, Neil. Thank you for coming over to talk. I hope you'll feel better with that off your chest." I patted him on the arm, and he walked down the alley; it dawned on me that I didn't see a car nearby. Did he live close by? "Do you want a ride home?" I called after him, but he either didn't hear me, or ignored the offer.

I closed the door behind me, shaking off the chill. I considered having another cup of coffee, but I'd already had three today... adding a fourth didn't seem like a great idea. When I entered the bakery, Tess and Detective Fox had their heads close together, and judging by the blush on Tess's cheeks, I guessed it wasn't about Neil.

I cleared my throat loud enough so I didn't walk in on whatever lovey-dovey sweet nothings were being said. "So, good talk with Neil?" I asked Detective Fox. I knew he couldn't tell us anything, but a girl could hope.

"Thank you for convincing him to talk to me," the detective said. "He gave us some good information to work with. Will you want to pursue criminal charges for the vandalism? Since I have to file it in our investigative report, the prosecutor will want to know if that's an avenue you want to go down."

"Vandalism?" Tess asked. Having been left out of the conversation with Neil, she had no idea what he'd confessed to.

"The window," I said, motioning to the front of the bakery. Tess said nothing, her mouth forming an "O" in understanding.

"No need for any charges; Detective. I'll need a copy of the police report for insurance, but I think Neil's been through enough with this whole ordeal." I replied, then attempted my best puppy dog expression. "I don't suppose..."

"You're not getting any information out of me, Ms. Howard."
Oh, beans!

I shrugged as if this wasn't disappointing news, and looked to Tess. "Did you already show him?"

"I was waiting for you, actually." Tess motioned for us to follow her back to her office. Her little space heater was chugging along, and I appreciated the warmth. I wasn't sure how to explain how we obtained these badge photos—I certainly didn't want to get Celeste into any trouble—but this was big news, especially after hearing what Neil had to say.

"Now, before you get cranky with a certain someone for involving herself in things you feel she should stay out of," Tess said to Detective Fox. He glanced at me, and I placed a hand on my chest, as if asking "Who, me?" He snorted and nodded for Tess to continue.

"We think this might be useful to your investigation." Tess woke her computer up to display the image with the wig on. "Meet the infamous blonde nurse of Willowhaven." She waited a few seconds, giving him time to study the picture. Detective Fox pursed his lips, like he'd just consumed an entire box of sour candies.

"OK," he said. "And…"

"And this is who she is without her miss blondie wig," Tess said, clicking to remove the hair. Detective Fox sucked air in through his teeth, which was a very satisfying reaction.

"Is that…"

"Olivia Birch from Willowhaven." My words bounced off the walls of Tess's office, echoing back to me. It sounded so odd saying that out loud, finally knowing who the blonde woman was. "No wonder she ran from me at the grocery store," I said without thinking.

"Excuse me?" Detective Fox eyed me, knowing full well he wasn't going to like the explanation. Tess snickered and I narrowed my eyes at her.

"Kendall was at the grocery store and saw this woman," Tess started to explain. "She took off once she got a good look at her. Kendall might have taken a slight detour home that evening," Tess said matter-of-factly.

"A detour, huh? Is this how you found the missing badge?" Detective Fox asked. *Well played, sir.* He apparently knows more than I thought…not that I doubted him.

"The one I returned to Celeste? Yes." He didn't need to know the adventure I had *before* I decided to hand it over. "What I can't figure out is, how has no one seen this blonde version of Olivia? We've asked a handful of people, and no one remembered seeing her," Tess flicked my arm, likely upset that I lumped her in with my investigation. "Ouch!"

"So, you followed her…where? Her house?" Now the good detective seemed interested in my side quest.

"The apartment complex off Forrest Avenue. She parked there, but I didn't see which unit she went into. And when we—I—went back to see if I was imagining things, that's when I found the access badge, in the same spot where her car had been parked."

"Do I want to know how you got the hair sample?" He asked, rubbing his forehead as though a massive headache were coming on. I suspected that headache was me.

"I…got lost in Willowhaven," I said. "The hairs were sticking out of a jagged corner of a filing cabinet. Since I started feeling like I was making things up, it seemed like proof—to me, at least —that I wasn't chasing some phantom." I shrugged. I omitted the information about *where* I found it; Detective Fox was on a need to know basis, and I didn't feel like that would help or hinder his work.

"Is there anything else you'd like to tell me, since you have my undivided attention, Ms. Howard?" I could hear his patience wearing thin. I felt bad, truly; it wasn't my intention to make his life difficult.

I tilted my head and tapped a finger on my chin, thinking. "I don't think so…nothing that you'll confirm or deny, anyway." I grinned at him. I really wanted to ask him about that man from the funeral.

"Out with it, you look like you're dying to say something," he said.

"I talked with Sebastian; he mentioned you were asking him about Prudie's early life. I was just wondering why?" I held up a hand before he could admonish me for asking something he likely couldn't answer.

Now it was Detective Fox who looked like he was dying to say something, but I knew he wouldn't do anything to compromise the investigation, especially now. He rolled his shoulders and sighed. "It's something we're looking into. I cannot share more than that." I'd have to be satisfied with that response.

***

It was dark by the time Detective Fox left. Just one of many traits of our Midwestern winters. Tess and I made sure both shops were locked up before heading back to the apartment. Tension blossomed between my shoulder blades as a muscle I didn't even know I had started twitching. *Was it too late to ask Santa for a massage appointment for Christmas?*

"Well, at least we can rule Neil out of our list of suspects," I said.

"True. And I guess the blonde nurse, since now we know it's Olivia," Tess called from the kitchen. "You want any cocoa?"

"No thanks, I'm good," I replied. "I can't believe he broke the window. I mean, I can…but…I just wonder what kind of information they had on him."

"You still haven't filled me in on that conversation," Tess said as she sat on the couch. Her legs were tucked under her and she had one of my many fuzzy blankets wrapped around her shoulders.

After activating the fireplace with the little remote—who would have thought we'd live in an age with remote-controlled fireplaces?—I explained everything to her, just as Neil explained it to me. Tess sat quietly and sipped her hot cocoa.

I added these updates to the notebook. I was losing hope that we'd ever figure this out; Detective Fox who is, I'm sure, great at his job, was moving too slowly for my liking. It was hard to know where they were at with the investigation, which is why I felt compelled to keep searching for answers.

"I got the all clear to return to my apartment," Tess said. She sounded a little bummed out.

"You know you're welcome to stay as long as you want; I really don't mind."

Tess grinned, "Yes, I know that. But you also need to take time for yourself…besides, you need to get your love nest set up so you and Sebastian can have date nights without a pesky third wheel hanging around." She wiggled her eyebrows. I rolled my eyes, but laughed; she was right, I was looking forward to having more date nights with Sebastian.

"When do you think you'll be heading back?" I asked. "I just want to make sure I'm here when you guys ditch me."

"Probably tomorrow. I don't feel like wrangling a cranky cat." Tess rolled her eyes. I only just realized Mittens McGee had been scarce all day…likely sleeping under the bed as usual. At the thought of sleeping, a yawn escaped me.

"I know it's super early, but I am going to play the old lady card and head to bed," I said, yawning again.

Tess nodded in agreement. "Yeah, I was thinking about that, too."

I turned off the fireplace and checked the lock on my door. Not that I was worried about someone coming in, but…it'd been a weird few days, I didn't want to take any chances.

Just as my head hit my pillow, my phone buzzed with an incoming message from Sebastian.

Hey there, do you have a minute to talk?

I yawned again, but figured it'd be a good time to update him about the day's events.

Yeah, sure - give me a call. I have some
news for you.

It barely took a full minute for my phone to vibrate with his call.

"Hey," I said, trying to hide the tiredness in my voice.

"You OK? You sound tired."

"I am…it was an eventful day," I replied with a slight laugh. "You'll never guess who showed up at my dumpster?"

"Not the trash pandas?" Sebastian guessed.

"Neil." I proceeded to tell him the whole story. "Oh, and we figured out who the blonde nurse is," I added as an afterthought.

"You what, now?" he asked, and I thought there was a slight sense of admiration in his tone.

"I'd like to take credit for that last part, but it was all Tess." I explained how Tess thought to use clip art of a blonde wig to see if anyone looked familiar. "Fortunately Detective Fox was already here talking to Neil, so we were able to clue him in as well."

"Wow," he said. "You *have* had a busy day."

"Your turn…what's new?" I asked, stifling a yawn. I climbed out of bed and started pacing my room in an effort to keep from dozing off.

"Mr. Knox called me with some…well, shocking news, if I'm being honest. I don't know if I've truly processed it yet." Sebastian said. "Apparently he had a visitor at his office yesterday, demanding to see Grams's will. Since he's under no legal obligation to show him—and if he really wanted to look at it, it's a public record—Knox tried to send him away. He had to call security to have him removed." There was a long pause after this, and I wasn't sure if I should say anything, or wait for Sebastian to continue.

"Well this is an unexpected turn of events. What in the name of beans could anyone want with Prudie's will?"

"He's contesting the will," Sebastian said.

"That's absurd. I suppose he's also claiming to be some long-lost relative," I scoffed. I didn't actually know how often that happened; if the entertainment industry was anything to go by, it was almost every funeral of a wealthy person. I noticed Sebastian hadn't responded. "He's not some long-lost relative, is he?"

Sebastian sighed. *Uh-oh...* "Jay claims to be Prudie's son."

"I'm sorry...what? Is this guy delusional?"

"I know how it sounds, but Mr. Knox has to look into it. Jay claims he tracked Prudie down through genealogy research," Sebastian said, doubt clinging to every word.

"I suppose that's possible...he did mention he was from Cincinnati." I realized I'd said this out loud, and winced, hoping Sebastian wouldn't think I was jumping right into believing this tale.

"It hurts my brain to even think about it. I'm not even worried about the will—that's the last of my concerns. I just don't know what Jay's angle is. And why come forward so soon after her death—doesn't that seem suspicious to you?"

I had to agree, if Jay visited Prudie before she died and promised she'd write him into the will, he'd have every motivation under the sun. But we saw the will as it was filed with the probate court; there was no mention of any beneficiary besides Sebastian. I wondered how this would impact the investigation; before I could get the words out, Sebastian beat me to it, saying Knox has already contacted Detective Fox. I didn't envy the detective in the least.

Chapter Twenty-Seven

THE CONTRACTORS WERE BUSY POUNDING AWAY, INSTALLING THE new window for the bakery. I'd left a key with them so they could get started as soon as possible…I just didn't consider that it would be four o'clock in the morning. I should have been used to that hour, but the last few days of being closed spoiled me with sleeping in a bit.

The news Sebastian shared yesterday also made it difficult to relax, and it took forever to fall asleep. I still couldn't understand why Jay would be coming forward, especially in the middle of a murder investigation. Unless he didn't know about that…but it'd been in the papers ever since it happened. It'd be pretty hard to avoid the gossip mill even for an out-of-towner.

Showered and caffeinated, I decided to head downstairs and do some baking. With luck, they'd have the window finished by the end of the day and I could reopen the bakery tomorrow; I wanted to be prepared. Tess would also be heading home and that left me with mixed emotions. While it was nice not coming home to an empty apartment, I was also looking forward to having my home back to myself. Not that Tess—or Mittens McGee—were any trouble, quite the opposite...I hated to admit I might actually miss having that furry rascal underfoot.

The banging and pounding was much louder downstairs which made me glad I grabbed some ear buds; I hoped some loud, festive Christmas tunes would drown out the racket coming from the front of the bakery. I surveyed the pantry to see what ingredients were on hand, pulling a little of this, and a bit of that from the shelves. I grabbed some cranberries from the fridge as well as the other cold ingredients, and got to work.

Just as I finished cutting the butter into the mixture, my phone rang. I sighed heavily, a little annoyed at the interruption, especially because I didn't recognize the number. Thinking it might be the insurance company calling me back about the police report, I connected to the call.

"Ken? It's Seb," the male's voice on the other end of the phone said.

"I almost let it go to voicemail, you know," I said as I moved to a more quiet location. Sebastian knew I preferred to be prepared when answering the phone; if I let it go to voicemail, I had more time to actually think about what the caller needed rather than just winging it.

"Yeah, sorry about that. I have you on speaker phone," he announced. I appreciated the heads-up...one never knew when one might feel a little like swearing. "I'm at Mr. Knox's office. I figured this would be easier than trying to explain it all later."

"Ah, well, hello to you both. What's up?"

"Mr. Knox did a little more research into Jay's claims about being Prudie's son. Turns out he's right."

I sucked in a breath at this news, uncertain what it meant for Sebastian. "And...?" I asked.

"When Jay came in, he said he'd matched using some DNA test from a genealogy website. I made a few calls to some folks who specialize in this kind of thing, and they were able to see the match." Mr. Knox spoke now, explaining how he discovered their connection.

"I completely forgot Grams did one of those a long time ago; she used to be very interested in building out the family tree, but just stopped one day. I thought it was around the time she went into Willowhaven," Sebastian explained.

"My guess would be that she realized her past would come out if she kept up with it," Mr. Knox said.

"Wow, I've heard of kids finding out they're adopted or the product of an affair that way, but not the other way around… though I suppose it makes sense. So what happens next?"

"Detective Fox met with us to discuss things; we reviewed the inheritance laws with regard to biological children who are adopted. Since there was a legal adoption of Jay, that severs all ties to biological parents; he is not entitled to anything from Prudie's estate, unless she specifically called it out in her will."

"I don't recall seeing that when we were reviewing the documents in your office, Mr. Knox," I said.

"That's right, it wasn't called out in her Will. She did leave a Letter of Intention with me—not legally binding, mind you—that did specify "if anyone comes forward claiming to be a biological child, they are not entitled to any portion of the estate." I am guessing when she filed this with me, it was after Jay spoke with her."

"More like threatened her," Sebastian muttered just loud enough for me to hear.

"Doesn't it seem odd to you that someone would come forward like this, so soon after their parent died? Especially since there was no relationship whatsoever…estranged or otherwise?" I couldn't move past this particular detail.

"That's something Detective Fox is looking into," Mr. Knox replied.

"And something *you* need to forget about," Sebastian added. "This is not your puzzle to solve anymore."

I glared into the phone; did he think this was a game to me?

"I can feel your look right now," he said, clearly unamused. He knew me far too well. "Seriously, Kendall. Mr. Knox said Jay was furious when was escorted off the property; I can only imagine how well he'll take the news he's not getting one cent of Prudie's estate. I don't know what he might do. I—I already lost Grams, I can't lose you, too."

Mr. Knox said he'd be contacting Jay this afternoon to inform him of this outcome; he advised me to keep a watchful eye out for anything—if Jay came around, I was to immediately contact Detective Fox. "He knows you're close to the Shaw family and he knows where you work; there's no telling how he may lash out." We said our goodbyes and I ended the call.

Mr. Knox's words sobered me, and for the first time, I truly felt nervous.

AFTER RUINING the second batch of dough for some hand pies, I gave up. I chucked the offending dough into the trash, cleaned up my mess, and stomped up the stairs to the comfort of my apartment. Sliding my feet into my fluffy panda slippers, I smiled at their little faces staring up at me...so innocent to the nastiness of the world. The Christmas lights on my little tree put me at ease as I wrapped myself in a blanket.

I must have dozed off at some point because I startled at a tap on my shoulder. When I checked the time it had been almost an hour. Peeking through one eye, I saw Tess staring back at me, amusement on her face. Hopefully I hadn't been snoring...or drooling. Instinctively, I wiped at my chin, just to be sure.

"I didn't want to bother you, but after about 45 minutes I just wanted to let you know McGee and I are getting out of your hair. I really, really appreciate you letting us stay here."

"Can I hug you, or would that be weird since I'm still not quite awake yet and might have drool on my blanket?"

"Well you just made it kind of weird, so you may as well do it anyway." Tess laughed, and I gave her a quick squeeze.

"I meant it, you know; you're always welcome here any time... both of you." I heard a meow and realized Tess had Mittens McGee in his travel carrier; he normally hated it, but it seemed like he sensed they were going home. I crouched down and scratched his head through the grate. "And you behave or else I'll have Santa take back your presents." Tess eyed me with suspicion, likely wondering which marble I had lost to make me buy a cat not one, but several, Christmas presents.

I felt a little silly as I walked them both to the door to say good-bye, but it seemed rude if they just left without a fuss. I closed the door behind them, breathing a sigh of relief—and, if I was honest a twinge of guilt—to have my own space back.

BY EVENING, the pounding from downstairs had stopped. The contractor left me a message informing me they completed their work, and the bakery was ready for business once again; I felt tears prick the corners of my eyes, so grateful to get back to normal. At least, I hoped things would be normal.

Relief set in as I realized the day was almost over and nothing unusual had happened in terms of unwanted visitors. I'd left instructions with the contractor to call me immediately if there was anyone lurking about, but no such call came. I settled back onto the couch and rested my head against the cushion.

I still couldn't believe what Mr. Knox discovered about Prudie. An unwed mother, in her time, was seen as taboo; I wondered if she was sent away by her parents until she had the baby, or if she just hid herself away from the world on her own...and to never tell a soul about it, even into adulthood. I couldn't imagine carrying that kind of secret to my death. But Jay found out, and seemingly tracked her down. I wondered how he managed to find her so easily. I shuddered, thinking about him confronting her; what she must have been thinking and feeling.

And there was still the question of who actually killed Prudie? Was it Jay, ensuring he'd receive what he felt was rightfully his inheritance? Or did Olivia do it, trying to get her hands on any valuables she could find after learning about the safety deposit box? And was Neil telling the whole truth about not being involved in her death...he had the means and opportunity, but did he have a motive? Money and greed can drive people to do some pretty awful things. Heck, I was sure at some point I was considered a suspect; aside from the hand pie being the last thing she ate, Detective Fox's questions about the bakery being successful sure felt like I was under suspicion.

A headache was blossoming between my eyes; I closed them, waiting for the thoughts of death and greed to dissipate. Sebastian and Mr. Knox were right—this wasn't my puzzle to solve any more, and I needed to leave it to Detective Fox. I sighed in resignation, feeling a sense of disappointment in myself; for letting Sebastian down...for letting Prudie down. I could hear Gran Lottie's voice in my head, *Getting yourself into trouble would be the real disappointment. Keep your nose clean, Peach.*

Chapter Twenty-Eight

I WAS UP AND OUT OF BED WELL BEFORE MY ALARM WENT OFF, excitement pulsing through me, despite being up well past midnight. I had gone back down to the bakery after talking with Sebastian to get my mind off of Prudie's case—the fact that there wasn't much I could do at this point—and made sure the decorations in the window were spruced up. I added extra twinkle lights, extra fake snow, and made sure there would be plenty of holiday cheer for folks who came in. I also had a feeling I needed to make some extra scones, hand pies, and tarts, so I whipped up about a dozen of each.

The sun was shining; a fresh layer of snow carpeted the ground and sparkled like a thousand diamonds. It was crisp and a bit windy, so I made sure to have extra hot drinks on hand for anyone who stopped in. The display case was well-stocked, and I was ready to welcome people back to City of Pies.

By the time Cayden arrived, there was a line around the side of the building. They flipped the sign to Open and a steady stream of customers made their way in from the cold.

"Wow, the window looks amazing!" Cayden said as they

worked to keep up with the demand of coffee and tea. "Did you even sleep last night?"

"Eh, who needs sleep!" I laughed, though I was sure my body would regret my actions from the night before. I took another long sip from my coffee mug, savoring the aroma of warm vanilla and cinnamon.

The bakery was so busy, I didn't even hear Tess come in. At about ten o'clock she stepped into the bakery from the bookstore, stretching.

"How was your first night back home?" I asked. I imagined it had to be more comfortable than living out of a suitcase for several days. Especially when you weren't on a fabulous vacation somewhere warm and scenic.

"I slept pretty well until a certain feline started warbling," she said, rolling her eyes. "When I checked on him, he was sitting at the front door making pathetic sounds."

"Sounds like someone missed Auntie Kendall!"

"More like, someone missed getting treats at all hours of the day," Tess huffed. "I think my cat needs to go on a diet now." She narrowed her eyes at me, and I shrugged as though I had no idea what she was talking about.

"Do we have any more cranberry scones?" Cayden asked. "We're down to our last half-dozen. And apple hand pies."

People kept commenting on how much they'd missed stopping by for their morning treats, and they certainly made up for it by wiping out our inventory almost within the first few hours.

"I have some dough in the fridge, I'll go make some more. Anything else besides the scones and hand pies?"

"Maybe some more pumpkin tarts, too." Cayden confirmed how many we had left in the case, and I agreed we likely needed about a dozen more.

I disappeared back to the kitchen, waiting for the ovens to pre-heat. My heart swelled with pride at how many customers came in this morning. It felt like I'd truly made an impression on the community, where people made City of Pies a part of their daily routines.

Reveling in my delight with the day's turn out so far, and Christmas music blaring from my little bluetooth speaker, I didn't even hear the bakery phone ring.

"Hey, Kendall? There's someone on the phone who wants to place a special order. I know we don't normally do them so close to Christmas, but they wanted it as a surprise for their mother's 90th birthday," Cayden spoke through the doorway. "He said they got the recommendation from Willowhaven and heard nothing but rave reviews."

I sighed. Cayden was right; it was already the 21st. This close to holidays I rarely made exceptions for special orders, but with the bakery being closed, I couldn't really afford to miss out on the income.

"As long as it's under five pies, go ahead and take it," I confirmed. Cayden knew how much time went into each item made, so I trusted them to make the right call if the order was placed. They nodded in agreement and I went back to forming the dough for scones.

After the last tray was in the oven and the timer was set, I stepped back into the bakery to check in with Cayden. I grabbed a soapy rag to wipe down tables and chairs, making sure there were clean spots for folks to sit. It was a bit after one o'clock and I realized I hadn't eaten anything since the night before.

"I'm going to walk over to O'Devlin's and get some lunch. You want anything?" I called out to Tess and Cayden. There was a lull in foot traffic, so I didn't feel bad about leaving Cayden on their own. They both jotted down their orders and I bundled up before heading outside. The cold bit into my face, wind whipping my scarf behind me. I shivered and waddled across the icy street into the welcoming warmth of the pub.

Arms filled takeout bags of delicious-smelling food, I pushed through the door to the bakery depositing the takeout bags on an unoccupied table.

"Come and get it," I said.

Tess and Cayden found their orders and tucked in while it was still warm. My Scotch Eggs were piping hot, and I almost burnt my mouth taking a bite.

"So how big was the order?" I asked Cayden.

They held up a finger as they chewed a bite of sandwich. "It was only three pies," they said. "And normal flavors: blueberry, apple, and pumpkin. Nothing that seemed too unreasonable."

I nodded in agreement. "When do they need them?"

"Tomorrow, actually. Here's the address; they said they'd pay you when you delivered them."

I frowned at that; I liked to get at least half up front, just to ensure they were serious about the order, but I reminded myself that beggars can't be choosers; I needed whatever revenue I could generate after being closed.

Cayden noticed my frown and said, "I know how you feel about that, but I figured with just three pies, it wasn't too risky." They had a point, I had to agree.

Finished with lunch, business started to pick back up later in the afternoon. Shortly before closing, Sebastian sent me a text.

> Hey there! Hope all is well at City of Pies
> today. Congrats on reopening!

I smiled and tapped out a reply that the bakery had been bustling all day, and there was nothing out of the ordinary to report.

> That's great news! Fox told me they
> informed Jay about the will. He was livid
> and threatened to sue...not sure who he
> was planning to sue...

Well I'm glad he didn't come around here to cause trouble. Gotta go, another wave of customers stopped in! Talk later?

Sebastian agreed to call later, and I got back to work. The last few hours went by in a flash, and I was exhausted by the time I flipped the Closed sign around and locked the door.

"Well that was a productive day!" Cayden said happily as they put on their coat. A fine dusting of snow was coming down, the crystals glittering in the glow of the street lights that kicked on.

"Thank you so much for your help, I know I wouldn't have been able to keep up without you! I'll see you tomorrow!"

I dragged myself up the stairs to my apartment, appreciating the fact I'd left the Christmas lights on. It was like walking into a scene from a greeting card: the warm glow of lights reflecting off wonky-shaped ornaments, the short stubby tree almost leaning under the weight of the decorations. I sighed, thankful for the comforting welcome.

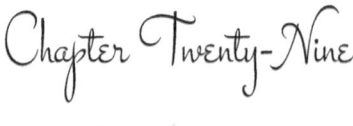

Chapter Twenty-Nine

DESPITE BEING AN UNHOLY HOUR OF THE MORNING, I FELT refreshed when I woke. I wanted an early start so I could prepare enough batches of dough for the bakery, as well as make the pies for the special order.

When Cayden mentioned the order was for today, I wasn't too thrilled about it; with the bakery back open, it was hard work keeping up with the stream of customers—which I hoped continued today— let alone making time for a special order for multiple pies. Luckily Cayden recognized how important any opportunity for income would be at this point; they were right, it was a small enough order that it wouldn't pose too much of a hardship. Besides, how could I turn down the chance to help a family celebrate their loved one? At that age, every birthday became a milestone and deserved to be celebrated.

No new snow had fallen overnight, so the sidewalk and roads were clear. It was still breezy and cold, and even with a sweater and the ovens heating up, there was still a chill that seemed to linger throughout the bakery. I checked the window to make sure no more funny business had occurred, though I would have noticed something on the security footage if someone was within range of the camera. Nothing seemed amiss, and the door was still locked, so I chalked it up to a drafty old building.

After making up a few dozen scones and hand pies, I set aside some ingredients for muffins. They'd come in handy if the rush of customers kept up today; easy to pop in the oven and quick to bake. The back door opened as Cayden stepped through, shucking off their coat and scarf.

"Seriously, why does it get so cold here?" Their teeth were chattering and I smiled.

"You can thank Canada for that," I said. Cayden looked at me, confused. "The cold air…" I waved a hand to indicate the air around us. "It comes down from the North."

"Yeah, but there's like a whole state between us and Canada. I figured it would lose a little bit of that frigidness by the time it got here." They shook their head and added, "It's kind of disre-spectful."

Having lived in the Midwest my whole life, I suppose I was used to it. I couldn't imagine living someplace that didn't experi-ence all four seasons, or have an actual winter for Christmas. Palm trees and sand did not seem conducive to Santa's sleigh or reindeer hooves.

Kneading the dough for pie crusts, I hummed along with the Christmas music playing from my little speaker. Even though we hadn't solved Prudie's murder, I felt a lightness that had been missing for a while; Detective Fox had new leads to follow, and it seemed like it was a pretty cut-and-dry case of greed and maybe a bit of revenge. I didn't know how Jay approached Prudie about her will; was he feeling bitter from the abandonment? Was he angry about it, maybe voicing that anger and directing it toward Prudie? Even if Jay did come forward with his side of the story, I wouldn't trust him to tell the truth. That may not be a fair judgement of a man I didn't know well, but anyone who would confront their birth mother in a nursing home just before she died wasn't exactly saintly in my book.

The ringing of a phone and Tess's voice jostled me from my thoughts as she poked her head into the kitchen before heading to the bookstore. She waved at me, and raised a coffee mug, splashing some over the edge.

With the pies in the oven it was time to open, and I smiled as I noticed several of the regular customers already lined up outside. I hurried to unlock and open the door for them, letting them into the warmth of the bakery. Cayden was busy filling the display case with the scones, some of the residual heat fogging up the glass.

I scurried behind the counter to get their drinks ready while Cayden helped with their baked goods. The scones flew off the tray, and within the hour we were already on the third batch. I'd need to bake some more at this rate, so I disappeared into the kitchen for the next few dozen, hoping this would at least last until noon.

There was a lull in customers around ten o'clock, and Cayden peeked into the kitchen. "We've been busier the last two days than we had been last month! And this day isn't even half-over!"

"I'm a little afraid to say this out loud, but I wonder what caused the spike? I didn't miss anything in the paper or on social media, did I?" I was forever behind the times when it came to keeping up with the latest news in town; unless the gossip brigade stopped in, I was usually in the dark until days after whatever hot topic had passed.

"I haven't seen anything, and no one has mentioned any news. They just know you're an amazing baker and missed stopping in!" Cayden said.

Tess wandered over to the counter, refilling her coffee. "Morning, friends," she said more upbeat than I'd heard her in a while.

"Someone's in a good mood this morning," I wiggled my eyebrows at her, and she smacked me on the arm.

"That was Jordan on the phone, he's taking me to lunch today," Tess beamed as she spoke.

Cayden and I made very mature "oooohh" noises in response. This garnered another smack on the arm from Tess. *Rude.*

"I hope things aren't too hectic for you when I deliver that pie order today," I said to Cayden. "I shouldn't be too long." I studied the address on the order form. It wasn't one I was overly familiar with, but Millwood was such a small town, I was sure it couldn't be too far.

"Shouldn't be a problem," they said as a few more customers stopped in for hand pies and coffee.

We chatted a bit about the weather, about having every intention of saving the hand pies for a late afternoon snack but never sustaining the will power to keep from eating them as soon as you get back to the car, and about warm beaches and sunny skies. A vacation sounded heavenly, but not something I could afford right at the moment. *Maybe next year...*

THE NOON HOUR FLEW BY, and I made sure the pies were cool enough to box up. I still had a bit of time before I had to deliver them, so I ran upstairs to grab a quick bite of lunch. Tess and Jordan were having a later lunch, so I didn't feel too badly leaving Cayden on their own.

Stomach satisfied with the peanut butter and jelly toast and hot tea, I made sure I looked presentable enough to be seen in public. In the bakery I was always tidy, with my hair up and out of the way in a hairnet, but flour and fruit filling always seemed to find the places my apron didn't cover well. Some days I considered wearing a full body suit, but the hot flashes would probably be the end of me. And let's not mention the times I forget to remove the hairnet before going out in public.

I boxed up the pies, placed the stickers on the boxes as well as any reheating or refrigeration instructions, and grabbed the order form with the address. As old fashioned as it may be, I still used carbon paper to write down the orders; I kept a copy for my records and a copy went with the order for the customer's reference. There was also a discount code for future orders, which I knew people liked.

I slipped into my coat and gloves and grabbed my keys to start the car. It'd been a few days since I'd driven the Beetle, and I was worried she might fight me on going anywhere. Fortunately after some sweet words and gentle patting on the dashboard, she roared to life, sputtering only once. I waited inside the bakery while the car warmed up, and carefully carried the pies to the car. I arranged them on the passenger seat, lovingly placing the seatbelt around them. The first time Cayden noticed this, I teased that it was because they were like children to me; in reality, it just helped keep them from sliding across the seat onto the floor…or into my lap.

"OK, I'm heading out!" I called to Cayden in the bakery. They were busy waiting on customers and just waved a hand in acknowledgement.

I tapped my phone to life and searched for the address; I just needed a visual of which streets I'd be turning on, and didn't have the luxury of GPS in my car. I puttered down the alley and made my way to the destination.

THE HOUSE WAS UNASSUMING; it was an older style brick home, two-story, and had large windows in the front. They looked like perfect Christmas tree windows. If I ever moved out of the apartment, I'd get a house with windows big enough to view my tree from the street. Very important house-buying criteria, of course. The walk was freshly shoveled from yesterday's snow, and chunks of salt looked like they'd been haphazardly tossed across the concrete.

There didn't seem to be a doorbell, so I tried to knock the best I could without dropping the pies. No one came to the door, so I tried again, this time using my foot; much louder this time and it actually resulted in a voice calling out that the door was unlocked. I shifted the pies so I could see the doorknob, and—successfully, I might add—managed to open the door without any fruit pie fatalities. It took my eyes a few seconds to adjust to the light as I closed the door behind me, but the interior of the house looked a bit dated, but clean and inviting. I debated whether to call out a hello, but a distant voice beat me to it.

"Hello?"

"Uh, hello! I'm Kendall from City of Pies. I've got your order."

"Oh, great! You can just set it on the dining room table in the other room," the woman's voice said. "Sorry I'm not helping you, but I had a few last minute dishes to whip up for the party, and apparently have been designated to clean-up duty." The woman laughed lightly, but it didn't sound genuine.

On my way to the dining room, I walked past the kitchen doorway, where I saw a woman at the sink, sweater sleeves pushed up to her elbows, the dark dress pants without a wrinkle. Her dark hair was pulled into a neat bun at the nape of her neck, not a strand out of place. I couldn't tell from this angle, but I'd bet money she was wearing pearls.

"No problem at all, let me just set these out for you and…oh, shoot!"

"Something wrong?"

"I was in a hurry when I left and the serving utensils are still on the counter. I'll just call over to have someone bring them to me," I said as I was already dialing Tess's number. I hated to interfere with her lunch plans, but I couldn't pull Cayden away from the bakery. I stepped outside to get some fresh air—it was like a sauna in there. Or maybe it was just me.

"Hey, Tess, sorry to bother you...but I walked off and forgot the serving utensils at the bakery. Can you run them over to me?"

"Sure thing. Jordan just pulled up, so you have great timing!"

I explained where I'd set the bag of items and mentioned the address was on the order pad by the register. I heard the bag rustling and a distant bell jingling, which I presumed was the bookstore's door. I thanked her profusely, and said I'd be waiting in the house but keeping watch for them.

I went back to the table to remove the pies from the boxes. As I was busying myself with folding the boxes up, I felt something hard press against my back and heard a click of what I assumed was a gun. (I am not a gun person, I don't make it a habit of knowing what they sound like or feel like, but this situation was definitely giving me gun vibes.)

I opened my mouth to speak, but all that came out was a slight squeak. I clamp my mouth shut as quickly as it flew open. Rolling my lips together, trying to think of a way out of this, I did what I do best...I started rambling. Or tried to start rambling; every time I opened my mouth to say something, they pressed harder into my back.

"Stop trying to talk," the woman said. "This will be easier for us all if you just keep quiet."

I debated that. I didn't see how any of this would be easier on her, regardless if I was quiet or not. I could only hope that Tess would realize something was up if I didn't greet her at the car right away. I shifted my leg a bit as my foot was starting to cramp, which resulted in another forceful nudge with the gun.

"Ow," I said. "Is that really necessary?"

"Shut up."

"Are you trying to rob me? Because if you are, just take the pies and whatever's in my bag. I'm a bakery owner, I don't have much dough," I paused wondering for the first time if using humor as a defense mechanism was a good idea. I'd never been held at gunpoint, this was a first for me.

"Would you stop," she said, nudging me with the gun. "Talking." *Nudge.* "Now." *Nudge.* The woman's voice sounded taut, as though she were gritting her teeth.

"Sorry," I whispered. I was nervous and couldn't stop myself from replying. Sweat was prickling my forehead. I never imagined this happening on a pie delivery of all things. I was trying to figure out why…was it a simple robbery? How much did they think I had on me when I made deliveries?

Knowing I had no chance to wrestle that gun—or whatever it was—away, I did the only thing I could think to do. I lowered my eyes to the table where I'd sat the pies earlier, judging the distance; if I could reach the edge of one, I might be able to pull it off the table. I hated to waste a pie like that, but I had to try something.

I moved my hand closer to the pie tin, my fingers just grazing the edge. *Shoot! Not close enough to get a good handle on it!* I tried to shift my weight a bit without the woman noticing. With my index finger and thumb, I grasped the edge of the pie and froze: what was I going to do with this? I couldn't smash it in her face, I knew I wasn't quick enough for that. I had to hope knocking it to the floor would be enough.

Taking a deep breath, I yanked the pie off the table and let it fall to the floor beside me. Blueberry filling oozed out from the overturned pie tin, shards of crust scattered around it, staining the cream colored carpet. I looked down and saw her nicely tailored pants were now tainted with blueberry pie filling and bits of crust. The woman bursts into a laugh that's so shrill it makes me wince. My heart skipped a beat as realization of who this woman was hit me like that pie hit the floor: Olivia.

"Can I ask you something?" I tried to keep my voice even, to not let fear or anxiety give away my mental state.

"What?" The woman—Olivia—barked.

"Why the blonde wig?" As soon as the words left my lips, it almost felt like the air was sucked out of the room. Not a sound. Not a movement from the woman behind me. "Ah, didn't know I figured that out? I'm not the only one, you know."

"Your dumb friends? Not that worried," she said.

"What's the deal with Neil?"

"What about the bumbling idiot?" Olivia spat the words as if they tasted bitter in her mouth.

"Why involve him? He seems harmless enough. Or did you need someone to do the dirty work for you?" I shrugged my shoulders, playing dumb. I wasn't going to let on that he already talked to Detective Fox; she could learn that the hard way.

Before Olivia could say anything, my phone rang. She growled and firmed her grip on my arm, preventing me from answering it.

"You know if I don't answer it, they'll think something is wrong," I said. "They'll probably come to the door...you don't want that, do you?"

Olivia seemed conflicted about this: if I answered the phone, my voice might give away something was wrong, or I could blurt out that she was holding me hostage; if I didn't answer, they'd suspect something was wrong and try to come inside. Either way didn't seem like a good outcome for her...or me, really. I could hear her swallow hard, taking deep breaths. Was she nervous? Eventually there was a knock on the door.

"Damn!" I heard Olivia swear.

"Hello?" a voice called out, and I immediately recognized it as Tess. I was equal parts relieved and terrified—I didn't need her stumbling into this mess.

"Who is it?" Olivia asked, trying to mask her frustration.

Tess's voice reached my ears again. "Uh, I'm here with the pie utensils, for your pies Kendall asked me to bring them..." she continued explaining how I'd called her.

A jiggle on the handle caused Olivia to tense; another jiggle on the handle and I felt the pressure from the gun ease slightly.

Tess called out one more time, asking if she could come in. Olivia seemed exasperated by this point. She stuttered a response, but it wasn't coherent. The gun lifted away from my back and I knew it was now or never. Steeling myself with a steady breath and a silent prayer, I shoved my elbow as hard as I could into Olivia's side. As Olivia cried out in pain, I cried out in terror. "She has a gun!"

Time seemed to stand still at this point, everything happening all at once but felt like it was moving in slow motion. As soon as the words left my mouth, the front door flew open. Detective Fox was positioned in front of Tess, legs hip-width apart, a gun raised. I threw my hands up in the air and moved aside so he could see Olivia.

Before I had a chance to move, however, she cracked me on the head with the butt of the gun, sending me to the floor in a crumpled heap. I wasn't knocked out, but it stunned me enough that I wasn't able to react when she started running for the back door. Detective Fox sailed past me, grabbing Olivia just as the fresh air and a taste of freedom were ripped away from her.

Tess ran over to me, her face a picture of fury and fear. She turned my head slightly to reveal a very nasty cut that will likely require medical attention.

"Do you want me to call an ambulance, or do you want us to drive you to the hospital?" Tess asked.

"Can you call Seb?"

A smile crossed her face. "Sure," she said.

⬤

OLIVIA KICKED and struggled with Detective Fox while he tried to restrain her with handcuffs and keep her in a chair until the backup he called could arrive. He was trying to ask her questions, and she seemed confused that he knew as much as he did. Within minutes, his reinforcements were there, tires screeching to a halt on the street. Two officers entered the house, both had their hands on their service weapons, but they were not drawn.

I tried to keep from passing out—not so much from the wound, just the shock of it all—and heard a muffled pounding on something. I glanced to the front door, which was still open; no one was there. I leaned forward to look at the back door, but the door frame was empty. The pounding noise grew more frantic, enough that Detective Fox also heard it. He motioned for one of the officers to check it out, which caused Olivia to grow more agitated.

Bracing myself along the wall, I hobbled my way to the kitchen to see what was going on. The officer was listening intently, placing his ear to each wall or door. The pounding and scuffling noise happened again and the officer threw open the pantry door, his hand on his weapon. Another officer had his gun drawn too, just in case.

A man tumbled forward out of the pantry and I gasped when I saw him.

"Jay!"

Chapter Thirty

ONCE DETECTIVE FOX WAS SATISFIED SEBASTIAN WOULD DRIVE ME straight to the hospital, he drove away with Olivia in the back seat, glaring at me. Jay was placed in another police car and taken to the police station for questioning. My head hurt too badly to make sense of it all right then, so I was thankful when Sebastian gently ushered me to his car and made sure my seat belt was fastened. Tess took my keys to drive the Beetle back to the bakery; she hated driving it because of the manual transmission, "grind it 'till you find it," was her motto.

"I wasn't snooping, you know," I said defensively.

"I didn't think you were, Ken."

"Did she say anything? I was kind of zoned out for a while back there once Detective Fox had her." While I didn't pass out, I definitely let my mind roam elsewhere…happier places, like my kitchen, or being smothered with puppies. Or with Sebastian.

"She clammed up," he said. "Once Fox read her rights to her, she closed herself off. Probably a smart idea."

"And Jay?"

"I don't even know where to go with that." Sebastian said, his voice low. "Detective Fox made sure we weren't near each other."

Sebastian and I were both quiet the rest of the way to the hospital. The throbbing in my head made it difficult to talk. I leaned my head back against the head rest and sighed.

ONCE IMAGING HAD BEEN COMPLETED and it was determined there was no brain injury, the emergency room nurses cleaned and stitched the gash on my forehead. They said I was lucky it wasn't a few centimeters over where my temple was, or there could have been a far worse outcome. I think I dozed off at some point, closing my eyes to block out the brightness of the overhead lights but managing to fall asleep; the nurses were impressed and never had someone doze off during stitches.

"It's a day of firsts," I joked. "I've never been bamboozled by a pie delivery before."

They prescribed a couple medications for me—one for pain, and one to help reduce the risk of seizures—and sent me on my way. When we were exiting the parking lot, Sebastian asked if I needed anything else.

"Ice cream," I said, matter-of-factly.

"It's freezing out, and you want ice cream?" Sebastian asked. "Did they check your head to make sure you weren't knocked silly?"

"Hey, I was just held at gun point today. I had to waste perfectly good pies, and lose out on a special order. I think I deserve some chocolate ice cream. With hot fudge. And peanut butter cups." I crossed my arms in front of my chest and huffed, as though I had the last say in this discussion.

A few minutes later, I was tucking into a delicious sundae.

"Just don't eat it too fast, or you'll get a brain freeze," Sebastian warned...too late, it seemed. I screwed my eyes shut and pounded my fist on my leg.

"Do. Not. Recommend. With. Head. Injury."

We were back at the apartment and the anticipation of collapsing onto my couch was enough to make me cry.

Sebastian made sure I had everything I needed before he left again to pick up my prescriptions. I settled into my little nest of blankets and pillows and marveled at how weird the day had been.

The chime of an incoming text message made me cringe, and I turned down the volume.

> Do you think you'll feel up to breakfast tomorrow morning?

I smiled at Tess's message as I tapped out a reply, which took a lot more effort than I expected.

> Sounds good. Turning in for the night.
> Thanks for everything today xx

> Duh, we're besties. I would fully expect you to save me from a hostage situation. Get some rest.

Sebastian returned with my medications, but I was already fast asleep. I woke only once in the middle of the night for some water, when I glanced over, Sebastian was asleep in the recliner, my panda slippers dangling off one foot.

THE MORNING LIGHT streamed in through the living room window, revealing another coating of fresh snow. That tingle of excitement filled me as I looked out, the world looking like a snow globe.

"Morning, sunshine." Sebastian yawned and stretched, trying to work out the kinks in his neck from sleeping in the worst possible chair.

"Good morning," I smiled. "Thanks for keeping me company last night."

"I just wanted to make sure your head was alright. Can I get you anything?"

"Nah. I'm going to take a shower, I think. Oh, Tess mentioned something about breakfast this morning, but never said what time. Would you want to find out? Obviously you're coming along...I mean, if you have time."

Sebastian shooed me to the bathroom and told me to take my time getting around and he'd sort things out with Tess.

A blissful 45 minutes and a drained hot water heater later, I felt well enough to be among the living. My head still hurt pretty bad—it was a challenge to wash my hair without getting too aggressive with it—but I think I managed. I grabbed the medication from the counter and read the dosing instructions before washing the pills down with water.

"Alright, Tess said to meet her at O'Devlin's around nine-thirty. I'm going to run home real quick, but I'll meet you guys there." Sebastian kissed me gently on the head, careful not to put too much pressure on anything that might cause pain.

"Sounds like a plan. See you in a few!"

I puttered around the house a bit, straightening a few things up, putting the blankets and pillows away from last night. Every time I caught my reflection in a mirror I stopped to stare at my head. It didn't look too scary; the stitches were neat little rows and not too obvious unless you really looked for them. The area around it was red, though, and looked angry. It was tender to the touch, and in such an odd place it was hard to avoid sometimes. I wondered if this was how Neil felt with his head wound? I laughed, thinking how that seemed to be Olivia's go-to method of dealing with unwanted visitors.

I bundled myself in one of my coziest sweaters—light blue with big white stars—and waited patiently to make the short trek across the street for breakfast. My stomach rumbled at the thought of food, and I realized I hadn't eaten anything since early yesterday afternoon, besides that amazing hot fudge sundae.

Cold air smacked me in the face as I left the warmth of home. The snow had already been cleared from the sidewalks and streets, even up to each business's door. I was thankful for the short walk; even with the sun shining, the wind was whipping around and chilled me to the bone.

It took a few seconds for my eyes to adjust to the darkness of O'Devlin's compared to the bright white snow outside. I surveyed the front room, looking for any familiar faces, but my friends hadn't arrived yet. I noticed the corner booth in the back was available and mentally fist-bumped myself. It was the best spot to be away from the gossipy ears of Mill Street. Austin, the owner, called out a greeting from the bar; I motioned toward the empty booth, and he gave a thumbs-up.

Not long after I was seated, Austin brought some water and menus to the table.

"I'm not sure how many will be here today," I said.

His gaze snagged on the wound on my forehead, winced. "Ouch, that looks painful."

"Definitely not my idea of a good time, that's for sure." I chuckled, hoping we could avoid talking about it. I wasn't entirely sure if I could say anything, since I was pretty sure it had something to do with Prudie's case. Thankfully, Austin simply nodded and said he'd be back once my friends arrived.

My stomach growled loudly as I waited. O'Devlin's was known for their amazing food, and their breakfast was no exception. Everything was set up buffet-style, with all manner of delicious options, or you could order a full Irish breakfast if you didn't plan on eating for the rest of the day. You could choose from mimosas, a Bloody Mary, or a good old pint of Guinness to get you ready for whatever the day threw at you, or you could be sensible and opt for coffee, water, or juice. I knew I couldn't drink while taking the medication, but a nice strong Bloody Mary sure sounded good.

Finally Tess walked through the door, and I waved her over. I was surprised to see Detective Fox following close behind. Sebastian arrived about a minute later.

"Cayden coming?" I asked as everyone got situated in the booth.

"They already had plans with Max today," Tess said.

Austin came back as promised, with waters for the table and to take drink orders. We all knew we'd be getting the buffet, so he told us to help ourselves. I loaded a plate with scrambled eggs (Robin, the owner's wife, once drunkenly shared the secret to their velvety, creamy scrambled eggs with me and I was surprised to learn it was butter), bacon, and a couple of O'Devlin's potato pancakes.

I savored the perfectly cooked bacon and sipped my coffee, waiting for everyone to enjoy at least a few bites of their breakfast before jumping right into conversation.

"So," I said, trying to think of how to ask what happened to Olivia without coming right out and asking. Detective Fox was eyeing me, humor crinkling the corners of his eyes.

"It'll all be in the paper later this afternoon, so I don't feel out of line discussing this with you. We have signed confessions from all parties involved, and their lawyers have agreed to let me discuss this with you. Besides, you and Sebastian have a vested interest in this outcome, all things considered." The detective took a sip of coffee before continuing.

"Olivia will be charged with confinement for holding both you and Jay at the house," he said. "When we started to question her about things surrounding Prudie's death, she refused to talk without a lawyer, which I would expect. There was a brief moment when we thought she might crack, telling her Jay already spilled the beans, but she wouldn't talk."

We all nodded our heads, understanding there wasn't really anything they could do to force someone to talk.

"And what about Jay?" Sebastian asked. He sounded cautious, almost like he didn't really want to know the answer.

"Jay really did tell us all there was to know," Detective Fox said. "He explained how he discovered the connection to Prudie, and tracked her down to Willowhaven. He assumed since she was in a nursing home, she wasn't doing well health-wise, and thought he could work his way into her will. He said he actually dated Olivia for a while before approaching Prudie, trying to get a feel for things. He claims he never told Olivia his connection to Prudie, just that he was researching places for his aging parents. When we asked Olivia about this part, she did mention they dated. She seemed a little sad when she realized he was just using her for information."

"Huh," was all Sebastian said.

"Jay eventually found out Olivia was diverting medication from Willowhaven, when he mentioned it to her, he made a deal with her: she helps him get to Prudie, or he goes to the authorities about the medication she's been taking."

Tess blew out a low whistle. "Blackmail," she said, as if it was the most common thing to happen in Millwood.

"So she was the one behind the missing medications. Celeste mentioned it a couple times. She wasn't sure if it had anything to do with the missing badge."

"We arranged a public defender for Olivia, and then she began to open up about everything. The wig allowed her to get around Willowhaven virtually unnoticed…until a certain someone ran into her at the market," Detective Fox smiled at me.

"Hey, I needed meatballs…she just happened to be there." I

took a bite of bacon and chewed, waiting for the detective to continue.

"Do the medications she was stealing connect her to Grams's death?" Sebastian asked quietly.

Detective Fox shook his head no. "In fact, what she was taking had nothing to do with any of the residents." He seemed a little put out by that fact.

"So where does Neil fit into this whole mess?" I really felt bad for the guy, if he wasn't directly involved. I hoped he wasn't.

"Neil was in the wrong place at the wrong time. As you know from talking to him, he admitted to wanting to steal from Prudie. He overheard them talking about the safety deposit box and valuables, and thought if he could pawn the jewelry, he could get out from under some financial trouble. He went to her room that night and chickened out, but heard voices from inside the room. When he entered to check it out, he was attacked."

"By Olivia and Jay?" I guessed. Detective Fox looked at me through narrowed eyes but continued.

"Yes, they attacked Neil. They also blackmailed him to keep quiet; Olivia knew he'd recently been divorced and his ex-wife took him to the cleaners. Tried to convince him to be on their side and they'd make it worth his time."

"And what about Grams?" Sebastian asked. I squeezed his hand for support; I couldn't imagine how hard this was to listen to.

"Once we finally got Olivia to talk, we got the full story. It went exactly as planned—except for Neil. Jay convinced Olivia if she helped him, he would give her a large sum of money from whatever he inherited. She agreed, and was to supply the drugs that ultimately killed your grandmother. She administered the medication; normally it wouldn't have been fatal, but since she'd been sick with a respiratory illness and was still weak..." Detective Fox trailed off, not wanting to go into too much detail. Sebastian inhaled a shuddering breath, but nodded for him to continue.

"Jay was startled by Neil coming into the room, so he knocked him out. He claims it was just a reflex, but I'm not so sure. Olivia then used the same drug on Neil to sedate him. They're lucky Neil pulled through, otherwise they'd have two deaths on their hands."

There was a lull in conversation as we all tried to process this information. Reflecting back on the notebook, the pieces were all there; we had them all in the box, but there were a few out of place. Honestly, Jay was kind of a wild card in this whole mix. I thought for sure he'd killed Prudie.

"And I suppose I was part of their game, too, when they placed that pie order...to lure me to them, somehow?" I asked. I hadn't really thought about it until now, but that made the most logical sense.

"Right. Get you alone, single you out, keep you quiet by whatever means necessary."

I shuddered. I could have been another victim.

"And Jay being tied up in the pantry?" Tess asked.

"Olivia found out he wasn't getting anything from Prudie's estate, so she turned on him." Fox shrugged. "Oldest story there is when it comes to couples in crime."

"Yeah, look how that turned out for Bonnie and Clyde."

Epilogue

SOLVING A MURDER WHILE STILL TRYING TO RUN A BUSINESS DIDN'T leave much free time for present shopping, and we all agreed it would be good to use Christmas Eve and Christmas Day to decompress. As much as we had to celebrate—and as much as I wanted to celebrate—I spent a very quiet, cozy holiday at home. Sebastian wanted some space to try and make sense of things; I suspected it takes a person a lifetime to process a tragic event like that, and even then I was willing to bet we went to the grave with some unresolved feelings. Still, we wanted to honor Prudie's memory and what better way than a gathering of best friends? Tess and I had made reservations for New Year's Eve at the new Greek restaurant that just opened, and I was already looking forward to sharing laughter and memories with everyone.

Just as Detective Fox had warned us, there was an article in the local newspaper regarding the case. The scales of justice could never truly be balanced, I don't think; how is there a suitable punishment for taking someone's life? Nothing seems big enough or severe enough, yet in committing that one act, Olivia sealed her own fate and perhaps that is punishment enough.

Since everything came to a head just in time for the holidays, sentencing wouldn't happen until after the first of the year. The article painted a solid picture of the events as we all remembered them, and even shed some light on a few things I still wasn't sure about.

Roberto was cleared of any wrongdoing once reports showed his badge being used during shifts he wasn't working.

Neil didn't face any punishment, at least not from the legal system. Celeste and Issac mentioned Willowhaven may do their own investigation, but there really wasn't anything to pin on him. The key they found on Neil the night Prudie died was a blank, planted by Jay or Olivia to throw suspicion his way. As for the vandalism, the prosecutor is still reviewing the evidence against Neil to determine whether or not to press charges. I didn't really feel it was necessary, but I didn't have much say.

After agreeing to a plea deal, Jay was being charged with conspiracy to commit murder; he admitted to his involvement, though he never intended to be the one to actually harm Prudie. His intention all along was to find someone else to do that bit of dirty work.

And, naturally, Olivia was dealt the harshest charges of them all: first degree murder, felony drug diversion, and criminal confinement. I wondered if at any point she questioned what she was doing, if she felt it was worth it. Even now, hearing her laugh echoing through my mind that day she held me at gunpoint sent chills down my spine, and I doubted she felt much of anything at all.

DARKNESS STARTED to settle in as the sun set. Sebastian grabbed one of the fluffiest blankets I owned and, after ensuring I had my warmest pair of boots and my coat on, pulled me to my feet. He ushered me out the door and down to his car, arms full with two large insulated tumblers that smelled faintly of chocolate, the blanket, and somehow still managed to hold on to one of my mitten-clad hands.

"Can I at least have a hint?" I asked. I knew it obviously involved something outdoors, though I couldn't think of anything happening in town until the few days leading up to New Year's Eve. It started snowing earlier in the day and was coming down at a moderate rate, coating the ground in white fluffy snow. I burrowed into the heated seat, which I would be sad if we had to abandon.

"You'll find out soon enough." That was the only response I received before he pulled away from the bakery and the coziness of my apartment. Minutes later, we pulled into the parking lot of Frasier Tree Farm where I picked up my little apartment tree. I threw him some side eye, but he ignored me, making a show of finding a parking spot, though the lot was fairly empty. As Sebastian pulled around a corner bypassing the main parking area, I noticed a sign advertising sleigh rides and immediately forgot how annoyed I was about not being home. I let out a squeak as the realization hit what the surprise was and was bouncing in my seat, excitement pulsing through me.

"I'm not entirely sure what we're in store for, but Noelle stressed bringing a blanket and some hot drinks." Sebastian smiled at me, and I tamped down the urge to lunge at him and give him the biggest hug ever.

We trudged from the parking lot to the entrance of the tree farm, which looked like it'd been transformed into a twinkling fairy wonderland. Noelle met us at the gate and we followed her to the row of wooden sleighs, each one decked out in fresh boughs of evergreen, red velvet bows, and sleigh bells. We climbed into the first of three, which also happened to be the most decked out. This one had battery operated fairy lights draped across the front and back, and one of the farm hands was harnessing a medium-sized horse to pull us. I was in awe.

"Noelle, this looks so....magical! You set all this up?"

"Well, I had some help, but yes. When mom called me after I'd been laid off, she let slip that the farm had seen better days; people just don't buy real Christmas trees as much, and business was a bit slow. One of our employees also does woodcarving, so he was able to use some of our scrap wood to refurbish these old sleighs for us on the cheap." Her eyes sparkled with a sense of pride, it warmed me through and through.

"When I found out Noelle was offering sleigh rides, I knew I had to plan it, Ken. It's been so chaotic this last month and I just wanted you to be able to enjoy a little holiday cheer." Sebastian's eyes twinkled as he spoke and I thought I saw a little tear gathering at the corner of his eye. Which immediately made me cry. And then Noelle. What a bunch of saps we were.

Sebastian arranged the blanket around our shoulders and I leaned into him and rested my head on his shoulder. Noelle gave some quiet instructions to the driver and with a few soft clicks of his tongue the sleigh jerked into motion. We glided down a path which was lit with large blow molds of candy canes and illuminated snowflakes tacked to fence rails. The snow was still coming down, but since we were under the canopy of trees it filtered out some of the larger flakes. I snuggled closer to Sebastian, savoring every minute of this enchanting ride.

The whole world was quiet around us, save for the occasional encouraging noise from the driver, a snort from our guide horse, and the swooshing of the sleigh through the snow. Sebastian pulled out a small portable speaker from the tote bag and after a few taps of his phone the gentle strains of Frank Sinatra surrounded us. It was honestly the most romantic thing I'd ever experienced. "I can't believe you did all this," I said with admiration.

"I did have a little help from Tess," Sebastian confessed, but it didn't change my feelings. It had been years since anyone had surprised me with anything like this, and the sheer fact that it was something festive and full of Christmassy goodness just made it even better. I'd been teased a lot about my affinity for the holidays, being told it was an unhealthy attachment to nostalgia or that it was just an annoying obsession. And it was true to an extent; I associated the Christmas season with Gran Lottie, and it was one of my favorite memories of our times together. Seeing the amount of thought put into this, though, made me realize it was always a 'them' problem and not a 'me' problem.

I felt the sleigh slow a bit and heard the driver click his tongue again, and when I looked up, the trees seemed to part before us giving way to a clearing. More strands of lights and boughs of evergreen outlined the perimeter, and I noticed in the back was a small cabin that looked like a gingerbread house. Multicolored lights draped the roofline, and colorful gumdrops outlined the doorframe. Peppermint swirls made up a pathway to the door, which was guarded by two giant Nutcracker soldiers. My mouth had dropped open at some point and I was unable to say anything. I heard a laugh as familiar as my own and realized it was coming from inside the little cabin. I looked to Sebastian who just grinned at me.

"Can we go inside?" I asked the driver.

"Sure! I think Santa is expecting you," he said with a wink.

I climbed from the sleigh and had to keep myself from sprinting to the door. I waited for Sebastian to join me, and we pushed it open together revealing a fireplace crackling with real logs. The smell of the wood and warmth from the fire was heavenly. Next to the fireplace was an oversized green armchair complete with Santa. I glanced around, taking in the sights of the cabin some more; a tree decorated within an inch of its life stood in the corner, and a train set ran around the bottom of it. There were stockings on the fireplace that looked full, and candles and glittering ornaments placed around the room.

I heard a faint snoring noise from the corner, and looked to see a dog bed with the cutest cocker spaniel snoozing away; he was wearing an elf sweater and every time his leg twitched from his dreaming, the little bell on his collar jingled. I tried to resist cooing at him, but it was no use; I was just a soppy puddle of Christmas pudding standing in this room.

Santa finally spoke, breaking me from my thoughts. "Ho-ho-ho! Hello, Kendall!"

It took me by surprise that Santa knew my name…but, then again, it is Santa… "Hello Santa! This is an exceptional cabin you have; it's so cozy and festive!"

"Mrs. Claus will be pleased to hear that; she and the elves worked so hard to make sure it was just right." As if noticing him for the first time, Santa greeted Sebastian, "Well hello, Sebastian. I'm happy to see you!"

Sebastian grinned, "Hi, Santa. Good to see you, too." He looked like a kid dazzled by all the magic of Christmas, and it melted my heart.

"Now, Kendall, I know we're a couple days past Christmas… but I'm Santa and I make the rules. Is there a special Christmas wish I can help you with?" Santa smiled as he looked over the tops of his glasses, his rounded cheeks tinted pink. I couldn't be sure if it was make-up or natural…or from the heat. I was starting to roast in here, I couldn't imagine how he was able to stand it wearing that suit.

I took in the sights around me again: the cozy sleeping puppy, the decked out tree, the fire spitting embers into the chimney. My hand found Sebastian's and I interlaced my fingers with his. I turned to look at his profile and I knew right then that I was meant to be with Sebastian. It might not be forever, but I'd take it for as long as it lasted.

"Santa, I think you already have."

The End

Chewy Peanut Bars

MAKES ONE 9X13 PAN.

On occasion, you just need a tasty snack that scratches that sweet-and-salty itch. Sure, it takes a few shortcuts here and there, but the results are no less satisfying to sink your teeth into!

Base Ingredients

- 1 package yellow cake mix
- 1/3 Cup margarine, softened
- 1 egg
- 3 Cups miniature marshmallows

Topping

- 2/3 Cup corn syrup
- 1/4 Cup margarine
- 2 teaspoons vanilla
- 2 Cups (12 ounce package) peanut butter chips
- 2 Cups crisped rice cereal
- 2 Cups (12 ounces) salted peanuts

Directions

Heat oven to 350F.

In bowl, mix base ingredients except marshmallows at a low speed until crumbly.

Press into ungreased 9x13 pan. Bake 12 to 18 minutes.

Immediately sprinkle with marshmallows; bake 2 more minutes.

In sauce pan, heat corn syrup, margarine, vanilla, and peanut butter chips until melted and smooth.

Stir in crisped rice cereal and peanuts. Spread on top of base in pan.

Chill until set.

Acknowledgments

This book started as a glimmer of an idea during a training session, so thanks to Kait for the inspiration…That job ended up being eliminated, allowing more time to work on this passion project; how's that for kismet?

To the Geek Girl Pen Pal community and my Cold Manor peeps, you're the best found family a girl could ask for. And to the supportive authors across social media and in the Writer's Retreat Discord server, who offered encouraging words and allowed me to ask questions, I appreciate you.

To my Coffee and Cadavers book club friends, your encouragement was like a warm hug, often on the days I needed it most. Please be sure to tell me when you plan to read this as a group so I can come down with some illness and avoid turning five shades of red as you talk amongst yourselves.

To the two main staples in my playlist while I was writing: Tamar Berk, you're a lovely human and I appreciate your support and your music; Local H, thank you for not only having a few shows throughout the year to headbang some of the stress way, but for also inspiring the business names scattered throughout this book…still trying to work in a Heavy Metal Bakesale somewhere…

To my alpha and beta readers, a thousand times thank you! Misty, your support and feedback proved to be invaluable and I can't thank you enough.

To Maggie, who was on the receiving end of so man random texts while I was struggling with difficult characters and plot holes the size of Saskatchewan; who never once told me to leave her alone even when she was 9 months pregnant and just wanted her pants to fit right, thank you doesn't seem to be enough.

To my parents, parents-in-law, aunts, uncles, and cousins, thanks for cheering me on, and for telling literally everyone you meet I'm writing a book (even the grocery store staff). Uncle Phil, thanks for letting me ask you morbid questions and not thinking I'm a complete weirdo (we all know I am, it's not a secret). Mom, I promise you'll get your signed first-edition.

And to my husband, who is always my biggest cheerleader, my voice of reason and logic who talks me off the ledge, who feeds me tacos and tells me I'm pretty…you're the best, and I love you to the moon and back…with three trips around Saturn in between.

About the Author

Kim Beatty is a brand-spanking-new author who can't quite believe she wrote a book. She lives in the Midwest with her husband, classic cars, and a quirky sense of humor. When Kim isn't writing, she can be found wandering the streets of Chicago, rocking out at Local H shows, reading way past her bedtime, or trying to convince unsuspecting friends they should try Malört.

If you like cozy stories, relatable characters, a bit of small town life, and just a pinch of light romance, Kim's books just might be your next favorite!

Keep up with Kim by visiting her website and subscribing to her newsletter - www.kimbeattyauthor.com